34 Days

Anita Waller

ISBN: 978-0-9955111-6-3

For my wonderful grandchildren – Brad, Katie, Dom, Cerys, Melissa, Lyra and Isaac.

What is hell?
Hell is oneself,
Hell is alone, the other figures in it
Merely projections. There is nothing to escape from
And nothing to escape to. One is always alone.

The Cocktail Party (1950) act 1 sc.3
T.S.Eliot, 1888 - 1965

Chapter 1
Monday 9 March 2015
Day One

'Are the eggs done?'

Anna flinched as she heard the shout from upstairs, just as she flinched every morning at the sound of Ray's voice. This particular morning hadn't started too well; she'd knocked over her first cup of coffee and while she was cleaning that mishap she caught the edge of the sugar bowl, sending it shimmering spectacularly all over the floor. As far as wedding anniversaries, this one was not proving brilliant.

Ray came downstairs as she confirmed his breakfast was indeed ready and they sat down to eat after he had made a scathing comment about the stickiness of the tiles; he had no idea of her earlier traumas and without saying a further word he handed her the cards they had received.

She developed instant post-natal depression. That was the only explanation for the frustration she felt when she opened the first envelope to see the card that shouted in big, silver letters: *To Mum and Dad On Their Silver Wedding Anniversary.* And it wasn't really frustration, it was more frustrated amusement.

Caroline had written in her distinctive curly handwriting, *35 years! Amazing!* and Anna wondered yet again where her daughter's head had been when she went to buy the card.

Anna passed it across to Ray. 'Spot the non-deliberate mistake.'

He looked at the front of the card, opened it, and said, 'She's forgotten the kisses.'

She upgraded the post-natal to manic and reached for another card. As she slit the envelope, she knew she didn't really need to open it. It was from Ray; it would have roses on the front, and he would have written, *All my love, Ray xxx.*

She was wrong. It said 'Happy birthday, darling. All my love, Ray xxx.' Caroline had got all her genes from her father.

She passed Ray his card from her and watched as he opened it, read it without any of the words registering, and laid it by his plate.

'Very nice, Anna, very nice.'

The final card on the table was from their eldest, Mark. It had been written by his wife and it was really quite normal. *With much love to you both, from Mark, Jenny, Adam and Grace.*

There was no card from Tim, their second son and twin brother of Mark. Just for a second sadness touched her but she soon shook it off – this was Tim, after all. She had learned to accept Tim would always be one of life's mysteries and she loved him unconditionally no matter what he did. The lack of a card didn't mean he didn't care, it just meant he hadn't considered it important.

Anna gathered up the cards, moved into the lounge, and stood them on the sill of the bay window. The bright, early morning April sunshine bounced off the silver lettering on Caroline's card, and she smiled before stroking it.

Their daughter had been born late in their lives, and they had always jokingly referred to her as their little afterthought. The truth was she saved Anna's sanity. Mark and Tim were fifteen years older than Caro, and when Anna had realised she was pregnant, she was actually on the verge of leaving an abusive marriage.

The pregnancy had temporarily stopped the beatings, but it also stopped all exit plans. The cards standing on the window sill now seemed to mock that decision. She hadn't loved Ray for years.

'Bye, Anna!'

There was movement in the hall as he paused at the mirror to run a comb through his short, grey hair, then the front door slammed as he left for work. Bye, Anna.

The tears that filled her eyes took her completely by surprise, and she swept the cards off the sill, watching as they slid down the wall. Anger was building in her, and she forced herself to calm down by picking up the cards and replacing them. She was not normally an angry person, and the uncharacteristic action scared her a little.

A cup of tea didn't help – and why should it? She didn't really like the taste. *It's just the thing to do, isn't it? Have a cup of tea, and you'll feel better.* She put their few breakfast dishes into the bowl and stood for a while, letting the warmth of the water soak into her hands as she stared out of the kitchen window. Her head dropped, and her shoulder length, blonde hair fell forward on to her face; she allowed it to remain like that, shielding the tears that were changing her blue eyes to grey. Anna felt strangely at odds with herself, and the rest of the world on this early spring morning, and didn't really know what to do about it.

It was while she was washing Ray's mug – the one proclaiming him to be a Sheffield Wednesday supporter– that she had her Damascus moment.

Anna wanted to be alone. She wanted to make her own decisions, pay her own bills, and vacuum her own carpet. And wash her own dishes.

Her first tiny act of rebellion was to leave the dishes to drain. Ray always insisted they be dried immediately, or the dishwasher be emptied before going to bed.

Her second act was to go into the office and switch on the computer. This in itself wasn't an act of rebellion as she used it every day to manage the business – but she had never used it to look for her own accommodation before. There were many estate agents in the Lincoln area, and she automatically entered "Lincoln Estate Agents" into the search engine, waiting patiently to see what it threw up.

3

She shook her head, going back to the beginning and entering "South Yorkshire Estate Agents." If she was to escape this existence, then her new existence had to be of her own making.

Many times in their married life they had ventured into God's own county, and it had captivated her. Maybe it was the flatness of the Lincolnshire countryside that had led her to appreciate the spectacular beauty of the rolling hills around Sheffield and the cragginess and bleakness of the Peak District on its doorstep. She knew her path lay in that direction.

Anna was quite stunned by the price of the accommodation on offer – so much cheaper than Lincolnshire, so much more property for the amount of money she had. It soon became clear she would be able to afford a three-bedroom house in Sheffield but only a tent in the Peak District.

She had a significant amount of money from the sale of her childhood home following her parents' deaths, and Ray had decided they should save it for buying a *gîte* in France for their retirement. Well, she was retiring right now from this marriage; decision made.

Her face, attractive even at this pre-make up hour of the morning, became animated as she rang a few of the estate agents. She made appointments covering the next couple of days before ringing Charlie, her long-time friend. Charlie lived in Doncaster, with her huge bear of a husband, his two children from an earlier marriage, and three dogs. Anna guessed Charlie would be shocked when she learned of her plans, but shocked or not, she suspected she would stand by her and totally support her.

'Hey you! Couldn't you sleep?' Charlie's voice lifted her spirits.

'Hey you. It's not that early is it?' Anna glanced at the clock. 'Oh my God, Charlie. It's only half past eight! Have I woken you?'

Charlie laughed. 'No, you haven't. I just don't normally get telephone calls at this time in a morning.'

'Well, I needed to talk. So sorry, but I'm not really. Have you got a spare bedroom for a night?'

'Always. When do you want it?'

'Tonight. Don't worry if you can't. I realise it's short notice.'

'Anna, I can always put you in the shed if we haven't got a room.'

They both laughed. Dan's shed was glorious but far from hotel accommodation.

'Thank you. It's just me.'

'Good.'

'Good?'

There was a brief pause. 'I meant it would be lovely to see you on your own. We can have a good catch up.'

'Charlie...' Anna counted to three and chickened out of saying anything further about her decision. 'I'll be there around midday. That OK?'

'Looking forward to it. See you later.'

It was while Anna was sitting on the settee in her oh so perfect lounge – a side effect of owning a building company – that it dawned on her what issues were already starting to accumulate. She picked up her small mirror and smoothed the moisturiser on to her skin. The action was automatic, something she did every day. Ray expected it of her. She put the rest of her make-up back in the zipped purse and thought, *Sod it.*

The first of the issues was the children would not be best pleased. Mark, living some distance away in Leicester, now seemed to be quite removed, not just in miles. Jenny, his wife, had cooled her relationship with them, and they saw very little of Adam and Grace. She didn't think for one minute Jenny would be bothered about a Ray/Anna parting of the ways; her frostiness since she had married Mark had always disturbed Anna, but Ray had shrugged it off saying it was just her imagination. However, Jenny had been almost as much a daughter as Caroline, prior to the wedding day, and at times it really concerned her that they rarely spoke. Mark, however, her first born twin, would probably arrive within a few hours to tell her how stupid she was being.

She was not stupid.

Tim, currently sharing his life with Steve in Florida, would be far more laid back about it. He, too, was a long way removed from them, yet her heart ached for him at odd moments, and she knew if he actually turned against her, she would be devastated.

And then there was Caroline, her beautiful, scatter-brained, sensitive, loving daughter, who totally belonged to Ray. From the second she was born, he enfolded her into his soul, and she had willingly followed.

Anna had to send them letters. She would post them as soon as she had settled herself somewhere to counteract any possible manipulations by anyone, and then sit back and wait for the fall out that would have to come eventually. Telephone calls wouldn't do it; they would be too difficult.

If briefly occurred to Anna she was being cowardly, but so what? Suddenly, she realised just how much this new freedom could mean to her.

She could be a coward, she could be brave, or she could completely ignore all feelings.

But, she wasn't free to ignore these feelings yet. She had to plan.

Ray had a temper that frequently surfaced, and when it did, it was scary. Anna had never known him be abusive towards the children, partly because he worked long hours, and so didn't see too much of them in their younger years; yet, a number of episodes had occurred when she had seen, and felt, that anger.

Anna had always explained the bruises away by saying all the usual things – walking into a door, falling down stairs– classic phrases that anyone normal would have seen straight through.

She had stayed for the sake of the children, particularly Caroline. She had intended to leave Ray when the boys reached eighteen, but by that time, she had had their three-year-old daughter.

Having Caroline softened Ray, and he seemed to get the temper under control, but Anna had spent all their married life walking on eggshells. There was no doubt in her mind if she said she was leaving, he would lash out at the nearest thing - her.

So the sensible thing to do was to leave him a note, write to the kids, and eventually speak with Mark, Tim, and Caroline. She needed to disappear for a few weeks. She hoped Ray would get over his initial anger by then, and she could safely contact the children.

Except, they weren't children, were they? Caroline was now nineteen, and the twins were thirty-four years old. Not children; adults with homes and families of their own.

The cards on the window sill seemed to mock her thoughts. Anna glared at them, knowing she was being childish, and went upstairs to pack for the trip to Charlie's.

She left a note on the table for Ray. *Gone away for a couple of days, will contact soon.* She climbed into her Audi and left; Anna couldn't resist one final glance back at the house in her rear view mirror. The exultation hit her as she got on the A1, and she laughed aloud. She turned up the radio, listening as some woman from Birmingham tried to answer more Popmaster questions than another woman from Grimsby. Anna scored six on the first set of questions and nine on the second set, and felt in awe of Sarah from Grimsby with her score of twenty-four.

The packing of a bag had turned into packing three large suitcases. Anna knew with certainty she would never be returning. The original thought in her mind had been to spend a couple of days organising some sort of accommodation then returning home to finalise her plans, but she realised pretty quickly once she had left, nothing would bring her back. It wouldn't be safe to return.

Charlie's smile was wide as she opened the door and her arms. Her brown, curly hair was still wet from a recent shower, and her grey eyes creased at the corner as she smiled to welcome Anna. Anna hugged her and said, 'Hey, I scored nine on pop master.'

She laughed. 'Were the questions all on Rod Stewart hits?'

Anna gave her a small punch on the arm. 'Cheeky.'

Dan walked down the hall towards her. 'Yeah, if it isn't my favourite Lincolnshire yellow belly.' He was a huge man, warm and welcoming, and he held open his arms. His dark brown hair was tied back into a ponytail, so she guessed he had been working in his shed prior to her arrival. The brown eyes scrutinised her face closely; she wondered if he saw the tiredness behind her eyes.

She reached up to kiss him, and his hug enveloped her. 'Come in, sweetheart,' he said. 'We can't stand on the doorstep all day. The neighbours will start talking.'

He picked up the small overnight bag. Upon entering, Anna was engulfed by the love and warmth emanating from their home. A beautiful quilt hung on the wall in the hall, and Anna couldn't resist touching it. The pattern was a wonderful melding of reds, creams, and greens, and toned effortlessly with the rich cream of the carpet.

Charlie was a textile artist, and their home reflected her love of fabric. She worked out of a studio at the end of the garden, and Anna envied her. Her own house was pristine. And boring. Charlie and Dan's detached property was a riot of colour and sensory feelings that she had never known. She would from now on – she had always been denied the opportunity to stamp her own ideas on their home. That would change.

The evening passed in such a carefree way, and she felt so relaxed – up to the point when her phone trilled out *Maggie May*. She cancelled the call and returned it to her bag without commenting on the caller; Ray.

Charlie raised her eyebrows and looked at her but said nothing. Anna casually lowered her hand into her bag and switched the phone to silent mode. She took the proffered mug of cocoa from Charlie's outstretched hand and cradled it.

Then, Charlie's landline rang.

Anna looked at her friend and gave a small shake of the head. Charlie nodded and pressed the answering button. There was a small pause as she listened to the caller, and she said, 'Ray! Lovely to hear from you.'

There was another moment of silence. 'Sorry, she's not here. If she turns up, I'll get her to ring you, but she normally rings before dropping in on us.'

There was a further hiatus. 'Bye Ray, if she contacts me, I'll let her know you were trying to find her.'

She disconnected the call, and, to her credit, asked no questions. Anna couldn't expect to get away with that for long.

Anna finished her cocoa, and stood. 'It's been a long day – I'll head off to bed now, I think.'

'Okay.' Charlie turned towards her. Her round face was made even rounder by the smile she directed at Anna. 'Oh, by the way, happy anniversary.'

She recognised this as Charlie speak for, 'We'll talk tomorrow,' and she simply nodded her head.

The bedroom was particularly cosy, decorated in greys of varying hues, with mint green accessories. The quilt was grey satin, with touches of white, and again Anna couldn't help but stroke it. Anna logged the colour combination into her brain; this would be the colour scheme for one of her bedrooms when she had a house.

She expected to lie awake into the early hours, but she read a couple of pages, switched off the bedside lamp, and drifted off to sleep.

Chapter 2
Tuesday 10 March 2015
Day Two

The sky was overcast next morning when she drew back the curtains, and Anna stood for a while gazing out of the window. Although she wasn't really aware of what she was doing, she was feeding thoughts into her brain of what she hoped to have in her new home. It felt strange to keep mentally pushing Ray to one side, and she knew she was kidding herself that this brave new life was going to simply be a matter of deciding it was what she was going to do, and everything would be hunky dory.

Anna walked into the kitchen and was surprised to find Charlie there on her own.

'Okay,' she said, 'time to talk.'

'It's not easy to begin a conversation when you don't know what to say,' Anna responded quietly.

'Talk,' she repeated.

'I've left him,' Anna said.

Charlie nodded slowly. 'Well, that's a start.'

Anna sat down at the round pine table, and Charlie handed her a mug of coffee.

Her brain turned to mush, and she ran her finger down the beaker, outlining the shape of the pig which decorated it.

'He let you walk away?'

'He doesn't know yet. I didn't know till nine o'clock yesterday morning. When I rang you, my plan was for just a couple of days away to see what I could do about accommodation, then go back home and sort stuff. But, really, that's not much of a possibility. If I go back, I'll never leave. I know I won't. So that's why I've arrived with all my worldly goods in the boot of the car.'

'Oh my god!'

'Look, don't worry,' she said to a shocked Charlie. Her eyes were like saucers. 'I won't be staying here tonight, so you won't be involved. Just keep telling him you haven't seen me.'

As if on cue, Charlie's phone rang. It was clear it was Ray. She was silent as she listened to him speak and then she said, 'Ray, stop worrying. I'm sure she'll be in touch today, and as I said last night, if I hear from her, I'll ask her to ring you.' There was another short lull in the conversation before she finished with, 'Okay, take care. Bye, Ray.'

Charlie stood with her back to Anna for a few moments then slowly turned around.

'You have to contact him. He's really worried.'

Anna stared into the cup of coffee, as if the pig beaker held all the answers. It didn't.

'Charlie, if he finds out where I am...'

'He'll hit you,' she said softly. 'Again.'

She nodded. She didn't think she could speak. Anna had clearly fooled herself when she assumed Charlie hadn't realised what Ray was capable of.

'I've always known,' she said. 'Why do you think we're lying for you, covering for you now? And before you ask, yes, Dan knows as well.'

Charlie put an arm around Anna's shoulders and squeezed. 'Tell us what you want us to do.'

*****

The estate agent led Anna from one room to another, explaining everything she needed to know. The apartment was in the centre of Sheffield and available to rent. It overlooked the river, had its own balcony, and she absolutely loved it. The master bedroom was really large and even the second bedroom would comfortably take a double bed. The lounge was huge and open plan; Anna loved the kitchen that formed part of the large space. The shower room was off the entrance hallway, and the whole thing was perfect for her. They stood out on the balcony, watching the sun break through the murkiness, and she breathed a sigh of contentment.

'I want this one. No doubt at all. I liked the other one you showed me, but this is higher up the building, and I love the view, the peace – oh everything. When would I be able to move in?'

He smiled at her enthusiasm. 'I knew you'd like this one. You can be in here by next Monday, if we crack on with the paperwork. Will that suit you?'

'It most certainly will. Until then, I'll be staying at the Hilton, but you can reach me on my mobile phone. I can transfer any money you need back at your office. And if you can make it quicker...'

Anna shook his hand and said, 'Let's go back inside.'

She checked into the Hilton for the night, and rang Charlie who informed her she hadn't heard any more from Ray. They spent half an hour chatting about the new apartment. Charlie was a little bit stunned by Anna taking on a property so quickly, but she explained it was only a six month let, as she intended on looking for a house to buy during those six months.

'Anna,' Charlie laughed. 'You've turned into a bit of a whirling dervish. This isn't the Anna we know and love, this is someone else! You amaze me.'

'It had to be done.'

'Absolutely,' was Charlie's response. 'But, I think you're living in a parallel universe, if you think everything's going to be this easy. There's a small matter of the husband, to say nothing of three assorted kids...'

Anna laughed. 'Not really kids, Charlie.'

'They're your kids, and always will be. Age is irrelevant.'

She sighed. 'I know. Just give me tonight to feel giddy about this new home, and I'll tackle the problems tomorrow.'

'You'll ring Ray?'

'Yes.'

'Promise?'

'Promise.'

Anna rang off and studied the room service menu before ordering a sandwich and a drink. She wasn't hungry, but felt she should eat something – she really didn't want to wake in the middle of the night absolutely ravenous.

Her thoughts turned to Ray, and she wondered what he was thinking. Her note had been ambiguous, and he was bound to be feeling out of control – a new sensation for him.

Anna's feelings, however, were of being very much in control. She felt a growing sense of freedom which was in part scary and in part so exciting she kept giggling. She had experienced two days of escapism and liked it.

Chapter 3
Wednesday 11 March 2015
Day Three

The next morning, Anna went down to breakfast, taking an hour to eat, drink coffee, and relax. She checked in with Charlie, and found out Ray had rung around eight o'clock, and told Charlie he wasn't going to work until he had heard from her.

Control, control, control.

Anna booked for four more nights at the hotel to take her through Sunday night for a Monday morning check out, and went for a walk around the city centre. There was nothing she could do to help along the apartment – it had all been set in motion. She bought some jeans, a couple of tops, and some sandals. And a kettle.

Anna got back to the Hilton after four, utterly exhausted and needing a sleep. There were a lot of shops in Sheffield. She stood the kettle on the desk and recognised it for what it was – a symbol of the new life she was planning, and her first purchase for her new home. And then, to her surprise and utter delight, the room telephone rang; she had asked the estate agent to contact her at the Hilton rather than on her mobile phone as she knew she would miss it. He confirmed everything was going through, and she could collect the keys from them Friday lunchtime.

*****

Promise. The word reverberated in her head, and she knew she had to ring Ray. Her palms felt sweaty as she dug out the silenced mobile phone from the bottom of her bag. There were fifteen missed calls, mostly from Ray, but two were from Caroline and two from Mark. What was the most surprising were the two calls from Jenny, Mark's wife.

It took her five long minutes of holding the phone in her hand before she pressed the call button. He answered immediately.

'Where the fucking hell are you?'

She disconnected and lay down on the bed, shaking. It wasn't just her palms sweating now. Her phone lit up almost immediately with a call, and she left it to go through to voicemail. The next time she looked at it, there was a text. She opened it and read, 'RING ME.'

Anna buried the phone under the pillow. *Not on your life, pal, not on your life.*

She slept fitfully, not because she was hungry, but because she knew she had to face a new day, and the problems it would bring. For too many years she had been scared of Ray, even extending to having contact with him over the telephone. What she really found so worrying and frustrating was the fact nobody else had seen this side of him, this bullying, egotistical monster. Except Charlie and Dan, it seemed.

It was around four in the morning Anna realised maybe she had unwittingly put them in the middle of the catastrophe, just by being friends with them. She had no doubt Ray would turn up on their doorstep at some point, convinced she was staying with them. Anna had to protect them by telling him she was staying in a hotel, but she daren't mention Sheffield. She would be too easy to track down. She could make some throw away remark about Newark and staying in a pub. Hopefully, that would give her a few days' grace, before Ray realised he wasn't going to find her.

Chapter 4
Thursday, 12 March 2015
Day Four

Anna rang Ray at seven o'clock the next morning. She kept it brief, trying to remain in control, but it was hard. She told him she had left him, and it was for good. She let slip she was only half an hour away from him, so if there was an emergency she could easily be reached. He just had to text her with the problem. Anna said she would let him know the name of her solicitor, and that it wasn't a separation; she wanted a divorce.

Anna held the phone away from her ear as his language grew stronger and stronger, and his voice heightened in volume. Apparently, she was a fucking whore, and he wanted to know the name of the man she had run off with. He was going to stop her credit cards, stop their joint account from being accessed by her, and generally make life so impossible she would crawl back to him.

Anna let him rant on, and when he had finished, she laughed and disconnected. He obviously hadn't checked the balance of the joint account, her two credit cards were both in her name only, and the money from the sale of her childhood home was firmly in her own name, along with her wages from the business she had earned and not touched for the past fifteen years.

Did she need him? No, she didn't!

Anna felt so much better as she tucked into a full English breakfast. She decided it was amazing what a difference a good argument could make to your life, especially one you've won. Over coffee, she considered what to do next. Anna felt she should ring Mark, but knew how he would be with her; she needed space from him. The more worrying issue was the two missed calls from Jenny, his wife.

Jenny was a quiet, young woman, although Anna recalled when Mark had first introduced her to his parents, she hadn't seemed quiet then. She was a happy-go-lucky person, full of laughter, but it seemed, after they married, she had assumed a mantle of responsibility which, in some way, had squashed the spontaneity. Initially, she had shared a fantastic relationship with her son's girlfriend, and when that became a stronger partnership, Anna's own feelings towards Jenny deepened. But, marriage had changed her, and now Anna didn't feel particularly close to her daughter-in-law; Jenny always kept her distance, which was why the two missed calls puzzled her. She could only assume Mark had asked Jenny to contact her, to try pressure from all angles.

Charlie rang just after eight o'clock. 'He doesn't believe you're in Newark,' she said, as Anna answered the phone.

'What?'

'He doesn't believe you. He was here last night, pacing up and down, convinced you would be coming back here.'

'God, Charlie, I'm so sorry.'

'Don't worry about us, you just take care. In the end, Dan had a word with him, and virtually threw him out, but he's not giving up on you.'

'Right, I've only tonight in this hotel – I can have the key to my new address tomorrow afternoon. Then, he won't be able to find me. I'm vulnerable for the next twenty-four hours or so. I'll pack up my car Friday morning and leave here by nine, straight after breakfast. I'll go down to reception now and make sure they tell no one I am here, and then I've only got today to worry about. I'll have a drive out into Derbyshire for the day. I'm safe once I've left here, and I'm in my own place. I'll text you the address; you'll be the only one who knows it.'

'Just take care, and keep away from us for a couple of weeks. I'll come and see you Monday, if that's okay? You should be well settled by then, if you're having the key tomorrow.'

'That would be lovely. And once again, Charlie, I am so sorry you've become entangled in all this.'

She laughed. 'Oh, it's a pleasure, believe me.'

Anna went down to reception and explained she didn't want anyone to know she was there. She changed her booking to just that night, and told the receptionist she would be leaving fairly early the following morning. The information was logged into the computer, and Anna felt instantly at ease. She checked her silenced phone before she went out and was quite startled to see, yet again, Jenny had rung twice.

Maybe she would have to ring her. She somehow felt Jenny wouldn't be as censorious as she expected Mark and Caroline to be – perhaps she would even understand.

Today would be Jenny day – she would ring while out in Derbyshire, decision made.

Bakewell was beautiful in the early morning, spring sunshine. Anna walked along the river, watching children feeding the ducks and listening to parents exhorting them not to go too near the edge, remembering all the times they had been there as a family, first with the boys and then with Caroline. She loved Bakewell, with its quaint shops and general ambience. She walked around for quite some time before heading to a pub to have a meal.

Anna had bought more items for her new home and placed them all carefully on the seat next to her. The barman brought her lunch over and knocked one of the bags which fell to the floor. They laughed together as they picked up the assorted goods and replaced them in the bag. She grinned at him and said, 'Thank you,' before stacking the bag a bit more carefully.

That was the last laughter for some time.

After she had eaten, Anna took out her phone and stared at it for a while before going into favourites and pressing for the connection to Jenny. She answered immediately, giving Anna the impression she had been sat with her phone in her hand, waiting.

'Anna. I have to see you.'

'Jenny? That was quick! I'm sorry I've...'

'Anna. Stop talking and listen. I have to see you. Just me. Not Mark, not the children. Just me. Where are you?'

Anna faltered. 'Jenny, I can't tell anyone where I am. Ray...'

'I know. Anna, I'm on your side. I'll drive up now. Or, if you really don't want me to know where you are, we could both set off driving and meet somewhere in the middle. Whatever way we do it, I have to see you. Adam and Grace are with my mum and dad, and Mark is in Lincoln with Ray, so no one will know I'm meeting you. Anna, it's important. Please.'

She heard anguish in Jenny's tone and knew she had very little choice. This all felt so strange – they spoke very rarely, and whenever they did speak, it was quite impersonal. There was real emotion in the younger woman's voice, a vulnerability, and Anna stood. She said quietly she would go outside to finish the call, and Jenny made a small sound, almost like a sob.

'Jenny, please don't cry,' Anna whispered. 'Look, I will meet with you. What about Trowell Services on the M1? Have you eaten lunch? Can you set off straight away?'

'Anna, I haven't eaten since we got the news about you and Ray. But, I will grab a sandwich and eat it as I'm driving. We'll meet up in the coffee shop. Is that okay?'

Anna felt utterly flustered, and anxiety hung over her like a pall.

'That's fine, Jenny. And drive carefully. I'll see you soon.'

She moved quickly to the car park, and was soon on her way. Anna filled up with petrol in Bakewell and headed for the motorway.

*****

Anna arrived at Trowell first and went in to get a coffee while she looked for her daughter-in-law.

She didn't have long to wait; Jenny walked through the doors and spotted her immediately. She hurried across and held Anna closely for several long moments.

'Hey,' Anna chided gently. 'We can talk properly now. But, I do have to tell you that nothing you can say will make me go back to Ray,' she added, looking closely at Jenny, 'I don't think that's why you're here though, is it?'

She shook her head. 'No, it isn't. I'm here to talk to you, to have the most difficult conversation I'll ever have in my life, but I do have to do this. I'll go get us two fresh coffees.'

Anna watched her walk over to the counter and was struck anew by how pretty she was. Her long, blonde hair glowed, and she had a wonderful figure, despite having given birth to two babies. Her face, however, looked haunted; something was very wrong in her daughter-in-law's life. Anna hoped it wasn't anything to do with Mark. Her mind was careering madly through so many possibilities – an affair, domestic abuse, maybe even something wrong with one of the children.

She most certainly wasn't prepared for the truth when it finally spilled out of Jenny.

*****

Jenny carefully placed the two coffees on the table and sat down. Anna waited for her to speak, but the silence lengthened.

'You're starting to frighten me, Jenny. Tell me what's wrong. Whatever it is, I'm sure we can sort it.' Platitudes. And they both knew it was platitudes.

Jenny carefully lifted her mug to her mouth and then sat back in her chair.

'Anna, I promise never to suggest you return to Ray and it goes without saying I'll never disclose we've met, or divulge where you're living.'

'You don't know where I'm living,' she smiled. The tone of her voice was stilted and formal, and Anna's smile was meant to ease the situation.

'I will do,' she said.

'Jenny...'

She stood and muttered 'toilet' before moving quickly through the coffee bar. When she returned, she was clutching a bottle of water.

'Sorry,' she said. 'I've been sick.'

'Are you okay?'

'I'm not ill, just my stomach reacting to what I'm about to do, I think.'

She took a sip of the water and pushed her hot drink to one side.

'Okay, Anna. I need you to listen and wait until the end before we speak. I want you to think back to before Mark and I married, to when we bought that little flat in Lincoln. It needed a fair bit of work doing to it, and Ray did all the plastering, joinery, and such like for us. I did most of the decorating, because Mark was working away, and it gave me something to focus on while I waited for him to come home each weekend.'

She paused momentarily, clearly gathering her thoughts. Anna said nothing, just nodded. They were good memories. Those were the days of carefree laughter, paint splashes, love. Mainly love.

'A week before the wedding, I took a day off work to finish painting the bedroom walls, the last job needing to be done. I finished in the middle of the afternoon, and went to have a shower before heading home to Mum's. I walked into the lounge with just a towel around me, and Ray was there.'

This time, the pause wasn't momentary. It seemed to go on forever, and Anna reached across and touched her hand.

'Jenny?'

'He raped me, Anna. He fucking raped me.'

Anna felt a fog descend over her, and the hubbub of the coffee shop faded away. All sound stopped.

*****

'Anna! Anna!' Jenny's voice, frantic and urgent, broke through everything. Anna was on the floor, with a small crowd looking down at her.

'She'll be fine now,' Jenny said to the onlookers. 'She just fainted from the heat. Can we give her some space?'

The people started to move away once they understood she really only had fainted, and not died. She looked at Jenny's concerned expression and almost wished it had been death. What she had to face now was not going to be good.

'Can we go to the car?' Anna whispered, as she spotted a member of staff bustling over with a 'first aider' look on her face. Jenny nodded and helped her to stand. She felt woozy but tried to hide it as 'Sue, first aider' arrived.

They both reassured her Anna was okay, and they slowly left the building and headed for Anna's car.

'Right,' she said. 'Questions. Did you tell Mark?' She hesitated before throwing any other queries at her. 'Forget the rest for the moment, because if you had told Mark, everyone's world would have imploded.'

Jenny's face was etched with misery. 'I couldn't tell Mark. How many lives would have been destroyed, if I had? I would have lost him for sure, because we would never have been the same people again. I love Mark with everything I have, and I knew I could never tell him. And Ray knew that as well.

And then, there was you. I felt so close to you, Anna, and I would have lost you along with everything else I hold dear. Oh, I know I wouldn't have been held responsible, but my life would have changed so much it really wouldn't have been worth living.'

Anna reached out, and once again, took her hand. 'So you married Mark and found some sort of happiness.'

'Total happiness,' she emphasised. 'I steered him towards a job in Leicester so we very rarely saw Ray — it backfired, of course, because as a family, we hardly see you and my parents. But, Mark enjoys his job, I enjoy my work at the library, and the children are happy at school.'

Jenny opened her bag and took out a packet of tissues. She held one to her eyes for a while, and then turned to look at her mother-in-law. 'It happened just that once, Anna, and if you had stayed with him, it would have remained dormant forever.'

Anna waited.

Jenny screwed up the tissue and stuffed it into her sleeve. 'I thought you loved him. I couldn't hurt you by telling you, but everything's changed now. Now, I can tell you, but only you.'

'I don't understand. Why can you talk now and not then? Surely it will still spoil things between you two just as much as it would have then? And now there are the children...'

'I'm not going to tell Mark. I love him, I love the kids, and I love my life. But, I have to tell you, because we can help each other.'

Anna stared at her. Her brain felt disconnected. She had no idea what Jenny was talking about. How on Earth could she help her, if she didn't want Mark to know? Did she just want her as a confidante? Someone to talk it over with, because she had never been able to do that?

Jenny stared straight ahead, her mouth set in a straight line.

'I'll need you to alibi me, Anna, when I kill him.'

Chapter 5
Thursday Evening, 12 March 2015
Day Four

Anna stared at Jenny for what seemed like hours but was actually only seconds. Jenny's grey eyes turned towards her, the beautiful face emotionless.

'What did you just say?' Anna asked slowly.

Jenny repeated the words, and Anna reached for the door handle without speaking. She left Jenny inside the car and stumbled across the car park towards a refuse bin. She leaned on it, taking in great gulps of air. How could her life be falling apart quite so spectacularly? She didn't hear Jenny walking towards her, and was shocked to feel a hand touch her shoulder.

'Anna,' she said softly. 'There's more.'

'More?' Anna heard the pitch of her voice increase. How could there be more? This woman wanted to kill her husband! Just what did she consider to be 'more' than that?

'Come back to the car.' She gently led Anna across the car park. Anna's car had always been her haven; the luxury of it usually engulfed and comforted her. All that had now changed.

She sat in the driving seat and leaned on the steering wheel, too afraid to say anything. Her head was pounding, and she knew it was as a result of the words Jenny had spoken, clearly actions Anna had thought about for a long time. No wonder communication with Jenny had been, at best, sporadic.

She lifted her head and looked at Jenny. 'What do you mean? You said there's more.'

She nodded. 'Much more. Adam... Adam was born exactly nine months after our wedding.'

'No.' Anna heard the weakness in her own voice, felt the tremble in her limbs.

'Yes.'

'But…'

'Anna, listen to me. Within two weeks of Adam's birth, I had already sent off a DNA test. Clare, as you know, works at the laboratory. Sisters can be pretty useful in times of great stress. Although, to be fair, she didn't know who she was testing; she thought it was a friend of mine from the antenatal group. She used a toothbrush from Ray, a glass Mark had drunk from, and a regular swab from Adam that I took. The results were almost as I had suspected. They showed, without any shadow of a doubt, Adam's grandfather was really his father. However, what they also showed was absolutely no connection, no connection at all, between the DNA samples on the toothbrush, and on the glass.'

The silence in the car was deafening.

'So, Anna,' Jenny said. 'Just who is the father of Mark and Tim? It sure as hell isn't Ray Carbrook.'

'Of course they're Ray's children.'

It was said with desperation, and she not only heard it in her voice, she felt it in her heart. Her heart, which had broken many years ago when she and Michael took the decision to end their relationship. She stayed with Ray; Michael lived his life with his wife, newly diagnosed with multiple sclerosis.

If Anna had suspected her twins really belonged to another man, she had chosen to quash the idea. It was the only way to stay sane. She was very good at burying her head in the sand, and that was exactly what she did when she discovered she was pregnant. Buried it into the sand twice, to be exact, as it had proved to be a twin pregnancy.

However, it now appeared sand dunes and ostriches were completely out of the equation. She stared at Jenny and hoped the turmoil in her brain didn't reflect on her face. She knew it did.

Jenny smiled. 'Don't worry. I'll keep your secret. However, it does beg the question who the real grandfather of Adam and Grace is, and it gave me some comfort to know the person I thought was Adam's father, as well as grandfather, is merely relegated to father.'

Anna wanted to laugh, not in humour, but in terror. She didn't know how to respond; she couldn't share her secret with anyone.

Jenny put her arm around Anna and held her close. 'I know you've had a shock. Look, it won't be safe for either of us to drive home tonight. It's a long way, and our minds will be on anything but the road. There's a Travelodge over there. Let's go book in, and we can have a meal and discuss what happens next.'

*****

The room was comfortable – they had opted to share one – and Anna curled up on her bed and let her thoughts roam. She had started something big, something already out of control, the day she walked out on Ray. And yet, deep down in her heart, she didn't regret it. She was starting to live, to see what freedom could be like. And she had bought a kettle!

Jenny had a shower, and Anna thought how terrified she must have been that afternoon after her shower in the flat. Terrified of Ray, terrified of losing Mark, just terrified.

And she had paid for that. Her whole life was one long secret only Anna knew; no wonder she wanted to kill him. Or said she did.

Anna sat up with a jerk as the earlier conversation flowed over her. Alibi. Murder. She knew Jenny hadn't really meant it, but even so, they were harsh words to say. One thing she did know, there was definitely no way she ever wanted to even be in the same room as that monster, let alone be married to him.

Anna fell back on to the bed and buried her head under the pillow. The tears came quickly, silently; she felt a hand touch her arm. 'Crying doesn't work. I've cried so many tears over that man. I hope you're just crying for yourself, and not for him.'

Anna shook her head. 'No, not for him. As a matter of fact, I think they're tears of relief. Jenny, tomorrow I move into my new flat, start my new life. When do you have to be home?'

'The children are away until Sunday. Mark is staying with his father for a few days while they look for you, and although he phones me, he's no idea where I am. The beauty of mobile phones,' she said with a laugh, and once again, for a fleeting moment, Anna saw the softness of the girl she had met all those years ago.

'Then come back with me. I'll tell you all you need to know, but not tonight. I feel drained, and I need my head straight. You'll be able to see my new home and know where I am, but I will be trusting you completely. If Ray ever finds me, I won't survive it.' Her words felt stark, but Jenny recognised and acknowledged the truth in them.

'He'll never find out from me. I owe him nothing,' she said simply.

They had a meal of sorts. Neither of them felt much like eating. They briefly put on the television, but by mutual consent, switched it off after the news and settled down for the night.

Anna didn't sleep much. Jenny's revelations had shaken her and things she had thought strange now became all too clear.

Anna had always known Ray was a violent man. She'd never suspected for one minute he was a rapist as well.

Chapter 6
Friday, 13 March 2015
Day Five

They got up at six, and were on the motorway back to Sheffield by 6.30, Jenny following her all the way. They drove straight to the Hilton, where they packed everything from Anna's room into her car, and went down to check out.

She thanked the receptionist and turned to pick up her bag. She heard Jenny ask about the availability of a room for that night, and she stopped her. 'You'll stay with me,' Anna said. 'We will manage somehow.'

The receptionist smiled. 'Just so that you know,' she said, 'we're always busy Friday and Saturday nights during the football season. Tomorrow is a home game for Sheffield Wednesday, so we will be extra busy, especially as they're playing Fulham. We get fans staying who don't want to drive back to London after the match. Let me know as early as possible if you do want a room.'

Anna felt sick. She hadn't considered the possibility of bumping into Ray by accident. She couldn't imagine him missing the match – he hadn't missed one all season.

'Jenny, let's get out of here.'

Realisation had hit Jenny at the same time. Mark was also a big Wednesday fan, although now lived too far away to see many matches, but they might just take advantage of being so close and decide the match was a must. Ray had stayed over a couple of times after matches when he had been entertaining colleagues, and he might decide to do the same for Mark.

They got in the car and looked at each other. 'He won't come until tomorrow, I'm sure. But, he might stay over. We need to stay indoors tomorrow, except for between two and five,' Anna said with a grin. She didn't feel like grinning, and she knew Jenny knew that.

'It's all very well you saying, 'stay with you,' but have you actually got a bed, any furniture at all?'

'I've got a kettle.' Anna put the car in gear.

*****

They finally got into Anna's new home just before one o'clock. They'd picked up emergency supplies such as tea, coffee, and milk (along with biscuits and other essentials), and Anna breathed a sigh of relief as she walked through her own front door.

She unpacked the kettle and gave it pride of place on her new kitchen work surface. 'Beautiful,' she said, and gave it a quick stroke.

Jenny was impressed. She wandered from room to room, and then eventually on to the balcony overlooking the river below.

'I love it,' she said. 'And thank you for allowing me to see it. I'll keep your secret, I promise. One day, you'll move back into Lindum Lodge, but until that day comes, this is you. I just know you're going to enjoy your stay here. And just ignore the fact it's Friday the 13th.' Jenny laughed as she came back into the lounge.

Jenny's reference to the home she had shared with Ray for so many years made Anna shiver. She would never go back there. That was her old life; she had walked away from that.

They unpacked the inflatable camping beds and sleeping bags they had bought and set up their beds for the night. Anna would go out on Monday – when the Sheffield Wednesday match was a dim and distant memory of two days – and order two beds, a king size for her room and a double for the smaller room, because she had a feeling this wouldn't be Jenny's only visit. But, for now, they would manage on camping beds.

They had sandwiches in their makeshift camp site for lunch, and unpacked the various bits and bobs she had bought in Bakewell before her world changed completely. Not only had Jenny flattened that world, she had made her friendship with Charlie and Dan into something different, because she knew she could never pass such a huge secret on to Charlie. It was Jenny's secret, not hers, and she could never betray that trust.

The flat already had carpets, curtains, and blinds, and by the time they had put everything away and set up their camping chairs, it almost looked cosy. They discussed what sort of lounge furniture Anna would buy, how to position it to get the maximum effect of the sun through the balcony doors, and then ordered a takeaway pizza for their evening meal.

It was while they were eating, Jenny said, 'Okay, now talk.'

Anna lost her appetite instantly.

She felt a shudder go through her, but she knew she had to tell Jenny something – her children had a different grandfather to the one she thought they had, up to that disastrous DNA result.

And Adam had a double whammy – he had a different father, as well as a different grandfather. Tangled webs...

Anna put down her pizza and turned to her. 'I met Ray, as you already know, when we were in our mid-teens, and we fell in love. We got engaged and arranged our wedding for two years later. We didn't have the money then that we have now, and it took a lot of hard saving. I took a second job as a cleaner to get a bit of extra money, and that was when I met Michael. He was about ten years older than me, married, with a child, who was about three at that time. His wife was a stay at home mother, but subject to bouts of illness, so they employed me to go in three times a week to do the cleaning. I actually enjoyed the job. It was a lovely house, and I saw a lot of Michael who worked from home. He was an accountant. One day, we started talking, and we never really stopped after that. We told each other everything, talking together was such a huge part of our relationship. And gradually, we fell in love.'

She paused for a moment and looked at Jenny. Her face didn't change; she was waiting for Anna to continue.

'The awful part of it was I still loved Ray as well. I was torn. Michael was so gentle with me, so loving, and Ray was exciting. And then, about a month before the wedding, Michael's wife was diagnosed with multiple sclerosis.'

Anna stopped speaking again while she remembered the awful day Michael had told her, and they made their decision to leave each other.

'We made love one last time, and I never went back to his home. They had carers in to look after her, and a cleaning company took on the work I had been doing. A month after Ray and I got married, I realised I was pregnant. In those days, dates couldn't be pinpointed with any degree of accuracy, not like today, and as I was carrying twins anyway, the date was pot luck, because twins tend to come early. I lived my life allocating those babies to Ray, not Michael. I never saw him again. I saw an obituary, when his wife eventually died, but I left well alone and didn't contact him. Then, a couple of years later, I saw he had died, leaving an only daughter. I can only assume it was cancer that took him, because the death notice asked for donations to cancer research. He will always be very special to me, but we made our choices many years ago.'

'And that's it? Did Ray never suspect?'

'I don't think so. He knew I had the second job, obviously, because it paid for our honeymoon, but I never let it come into our life. I have to say, Jenny, I regret not being with Michael. I believe, in your life, there is always one person who is so totally right for you. Michael was my soul mate, in every way, just as I believe you and Mark have both found exactly the right person.

'I gave my right person up and lived a life of being bullied, being scared, but being even more scared of leaving him. Ray was a good father, but a lousy husband, and I gave up my happiness really for the sake of my three children. They never went without anything, had amazing educations, and, more than all that, they loved their father. I felt I didn't have the right to jeopardise any of that.

'But, now, it's my time, and those ridiculous anniversary cards were the absolute catalyst, final straw, call it what you will. When I divorce him, I know I will have to see him, but that will be the only time. The thought of that makes me feel so sick, but there will be other people there, and I will be safe. I'll take Dan with me,' she finished with a laugh.

Silence permeated the room, until Jenny spoke.

'Don't divorce him, Anna. You won't need to. Trust me on this. I'll get Lindum Lodge back for you, you see if I don't.'

She held up a hand as Anna started to speak.

'Sssh. You don't need to know anything yet. Just don't do anything about a divorce. Might even be a good idea to let Mark, Tim, and Caroline know there's half a chance you'll go back to him, once you've had some breathing space. They will pass any information like that on to Ray. It will get him off your back for a bit, if he thinks that all he has to do is lay low for a while, and you'll run back with your tail between your legs. Are you okay for money? Has he stopped your cards?'

Anna laughed. 'I reckon I have more than half a million he can't touch, but he doesn't really know about that. It's all in my name. The only thing he does know about is I emptied the joint account simply by transferring the balance into my account, so he thinks I've got maybe £5000 from that, plus the money from the sale of Mum and Dad's house. I'm fine as far as money goes.'

'Good. I couldn't really have helped, because Mark would have seen money leaving our accounts and going to you.

But, you have my support in every other way. Ray is a bastard, and finally, he's going to pay for that.'

*****

They sat in their less than comfortable camping chairs for quite some time before moving into their respective bedrooms on their makeshift camping beds. Anna tossed and turned through most of the night, and heard Jenny get up to make a drink around three o'clock. Her mind was whirling.

There was sense in Jenny's advice about letting Ray think she might go back to him – it would take the pressure away, and he would just sit back with that sanctimonious smile on his face, waiting for her to scuttle back. She would have to contact Mark ostensibly, just for a chat, to explain what she was doing, and Mark would go straight to his father to tell him.

She would also have to talk to Caroline. Her daughter would always take Ray's side, but she still needed to tell her why she had left.

And then there was Tim. Her Tim. Of all her children, she had felt closest to him. She had taken a nasty beating from Ray when she had supported Tim during the dark days of him telling them he was homosexual. Ray had always found it difficult to believe any son of his could be gay, but all Anna cared about was Tim's happiness. She presumed he found it hard to tell them, because he knew what Ray's reaction would be, but she had guessed anyway. Anna felt she needed Tim now. She must contact him in Florida and just talk. She suspected Ray wouldn't have bothered telling him, but Mark might have rung him, and she knew Tim would be waiting for her call.

She mentally made a list of things to do through that long night, laughing at herself for thinking, at first, she could send them a letter. She had to speak to all of them and soon. Finally, around 3 am, Anna dropped off to sleep.

Chapter 7
Saturday, 14 March 2015
Day Six

Anna awoke to the smell of bacon sandwiches and coffee. Jenny stood by the side of her bed, holding a paper bag and a mug.

'Breakfast!'

'Where…?'

'Go down to the ground floor, out of the building, and turn right, then right again. There's a little café that does breakfasts. I got us bacon sandwiches and have made coffee. Come on, time to get up.'

It had been a long night, and the coffee and food went some way towards putting her head back in order. They stayed in the flat until after two o'clock, and then they drove out of the city centre until they found a retail park. Anna bought a television and stand, a laptop, a printer, an iron, a toaster, and sundry items all from the same retailer. They laughed when the sales assistants escorted them back to the car and loaded it all into the boot. A big tick for that electrical retailer! She also ordered a washing machine and fridge freezer, which they were more than happy to deliver and install for free.

And she also bought a fish tank. Throughout their entire married life, Ray had steadfastly refused to allow pets of any sort – one day, Anna and the boys returned from a trip to the local fair with a goldfish in a plastic bag. They stopped at the pet shop and bought a bowl, setting it up before Ray arrived home. They called the fish Eric, mainly because it reminded Anna of a special day she had spent with Michael. He had had a magnificent tropical fish tank with what seemed to be hundreds of fish. He had laughingly said he had named them all so she pointed to one and asked what it was called. He said

Eric. She pointed to another and asked its name. He said Eric. And a third, and a fourth. He had called them all Eric, to save confusion, he said.

When Ray came home, he scooped the fish out of the bowl, squashed it, and flushed it away down the toilet. He emptied the bowl and threw that in the bin. Pets were never mentioned again after that. So, now, Anna had an all singing, all dancing fish tank, with a wonderful lighting system, and next week, she'd have a fish!

The frivolity and happiness surrounding spending money on new items lasted until they arrived back at the flat, and reality hit them again. She had enjoyed her time with Jenny, and, really, it was the first time she had enjoyed her company since the day she married Mark. She was seeing a softer Jenny; unburdening herself had been good for her. However, she had to go back home the next day, and Anna knew she would be truly on her own then. Charlie was meeting her on Monday, but Anna now had secrets, secrets she had promised would stay with her.

They connected the television; a smart piece of equipment which had a built in DVD player and looked really good standing in the corner. Jenny scrutinised the room.

'I quite envy you,' she said quietly. 'This could almost be fun, if the situation ...' she broke off with a catch in her breath.

Anna moved across to her and held her. 'Jenny, you're not on your own any more. Now, there are two of us, and we can speak any time.'

'I know.' Anna felt Jenny sag against her. 'You have no idea how good it feels just to tell somebody, to acknowledge to myself that I needed to talk about it. I'll never be able to speak with Mark about it; it would be the end of my marriage, even if we stayed together. I've kept it to myself for too long, and I don't think Mark would ever see beyond that.'

'Jenny, it doesn't matter who the genetic father is. Mark is Adam's dad. Just as a matter of interest, did Ray never suspect...?'

She shook her head. 'I don't think so, but I've never spoken to Ray since that day. He rang quite a lot after Mark and I got back from honeymoon, but all his calls to my phone are now blocked. The ability to block calls is a wonderful thing,' she added with a smile.

They had a pleasant evening listening to the radio, feeling somewhat let down by the Saturday night viewing on the television, and were both in bed by ten o'clock. Anna slept better than the previous night, and Jenny was ready to leave by eight o'clock the next morning.

Chapter 8
Sunday, 15 March 2015
Day Seven

Anna went down to the car park with Jenny, and they hugged. 'Don't despair, Jenny,' she whispered as she held her daughter-in-law. 'We'll get through this.'

Jenny climbed into the driver's seat of her little silver Fiesta, closed the door, and lowered the window. 'Thank you for listening, Anna. And I'll leave you to see to the smoothing over of things. Start with Mark. He'll pass the message on to Ray, and Ray will back off. You will return to Lindum Lodge, when he's dead.'

She put the car into first gear and waved out of the open window as she drove off.

Anna felt sick. She absolutely loathed Ray with a passion, and deep down, she knew there would be no mourning if he was dead, but for heaven's sake! It had to be by natural causes, not by Jenny's hand!

She hadn't really believed for one minute Jenny meant it when she had said at Trowell she would need Anna to alibi her, but she wondered just how well she knew Jenny. When she first started seeing Mark, she had enjoyed getting to know her, but then it had been a very barren ten years, until this weekend.

Finally, Anna now knew why their friendship had deteriorated so spectacularly; limited to birthday and Christmas cards – oh, and anniversary cards. Anna wanted to bring her back, wanted to tell her not to do anything stupid. She had two children who loved her, and their upbringing and development was the most important thing. Hadn't she proved that? She gave up her freedom and her self-respect to make sure her children had the best possible start in life, and she desperately wanted Jenny to do the same and drop all thoughts of revenge.

Anna promised herself she would ring Jenny later, and then went back up in the lift and let herself into the apartment. She wanted to sort out furniture, but forced herself to put it on hold for a day. The football results had told them Sheffield Wednesday had drawn 1-1 against Fulham, and she suspected Ray and Mark would have stayed overnight in Sheffield to celebrate.

Wednesday had had a rocky season, and seemed to be finishing mid-table, but at least hadn't been battling relegation; she knew that would be cause for celebration in Ray's eyes. Anna couldn't take the risk of being spotted, so she stayed put. They had picked up a couple of store catalogues the day before, so she spent an hour or so reading through them, making a list of essentials, and thoroughly enjoying herself.

The call from Jenny broke into her semi-comatose state. She had started to nod off in the very uncomfortable camping chair.

'Jenny? You're okay?' Anna knew she sounded anxious. She was. Jenny couldn't possibly be home yet.

She laughed. 'I'm fine. Mark isn't coming back until tomorrow. They did stay in Sheffield last night, and are still there until this afternoon to make sure the alcohol is out of Mark's system before driving back to Lincoln. He overdid it a bit last night I think.' She went quiet. 'Anna, they stayed at the Hilton.'

Anna too went quiet. 'No... How lucky am I that I could move on Friday – my original move day was Monday, but they knew I was desperate to move in, and I got the keys for Friday. I would have bumped into them, wouldn't I?' She could hear the flatness in her voice. She felt threatened and scared, and Ray wasn't anywhere near her.

'Don't panic, Anna. We out-thought him. We took all necessary precautions to avoid even the possibility of seeing them. You need to stay put today until you hear from me, though. Mark is going to ring me when they get back to Lindum Lodge. By the way, I played the concerned daughter-in-law, and asked how Ray was doing and if he had any idea where you'd disappeared to; he hasn't. Mark did say he's starting to unravel, not eating much, drinking too much, and talking about you constantly, but he's really quite angry you're out of his control.'

'So, where are you now?'

'I've pulled in for a drink at Trowell, and have had a little walk around, just to stretch my legs. Mark rang while I was driving, so I've just rung him back – told him I was out in the garden doing some weeding and didn't have my phone with me. He's no idea I've been anywhere, so don't worry. I'll speak to you soon, after Mark rings to say they're home.'

'Ok, Jenny – and thank you.'

'You're welcome. We'll be fine, Anna. I promise you, we'll be fine.'

She disconnected, and Anna went to the kitchen area to make herself a drink. She took her chair out on to the balcony and sat for half an hour, just watching the comings and goings five floors below her. She decided to get some pots for the balcony area and a little table, with a couple of chairs – this would be her garden. She felt a sense of security living so high up and coded entry to get into the apartments added to that.

Eventually, Anna began to feel cold and moved back inside. She was debating whether to risk driving out to a garden centre when her mobile phone rang again.

'You're safe to go out now, they're home. And so am I.' Jenny's voice was a welcome sound.

'Thank you. Good journey?'

'No problems at all. I'm tired now, but I think that's more emotional than physical. And I'm missing Mark. I've been thinking... I suggest you ring Mark today. I know he's with Ray, but this will show Ray you're out of the loop; you don't know where anybody is. Make sure they don't know we've been in contact and let them think it's your decision you could be away for a short while, but it's just to give you a break, and you'll probably return soon. I think Mark will then convince Ray to let you come around in your own time. It will take away his need to find you, if he thinks you're going to play the prodigal wife sometime soon.'

'You're right. I'll do it later this evening. I'm going out now to buy some plants for the balcony.'

Jenny laughed out loud. 'Anna, you're priceless. You haven't got a bed or a sofa, but you're going to buy plants for the balcony. I love you, mother-in-law, I love you.'

'And I love you, daughter-in-law. Take care, we'll talk tomorrow. Don't forget, Charlie is coming in the morning, so if you ring when she's here, I may have to watch what I say. Night, sweet Jenny. Be good.'

They disconnected, and she went into the little bedroom to find the new telephone they had bought; she sat and read how it worked, then plugged it in and rang it to test it. Awesome. She decided not to leave her own voicemail message, but to use the automated sounding voice that came as standard with the phone. She texted Jenny the number, along with instructions to put it in her contacts as Mary, and to delete the text. Jenny confirmed she had done and then the new phone rang.

'Testing!' she said with a laugh, and she cut herself off.

Anna smiled and thought how like the earlier version of Jenny she was starting to sound. They could never go back to those days, but they could be friends again, provided Jenny refrained from killing her father-in-law.

Chapter 9
Monday, 16 March 2015
Day Eight

Monday was a strange sort of day.

Anna felt safe for the first time in a number of years. Ray was nowhere near her, and she had made certain of that by speaking to Mark first thing. Despite the circumstances and his clear allegiance to Ray, it had been lovely to talk to him. She explained to him she just needed time to be on her own for a while, and did he think his father would be okay with that? He seemed to think so, and actually told Ray while she was on the phone that a week or so away, and Anna would head back home. She heard Ray say, 'Let me speak to her,' but Mark stopped him. 'She wants time out, Dad. Give her that.'

Ray grudgingly acquiesced, but then he shouted loud enough for her to hear, 'Get yourself back here. And damn quick.'

Anna smiled to herself as she disconnected from Mark, because there would never be any chance of a return to that man, damn quick or otherwise. She had asked Mark how Jenny was, just to keep up the pretence, and he had just said her and the kids were fine.

She then rang Jenny, but had to be careful because she could hear Adam and Grace in the background. She didn't want them to know who was speaking to their Mummy, so they kept their conversation short. Anna said she would ring her again during the week and reminded her of Charlie's visit.

'Take care,' Jenny said softly. 'You're safe for the moment.'

Charlie arrived a little after ten o'clock, and they hit the shops after she laughed at the camp site. She brought Anna a gift; a quilt of some magnificence in golds, silvers, creams, and pale greens.

'This is for you and you alone,' she said. 'I've been working on it for a long time, and I knew you would like it. Now, all you need is a bed to put it on.'

They spent a lot of money in the morning, buying everything she could possibly need, and then went back home – Anna had very quickly come to think of it as home – to await the afternoon arrival of a washing machine, a fridge freezer, and two beds. The camp site in her lounge would have to continue for a while, but she would sleep better in an actual bed. The furniture shop had been very obliging with delivery when Anna explained she had been sleeping on an inflatable camp bed for three nights; the beds could be delivered immediately, the chairs and sofa would take a little longer.

Anna asked Charlie if she wanted to stay, but she had an early morning doctor's appointment, so she left around eight o'clock. Anna felt quite bereft once she had gone. She'd always been able to talk to her, and maybe one day she would be able to tell her about this nightmare threatening to overwhelm her, but that time wasn't yet.

Anna made her bed, with the lovely new bedding, and covered it partially with the quilt. It looked wonderful, and so her first real day came to an end. She went to bed.

Chapter 10
Tuesday, 17 March 2015
Day Nine

It was pouring with rain when Anna got up and the streets below her balcony looked slickly grey. Cars had headlights on, and she couldn't decide what to do. Go out? Stay in? For the Irish population in Sheffield, St. Patrick's Day was looking pretty grim.

Anna pulled the laptop towards her and sorted out the internet connection on it. She then did a bit more shopping, including a Waitrose home delivery shop and stayed on the internet for quite some time. She ordered a couple of books for her e-reader, several real books, and some DVDs to get her through what could be long hours of loneliness; all of this took her until lunchtime.

After lunch, Anna nipped out to the pet shop and bought her new friend, Eric the goldfish. He seemed to like his posh new home, so she fed him and left him to get on with living.

Her mobile phone rang. Ray. She felt so angry he had only lasted just over twenty-four hours; so much for giving her space. She ignored the call, and he didn't leave a voice mail. Anna figured if it had been anything important, such as a problem with any of the kids, he would have left a message.

It did, however, serve to highlight the fact she hadn't contacted Tim. Anna glanced at the clock and decided to wait a few more hours before ringing him. Time zones were so frustrating.

They had never visited Tim and Steve; Anna had deliberately chosen never to mention a visit, because she didn't think their relationship with their son would withstand the fall out. Ray had hated how Tim shared his life with another man.

They were good together, Tim and Steve. They had met at work, both doing virtually the same job with an IT company. Anna had recognised the attraction as something more than friendship a long time before they had announced one night they were moving in together and would officially become partners. She had seen Ray in some foul moods, but that night, after they had left, he exploded. It was, apparently, all her fault Tim had turned out *like that*, and when she protested, he hit her.

Anna had taken a proper battering that night, but Caroline, although still living at home, saw nothing. He was careful that way – always made sure they were unobserved when he used his fists. The next morning, Anna told her daughter she had taken a tumble downstairs. It was the first time she had to seek medical help, and although there were raised eyebrows at the hospital, there was nothing on her file to suggest she was a victim of domestic abuse.

Anna had healed physically quite quickly but mentally she changed. She tried not to rock the boat at all, and gradually things settled down. It was partly because Caroline grew older, and they couldn't insist she went to bed early so she would be rested for school next day, and partly because Anna herself switched off. Jenny seemed to have forgotten about them, and she felt with Tim's departure to be with Steve, followed by Mark and Jenny's plans to move to Leicester, she was becoming more and more on her own.

Anna sat on her camping chair and mused at how different things would have been, if Jenny had spoken up about what had happened with Ray. She understood her desire for revenge, but also understood how that in itself could be such a destructive thing. Anna tried to project her thoughts forward a year, to a time when she could be free of all of this, free to feel brave and not scared of her own shadow. She had made a start towards that, but it would take very little to send her tumbling back down that hole she had escaped from.

Anna actually started to feel a little concerned about the emptiness of her days. She had been used to being quite busy, running the administrative side of the business – she hoped the lads would get paid properly, but she doubted it – and the days were now long and full of very little! Anna needed something to do.

Anna thought about all the things she could do, such as knitting, crochet, reading, and baking cakes, and decided to set herself up with everything she would need for all of those activities.

She had a little chuckle, because her other love was football, but she didn't somehow see herself buying a season ticket for Wednesday. And at her age, she was a little old for joining a team. Anna would have to content herself with watching it on television for the time being and again she projected her thoughts forward a year, as she dreamt of a brighter future.

So, once more, she went shopping. She bought lots of crafty stuff, all the time thinking about the glory of Charlie's home that screamed handicrafts the minute you walked through the front door. She wanted to fill her home with handmade items, just as Charlie had.

Anna stacked the cupboard in the hallway with all the wool and other items she had bought and sat down in her camping chair with a coffee and a big vanilla slice. Since the Great Escape, she seemed to have eaten a lot of buns, and it briefly occurred to her visiting a Slimming World or Weightwatchers group might be an essential activity in the near future, to fill up a small part of her free time every week.

Anna had a mouthful of vanilla slice when her mobile phone rang. It was Tim.

'Mom? Come to us.'

The tears started to roll down her face. 'Tim – oh God, it's lovely to hear from you. I was going to leave it another hour before ringing you. I have to explain...'

He interrupted. 'You don't have to explain anything. Have you enough money for a plane ticket? Come to us. There's always a home here for you. A bolthole.'

The last two words hit her like a hammer blow. Tim knew. All the hiding of the bruises had been silly, Tim knew. Did Mark? Did Caroline?

'Tim, I'm fine for money. I will come, but it won't be yet. Maybe in six months or so, when my brain is back inside my head. I'm a bit all over the place at the moment.'

'Fine. We'll come to you.'

'No! Honestly Tim, I am coping. I have Charlie and Dan supporting me, and I have a new home. And I've bought some wool.' She burst into tears.

'Mom! Don't cry. We can be with you in two days, and we'll sort out what you're going to do, I promise.'

Through her tears and sniffles, she said, 'You can't come. You don't know where I am. I can't tell anyone. Not yet. I promise I will fly over and visit you. And stay for a while, until my brain stops hurting.'

'And I want another promise,' he said. 'Promise me you won't go back to him.'

'That I can promise. If you speak to Mark, he will tell you I am just having some time on my own, and then I'm going back to your father, but that is something I've told him to get your father off my back. He will stop looking for me, if he thinks I'm going home anyway. I'm not, I assure you. I may be crying, but it's not because I'm unhappy; it's because I'm talking to you and you're on my side. Keep my secret, Tim. Please.'

'You don't have to ask. I'll ring again in a few days, but if you decide you just want to come, a phone call to say you're on your way is enough. We have two spare rooms. Take your pick, Mom!'

She smiled at the slight American twang in his accent, said 'Love you,' and disconnected.

Anna pulled her purse out of her bag and took out the small photograph she always had tucked inside it. It was a picture of Mark and Tim, aged about twenty. As identical twins, many people couldn't tell them apart, but she could. Anna stroked a finger across the picture and saw the sameness; the short, dark blonde hair, the bright blue eyes, the smiles. Tim's face carried a tiny scar from a scooter handle, which had hit him when he was about ten, but the difference to her was more noticeable than that. Tim's smile was genuine, Mark's forced, and it had always been. Mark was the serious twin.

She felt so much better for having spoken to both of her sons. There was just Caroline now.

Chapter 11
Wednesday, 18 March 2015
Day Ten

Anna slept peacefully, and went over her conversation with Tim many times. She would go to visit him, but she knew she couldn't do it yet. Jenny was the worry in her mind constantly, and she couldn't just escape to America without resolving problems. And a potentially psychopathic daughter-in-law was a problem.

Anna had absolutely no idea how to deal with Ray raping Jenny and fathering her firstborn. None of it seemed real, and yet, she knew it was. Anna could quite cheerfully murder him herself, and yet, wasn't that exactly the attitude Jenny had adopted? Kill him! Get him out of our world!

She woke to the sound of the doorbell, followed by a banging on the door so loud, it frightened her. A glance at the clock told her it was only 7.05, and she knew Ray had found her. She huddled under the duvet and then the banging came again. 'Hello! Is anyone in? Waitrose delivery for you.'

She laughed nervously and shouted, 'Coming,' while grabbing for her dressing gown.

'I'm so sorry,' she said to the very young man standing at the door. 'I forgot I'd organised an early delivery.' Anna didn't bother tell him she'd forgotten the delivery altogether. She looked stupid enough standing there, with her hair all over the place, frantically trying to fasten her dressing gown. He didn't need to know her brain cells seemed to be closing down at a fair rate of knots.

'How did you get in?'

'I had two deliveries for here, and the other lady hadn't forgotten I was coming. She let me in.' She felt suitably chastised, and he went on his way after she signed his machine.

Anna put the kettle on while she was stashing away the groceries, and finally, the fridge looked a little better. It had been very bare up to this point. She now had bacon and eggs, so decided to celebrate having food in the apartment by making a cooked breakfast. She was also partly celebrating the fact the oven and hob had come with the apartment, because they were built in to the rather smart kitchen – it was one thing she hadn't had to buy!

It did make her smile that Ray would be cursing her not being there – he had no idea how to prepare food, but a little adversity in his life would soon teach him.

Jenny rang mid-morning to tell her Mark was now with her, and he clearly thought she would very shortly be with Ray. She sounded anxious. 'Anna, you wouldn't…?'

'Don't worry, Jenny. Nothing, and I mean absolutely nothing, would ever make me go back to that man. He's vile. I take it Mark has gone off to work?'

'Yes. The strain's gone now. He really does think it was a storm in a teacup.'

'It's a big teacup,' Anna said drily. 'I spoke to Tim yesterday. He's totally supportive of me, doesn't want me to go back to Ray, and wants me to go over to them in Florida. I've even got a choice of bedrooms apparently!' She laughed and heard Jenny gasp.

'But…'

'Jenny! I'm not going yet. I told him I needed to sort my head out first, and then I'd go out for a break and to spend some time with them. It's not going to be a permanent thing.'

'You didn't believe me,' she said slowly.

'Oh, I did believe you. You definitely wouldn't have made something like that up. I could have told Ray what you'd said, could have told Mark – and would have done, if I hadn't believed you. No, Jenny, I believe Ray did exactly what you said he did.'

'I don't mean believe me about that. You don't believe I'm going to kill him.'

She couldn't speak. She waited, and waited.

'I am, Anna. With or without your support, Ray is dead. Why do you think I said don't put a divorce in motion? You won't need to. You'll be moving back into Lindum Lodge, the business will be yours, and you'll finally have some peace. I've half the plan in place, and will probably need an alibi, but dead he will be. No doubt.'

The finality in her voice echoed down the line.

'Jenny, you can't! We need to talk properly. I…'

Jenny interrupted. 'Does he deserve to live, Anna? Does he? He's beaten you many times, and if he could get his hands on you right now, you wouldn't survive, I know you wouldn't.'

'Okay, stop right there. Do you realise what will happen? I don't doubt you will find a way to kill him, but the police always look at immediate members of the family first, and you and I are pretty immediate. You'll never see the children again, Mark will walk away for the sake of the children, and your life will be ruined. Don't let Ray do that to you again.'

'Right, I'll start to explain. You will be in Sheffield. With an alibi. I will be in Sheffield with you, and you will be my alibi, along with whoever we decide can give the two of us an alibi. As I said, the plan is half sorted.'

'I can't believe we're talking like this. This is stupid. We're not murderers. We're ordinary women, who are hitting a rough patch, and murder is not the obvious answer.'

'It is,' she said very quietly. 'I'll ring again tomorrow. Think further about this, and you'll see I'm right. While that man lives, you aren't safe. Love you, Anna, take care.'

'Love you, too,' Anna responded weakly, and disconnected.

*****

Caroline. Her beautiful daughter. In the first few days, she had called several times, as had Mark, but since then there had been silence from her. She was something of a pragmatist, and had probably accepted her mother wasn't going to answer, so she would just sit back and wait for her to call.

Caroline knew Anna well enough to know she would call, and yet, as Anna stared at her mobile phone, she felt scared. She really didn't know how she would be reacting to all this trouble befalling her beloved father, and Anna rather suspected she would be completely on his side, and she would be the Wicked Witch of the West. And North, South and East...

Anna felt sick. She looked at Caroline's name in the contact's list, pressed it, and almost immediately switched it off. She didn't know what to say to her.

She pressed her name again, and this time let it ring.

There was no answer.

Was that deliberate? Or did she genuinely not know she'd called her? And then Caroline returned the call.

'Sorry, Mum,' she said breathlessly. 'I was at the door when you rang. Have you gone back home yet?'

Anna laughed with relief. 'Slow down, young lady. No, I haven't gone 'back home,' as you put it. First thing's first. Are you okay?'

'I'm fine, just trying to keep Dad from hiring every private detective in the country to find you. But, I don't think you want to be found, so for the moment he's patiently waiting for your return. It won't last forever though, Mum. He'll get his own way, he always does.'

Anna was tempted to say, '*Not this time he won't,*' but instead said, 'We'll see, we'll see.'

'What do you mean?' She sounded puzzled. 'Surely...'

'There's no surely about anything, Caro; I'm taking time out to think about things.'

'But, Mark said...'

'I know what Mark said, but ultimately, it's my decision what I do with my life, not Mark's.'

'Oh.' Caroline sounded really perplexed now, and she was obviously trying to understand this strange woman who used to be her mother. Anna waited for her to continue, and she said, 'Can we meet?'

'Not yet, sweetheart. Your father may be struggling to understand what's happened, but I need to understand it as well, and I can best do that on my own. Tim asked me to go to him, but I said no. Give me a few weeks, and I'll meet up with you, but not at the moment.'

There was a long pause. 'Mum – I wouldn't tell Dad we were meeting.'

That was the moment Anna knew they hadn't really fooled any of their children. All three knew exactly what was going on in their parents' relationship, and she was beginning to see they all understood, to different degrees, exactly why she had left Ray. The exception was Jenny, who understood so much more.

'I know you wouldn't, sweetheart, but I still need more time to get over this break up. It wasn't planned, you know, it was all down to the anniversary cards.'

She laughed. 'That wouldn't be the anniversary cards he burnt on the bonfire, would it?'

'Sounds about right.'

'Look, Mum, I'm going now. My taxi's here, and I'm catching a train. Just ring when you can. I'm always here. Love you,' and they disconnected.

Relief washed over her. She'd checked in with all the kids, and so far, so good. That worry was out of the way, but the one on the back burner was Jenny. She felt at a complete loss with that particular issue.

Issue.

Murder.

Chapter 12
Thursday, 19 March 2015
Day Eleven

The number showing on her mobile phone wasn't one Anna recognised, and she almost ignored it. She hesitated and then pressed the answer button, prepared to tell them she didn't want to claim PPI, didn't want any new windows, and she certainly hadn't had an accident two years earlier she hadn't made a claim for. Unless the black eye and cut lip supposedly caused by walking into a cupboard door, which had been left open, counted as accidental.

It was Jenny.

Anna laughed and said, 'Well, you nearly got an earful for being a PPI claim company.'

'I'm not.'

'I know. You got a new phone?'

'Yes. There's one in the post for you.'

'I don't need a new phone! I like this one...'

'The one in the post is a number for use just between the two of us. I'll tell you when you can throw it away. And I'm going to make a point of ringing you every week, at least once, on your usual number. One day, I will have to tell the family I know where you are, so we have to leave clear evidence of communication between us. This number is ours, Anna. Don't give it to anyone else, not Charlie, not Dan, and especially not Mark, Tim, or Caroline.'

'But...' Anna felt bewildered. 'What's going on, Jenny? Are you okay?'

'I'm fine,' she laughed. 'Never felt better. I'm going to be away for a couple of days next week, because Adam is off to some outdoor retreat with school and Grace is going to a sleepover with her friend straight from school, so I have from nine o'clock next Thursday until three o'clock Friday free.'

'Are you coming here?' She felt a lightening inside her at the thought.

'No, not this time. Soon. Make sure you charge the phone, and always keep it charged. Ring me when it arrives; I've already programmed my number into it. No more questions at this time, Anna. We'll talk when our two special phones connect. Be brave.' She disconnected.

Anna felt a little sick.

And then the phone rang again, making her feel positively bilious. Ray. Be brave. Jenny's strange words echoed in her head, and she pressed answer.

'And where the fuck are you?'

'Away from you.'

'Well, I know that, Miss Smarty Pants.' His sarcasm left her unmoved.

'Ray, I can't come back yet. I need a break.'

'You've had one. Now, get back home. I'm struggling here. And where's the money?'

'Money?'

'Around five thousand quid, Anna. That money.'

'Oh, that money. Spent it.'

'WHAT!!'

The roar in her ear was deafening, and Anna laughed as she disconnected. She'd stopped feeling sick.

She sat down on her new sofa, clicked on her new television, picked up the new cross stitch design she was embroidering to hang on her new apartment wall, moved her new coffee table slightly to the left, and smiled. Spent it!

At the moment, life felt good.

*****

The new mobile phone arrived in the post, and it was fully charged. She went into contacts and saw one number, allocated to Maia.

She called the number, and when Jenny answered, she said, 'Maia?'

She laughed. 'I'll leave you to look up the meaning.'

'What name am I in your phone?'

'Kyra. Look them both up, Anna.'

'So, why do I have this phone?'

'I don't want communication between us to be traced. These phones are cheap, throwaway, pay as you go phones. I've loaded them with £20 each, and when things are resolved we can destroy them. I used cash to buy them and the top up, so they can't be traced to either of us. I'll be keeping mine on silent, because I don't want anyone to know I have it, but I promise I'll check it frequently. If you ring me, it will show, and I'll get straight back to you.'

'Jenny, you're scaring me.'

'Don't be scared, Anna. One day, you'll be happy again, I promise. It starts next week. Love you, my Kyra.' She disconnected before Anna could say anything else, and she looked in horror at the little phone still in her hand.

Jenny's words buzzed around her, and she made a coffee before sitting down. It was all very well to say, 'Don't be scared,' but over the years, it had been forced into her psyche to be scared.

Anna pulled the laptop towards her and looked up the names. Maia – brave warrior, and Kyra – strong woman. She deleted the website from her history, fully aware if anyone wanted to trace her web browsing, they could probably do so, notwithstanding the delete button. She suddenly felt as though she was drowning, and everything was spiralling away from her. Jenny sounded so confident, so different to the person she had met up with at Trowell, and yet, she felt out of control.

34 Days

Anna prayed for the first time in a while that night.

Chapter 13
Friday, 20 March 2015
Day Twelve

Anna looked in the mirror, and saw the same face she knew so well. Blue eyes, blonde hair – now needing a bit of a root touch-up – generous lips; it occurred to her she looked no different to the woman who had left Lincoln, but her soul was changed. The sun was shining, and she decided to walk into the town centre and maybe pop in to the Cathedral. She had been with Ray to Sheffield Cathedral on one of their trips to the city, and she remembered it being a lovely place; not massive as Lincoln Cathedral was, but beautiful in its own right. She would feel totally safe in there, and perhaps it would bring a little peace into her life.

Two hours later, feeling refreshed and much calmer, Anna walked back home, picking up a pizza on the way. She had cooked a full meal every day back in what she now thought of as her Lincoln days, and it had taken a while for her to realise she no longer had to do anything she didn't want to do. Hence the pizza. A slimming club might definitely be looming on the horizon!

Anna ate her pizza, picked up the newspaper and did the crossword, switched on Classic FM, and relaxed. She was almost asleep when she heard the doorbell. She put down the cross stitch which had almost fallen off her knee, and crossed to the door. She looked through the spyhole and saw a man standing there. She pressed the intercom. 'Can I help you?'

He leaned across and pressed the intercom outside her door.

'Oh, hi! My name is Jonathan Price. My wife and I live at number 83, and we thought it would be good to introduce ourselves.'

'One moment!' She opened the door and looked at the man standing there. He was tall, fit, and she suspected about her age. His dark hair was short, and he had the most beautiful brown eyes. His wife was lucky.

'Do you want to come in?' She sort of vaguely waved her arm backwards, and he smiled. Delicious.

'No, no! We'd like you to come to us, if that's okay. It's that one there,' and he pointed in the direction of their apartment.

'That would be nice. I haven't really met anyone yet.'

'Five minutes?'

Anna nodded, and watched him leave to make sure she knew exactly which door was his.

Well! Friday had just got better.

She quickly washed her face, replaced her lipstick and brushed her hair. Anna felt quite excited at the prospect of actually doing something different.

Jonathan opened the door and ushered her in. 'Come and meet my wife.'

The apartment seemed more spacious than hers on first sight, although she came to realise it was quite a different layout. It was very open plan, made that way to accommodate his wife's wheelchair.

'This is my wife, Melissa,' he said, and touched her hair. She smiled. 'It's Lissy, haven't answered to Melissa since the day I was born.' She held out her hand, and Anna briefly touched it.

'And I'm Anna, Anna Carbrook.'

'Please, sit down,' she said, and indicated towards the seating area. 'Jon?'

He turned towards them. 'Anna, what can we get you? Tea? Coffee? Wine?'

'Coffee, please, Jonathan.'

Lissy was strikingly pretty. Her dark brown hair was gathered into a high ponytail, and she had glasses pushed on to the top of her head. Brown eyes were turned towards Anna, and Lissy smiled.

Anna moved towards the sofa, and she heard the soft hiss of the wheelchair tyres as Lissy followed her. 'It's Jon,' she said. 'And welcome to Haddon Court. We left you alone until we figured you'd be settled. Do you like it here?'

'I love it. It's exactly what I need.'

'Me too,' she smiled. 'I fell in love with it as soon as we came through the door, and yes, we did have slight qualms about the lift, but we've lived here five years now, and there's never been a problem with it. This apartment is three bedrooms – one is a guest room and the other is my work room. It all looks very neat and tidy in here, thanks to our wonderful cleaner, but my work room is something else.'

'Work room?'

'I make children's clothes. One off, individual items. I have an internet shop, and it keeps me pretty busy.'

Jon interrupted. 'Far too busy.' He bent, placing a tray on the table with three pretty tea cups and a plate of scones. 'She works longer hours than I do. On the sewing machine all day and then sits at night doing the hand-work on the garment.'

Anna smiled at Lissy. 'Can I see? I have a seven-year-old granddaughter and a ten-year-old grandson. What age do you design for?'

'Up to age eight. After that, children tend to want what their friends are wearing – Adidas, Nike and such.' She reached into a smart patchwork bag, clearly made especially for the wheelchair, and produced a catalogue. She looked up at Jon who laughed.

'I know, I'll get something. The dress you worked on last night?'

She nodded, and he went into the room directly behind Anna. He returned with a dress on a hanger that simply took her breath away. It was a shimmer of rainbow, with hand-appliquéd tiny fairies floating around it.

Anna shook her head. 'This is amazing! Such skill...'

'It's for a five-year-old who is to be bridesmaid at her mum and dad's wedding. They wanted something really special for her, and we had lots of discussions about it. They came for a final fitting yesterday before the wedding in three weeks. Yes, it's expensive just for one day, but it will be a day to remember for all of them.'

'I need to bring my daughter-in-law to meet you. I don't see my grandchildren very often, as they live in Leicester, but I want a dress for Grace. Jenny will know best what Grace would like, so would it be okay if I bring her across next time she is here?'

Lissy laughed. 'Of course, but we didn't invite you around to sell you a dress. We wanted to get to know you, to let you know there's usually someone in here, if ever you need to have something delivered and you won't be in, and to offer you tea and scones. Made by Jon, as I'm no housewife, and never wanted to be.'

It was Anna's turn to laugh. 'I have a friend called Charlie who is a textile artist of some repute. She also doesn't "do," as she puts it. She says it traumatises her creativity.'

'Charlie Lewis?'

Anna nodded. 'You know her? Her name is actually Charlie Armitage, but she kept her maiden name for use with her work.'

'I know of her. Who wouldn't?'

'Then you must come across to my place and look at my quilt. It absolutely lights up my bedroom. Take a couple of hours off one day this week, and come have a coffee with me. I'd love to show you what I've done with the apartment.'

Unknowingly, Anna had just organised the means of their future alibi.

*****

She went to bed that Friday night, feeling a little more at ease with herself. It had been a good day. The three of them had talked and talked, with Lissy revealing a car accident in her teens had put her in the wheelchair.

It bothered neither of them; Jon had never known her when she could walk. They had met at a mutual friend's wedding, and followed that meeting up with a wedding of their own, some six months later. He clearly adored her, and Anna could see why. She was beautiful; long, dark hair, warm, brown eyes, and a smile to melt hearts.

Jon worked a lot from home, but had a solicitor's office in Paradise Square in the legal centre of Sheffield. He was clearly a very intelligent man; it shone out of him.

Anna slid into bed and remembered she had asked Lissy to come for coffee and see her quilt. She promised herself she would follow up on it, and she picked up her book. She was asleep before finishing the first page.

Chapter 14
Saturday, 21 March 2015
Day Thirteen

Although it was still only mid-March, the year was certainly warming up, and Anna sat on the balcony with coffee and toast for about an hour before deciding what to do with her day.

She felt she needed a job. It wasn't for financial reasons; it was for her. She needed some sort of purpose, a reason to get out of bed. Prior to her leaving Ray, she had worked every day running the business. Anna had initially started by just doing the accounts, but within a couple of months, she had taken everything on, from ordering bricks to doing VAT and tax returns. Ray had turned a room at Lindum Lodge into a state of the art office and paid her a healthy salary.

Anna had enjoyed the job; living with the boss was the downside.

She knew her strengths were administrative, but she was not altogether sure she would get a good reference! And, if she was being brutally honest, Anna wasn't sure she would have chosen office manager as her career path; it was very much thrust upon her.

The world, as they say, was very much her oyster now. Should she make pearls, or sink into oblivion? Anna leaned back in the chair and felt the warm sun on her face. Closing her eyes, she decided oblivion would do for the moment.

The peace didn't last long. Anna heard the letter box rattle, and she stepped back inside to retrieve her usual junk mail. It wasn't the postman but a note from Lissy saying thank you for the previous evening. She smiled – Anna liked both Lissy and Jon, and decided when she went out she would pick up a bunch of flowers for her. It had been a very enjoyable, if unplanned, evening.

She glanced at her new phone, which she hadn't taken with her to number 83, and saw that "Maia" had called at 6.43 pm.

Anna didn't know what to do. Call her on the iPhone? Call her on this phone? On the landline? It all seemed very cloak and dagger, and although she didn't believe for one minute Jenny would carry out her threat to kill Ray, she certainly seemed to be planning something.

Anna had always been very good at burying her head in the sand.

She tentatively pressed "Maia" on the new phone – decision made. "Maia" didn't answer, and Anna knew it was because she had to keep it silenced. She would just have to wait for her to ring.

She rang within five minutes.

'Good morning.'

'Good morning, Jenny. Everything ok?'

'Everything's fine. I won't be around Thursday, and so I thought I'd better remind you. I'm leaving all mobile phones in the house. Won't talk any more now, because I'm going to ring you later on your iPhone. We are now officially in touch although I don't know where you're living yet. I won't say we're in touch until it actually crops up, the longer we can sidestep the hassle, the better. Be good, talk later.'

And she disconnected!

Anna shook her head; Jenny was like a whirlwind. This was the girl she had known prior to their marriage but her behaviour was becoming more intense than she remembered..

She did a bit of a spruce up of the place – any room would look and smell better for a quick burst of furniture polish – and then she went on the computer.

Anna typed in "Michael Groves" and "Lincoln," and waited to see if anything would be thrown up.

It was, and she sat back with slight feeling of disbelief. She pulled up a couple of the websites his name had generated, and it was clear he was still in Lincoln. A little more work and use of her credit card gave her his address and phone number, and she sat back in shock. He had been so easy to trace.

It wasn't a shock he was still alive; she had deliberately lied to Jenny about that. She didn't want her trying to track him down and bring him into the equation in any way. His wife had died, and for all she knew he could have remarried. His business continued in his name, and the website stated he was retired. He had stayed in accountancy. When Anna had known him, Michael had worked for a company, but that had changed at some point, and he had formed his own firm.

She locked the knowledge away in her heart for the moment, made a note of his address and telephone number, and wiped the history from her laptop. She poured a coffee, didn't give in to the urge for a biscuit, and sat back on the sofa.

Jenny rang a few minutes later, and they had a light-hearted chat about everybody and everything. Jenny confirmed Ray was getting angrier with every passing day, but he really had no idea of her whereabouts and wanted her home. She added Mark had spoken to him on several occasions, and the thing that had really bugged him was the £5000 she had taken from their joint account!

Anna had known this would hurt him – and the transfer of the funds had been so easy. Their joint account could be used by both of them, and only needed one signature or one instruction. It had taken two seconds to move it to an account of hers that Ray couldn't access. 'Shall I send him a cheque for it?'

'That would be good,' Jenny laughed.

'The funny thing is, I didn't need it; I just did it because I could. When all this is over, and we're apart permanently, I'll reimburse him for half of it.'

Anita Waller

'You won't need to do that'. Her tone had changed. 'The man is going to die.'

'Jenny...'

'Anna, what he has done to the two of us, and unknowingly to Adam, has condemned him. He doesn't belong in our world. Only death will get him away from us. For certain he will never leave you alone for the rest of your life, even if you divorce him. He won't be able to stand the fact you've walked away from him. Look, I have to go now, because I have to get Grace ready for her night away tomorrow, but I will be ringing again over the next couple of days. On the other phone. Miss you, and I'll see you soon.'

They disconnected, and Anna shivered. The distance between them in miles was vast, and she couldn't talk her down over a phone. She clearly had something planned, and Anna didn't know what to do.

She walked by the river and up into the town centre, feeling very unsettled. She bought a bouquet of flowers for Lissy and another plant for her own balcony. A couple of candles in storm jars were added to the shopping, and she felt better when she began the walk back home.

Anna met Jon in the lift and handed the flowers to him. 'They're for both of you anyway,' she explained. 'You made me feel so welcome yesterday. And please tell Lissy I am in tonight, if she'd like to come for a drink. I might even manage a cake to go with the drink.'

His smile was awesome, and she felt like a silly schoolgirl, giggling as she entered her apartment. She clearly wasn't too old to appreciate a good looking feller!

Anna quickly put together a coffee cake and prayed that the oven worked – she hadn't actually done any baking in it yet.

It turned out to be very passable indeed, so she looked forward to her evening and hoped Lissy would be able to come.

66

She did, complete with some hand-stitching she needed to do on a jacket. 'Hope you don't mind,' she said, waving the garment around. "I need to have this finished for tomorrow evening.'

They chatted all night, and Anna watched with awe as Lissy's needle flew in and out of the fabric. She was really good company, and by the time she left for home, they had demolished most of the cake; she took the last small slice with her for Jon. Lissy had been thrilled by the quilt, and asked if Charlie would be coming over any time soon. She wanted her own version of a Charlie Lewis quilt.

Anna felt strangely reluctant to go to bed. It was as if she was waiting for something to happen, and yet had no idea what. She finally closed her eyes around two o'clock and slept fitfully. The quilt, and most of the bedding, ended up on the floor, and she felt completely out of sorts by the time morning arrived.

Jenny had a lot to answer for.

Chapter 15
Thursday, 26 March 2015
Day Eighteen

Jenny walked into Hartsholme Park feeling as if her brain was on hold. She moved with a stride completely unlike her normal gait. Her coat flapped around her jean clad legs, and it felt so strange because a long coat was not her normal clothing. The woman in the charity shop had said it suited her, but it felt uncomfortable. Her long hair was tucked up into a woolly bobble hat, and her face was devoid of make-up. She had bought some very plain reading glasses and sported them, although she would be glad when she could take them off; her vision was slightly out of kilter. She hoped she looked suitably non-descript; that had been her aim. The coat was a beige shade, and the hat matched it. People would remember red, or blue; she hoped they wouldn't remember beige.

The overlarge bag she carried held a clear, plastic bag, long, black, plant ties, duct tape, a new, ultra-sharp knife, a short jacket, and a stuffed dog. The dog was realistic, and she had smeared it with blood from a piece of liver.

Jenny wandered off the path and into the trees. She chose the densest part, and put the dog half buried in a pile of leaves. She pulled on some very thin leather gloves and waited.

Less than five minutes later, a woman walked down the path; she had a Yorkshire terrier on a lead, talking to the dog as she walked.

Jenny called out to her. 'Excuse me, can you help me please? My dog...' She pointed helplessly at the stuffed dog in the leaves.

The woman immediately left the path and spoke to her dog. 'Come on, Twinkie. This lady needs our help.'

She reached Jenny, looked at the dog, and bent down. Jenny slipped the knife out of her coat pocket and brought it down into the back of the woman's neck. Twinkie began to bark, and Jenny pulled out the knife before plunging it into the dog. He was silenced. The woman had had no time to scream; she made a gurgling sound as she overbalanced, and blood began to pulse out of her mouth. Jenny glanced quickly around her and took out the plant ties. Working in automatic mode because she daren't stop to think, she swiftly secured the woman's feet, then dragged her hands behind her. The lead was still attached to her right wrist, and Jenny left it there as she secured the ties. She slipped the plastic bag over the woman's head and wasted a few seconds sorting out the duct tape. She hurriedly sealed the base of the bag, but she knew it hadn't been a necessary part of the act. She was now scene setting. The woman was dead.

With her mind in overdrive Jenny frantically scanned the area around her. She saw no one. Just for a moment she couldn't move; the blood was congealing in the grasses and weeds and she began to feel sick.

She repacked her bag with everything and moved away from the path area, heading deeper into the woods. Her hands were shaking and she could feel sweat running down her back. She walked for five minutes and then took off the long coat and gloves. There was blood down the front of the coat and on the cuff of her right sleeve, but not as much as she had expected there to be. She put on her own short jacket, put the long coat and gloves into the bag, and stepped on to the path bordering the south side of the wooded area. She had seen nobody at all during the entire operation; her relief was palpable.

She headed back for the train station, had a brief wash in the ladies toilets and went home. As a form of punishment, she made herself walk home from Leicester railway station; in some twisted way she felt it was what she deserved. Part one was completed. She had set the scene for parts two and three. Her brain was no longer on hold, it felt disconnected.

Chapter 16
Friday, 27 March 2015
Day Nineteen

Anna heard nothing from Jenny until Friday night. When the phone rang she jumped. She was engrossed in counting spaces on the aida fabric, and it took her by surprise.

'Jenny?'

'I'm fine. I'm back now.'

'Back from where? Jenny…?'

'I'm back from Lincoln, and no-one knows I've been anywhere. I arrived home last night about ten o'clock.'

'Lincoln?' Anna could hear the steadily rising panic in her own voice.

Jenny laughed. To Anna, it sounded almost maniacal. 'Don't worry. He's still alive. For the moment.'

She exhaled slowly. 'So…'

'Tomorrow, I'm posting a parcel to you. There will be two letters, an empty envelope, and a stick of sealing wax in it. One is addressed to you, and you need to read that first, before deciding whether you want to read the other one or not. Either way, use the sealing wax to seal the second one. Destroy the one addressed to you. Before you touch the second letter in any way, you must wear gloves of some sort. I don't want your fingerprints either on the letter or the envelope. It's fine for your fingerprints to be on the empty envelope because that is the envelope I need you to put the letter in. Gloves, Anna,' she repeated.

'I don't understand. What have you done?'

'It would be better if I didn't say anything out loud. Just trust me.'

They said their goodbyes, but Anna felt as though some line had been crossed without her knowing what was on either side.

*****

She bumped into Jon in the hallway, and he said that Lissy wasn't feeling too well. They both went back to number 83, and he let Anna in; he then went off to the pharmacy to get Lissy some medication.

She looked dreadful. 'It came on very suddenly last night.'

Her eyes were red-rimmed, and her voice bore no resemblance to her normal timbre.

'Poor you,' Anna said with a smile. 'Wouldn't you be better in bed?'

She nodded. 'Yes, but I've too much to do. Jon is getting me something for through the night. I hardly slept last night, which, in turn, keeps him awake, so he's basically gone to get something to knock me out.' She began to cough, and her slender body shook with the ferocity of the attack.

'And that,' she said, when she could eventually speak again, 'is why Jon is off to the pharmacy.'

Anna moved to the kitchen. 'You have honey?'

'Cupboard to the right of the cooker.'

She moved things around until she found it, and then made Lissy a honey and lemon drink in warm water. She sipped at it gratefully.

'It does nothing to cure it,' Anna said, 'but it soothes. Get Jon to make you one, if tonight is bad. Is there anything I can do for you?'

She shook her head. 'I don't think so. Just sit and keep me company.' She pulled the dress she had laid to one side towards her while she sipped at her drink and located the needle secured in the hem.

They sat and chatted until Jon returned, and then she left them to each other. He was clearly concerned by her health, and as he walked Anna to her door, he said, 'If I need you, is it okay to ring you?'

'Of course. Do you have my number?'

'I know you gave it Lissy, so I'll find it and put it in my contacts when I go back in. Last time she was like this she had to go into hospital, and it was scary. Thank you, Anna,' he said, and kissed the top of her head. His concern was profound.

Anna closed her door and leaned against it. It seemed everything in her life at the moment was beset by worry.

Chapter 17
Saturday, 28 March 2015
Day Twenty

The parcel arrived Saturday morning and Anna's world disintegrated. It looked so innocent; a small box measuring around ten inches square, wrapped in ordinary brown paper with her name and address on it. No return address on the reverse.

She placed it on the coffee table and went to get the coffee she'd left on the side in the kitchen when the postman rang the intercom. She took a long drink of it and inspected the package with trepidation. Two letters, Jenny had said. And sealing wax. *Sealing wax? Who on Earth used sealing wax these days? And can you still buy the stuff?*

Anna pulled the package towards her and then pushed it away again. She would open it later. She needed to go to Lissy, make sure there was some improvement. Jon and Anna had both threatened her with A & E the previous evening, and she had said she would go if she was still as bad this morning.

It was a relief to see her smiling face. She hadn't smiled much for two days. 'I'm feeling much better. I've still got the cough, but I can breathe properly now, and I don't feel nearly as bunged up as I was. Thank you so much for all you've done, Anna. We're both so grateful.'

She grinned at her. 'You're welcome. You look tons better. Sleep well?'

'In comparison to the night before, I was in heaven.'

'Good. I'll leave you to rest. That's what you need now. Has Jon gone out? I'll stay, if you need me, but you really should sleep.'

'He'll only be two minutes. Go.' She made a shooing motion with her hands, and Anna laughed.

'I'm going. Call if you need me.'

Anna let herself back into her own apartment, and knew she couldn't put off the package any longer.

*****

Jenny had used lots of sticky tape and parcel tape. It took a while to actually open it, and when she did it was to see two white envelopes, a large brown envelope, a stick of red sealing wax, and a seal to press into the wax. *Clearly*, she thought, *you could still buy it!*

Carefully avoiding touching the second white envelope in any way, she opened the one marked "Anna" and began to read the handwritten letter.

My lovely Anna,

My quest for justice for my family, and for you, has started. My plan is to steer the police away from us and the rest of our family by making Ray's death look like a serial murder. To this end, I have to kill two people apart from Ray.

What was left of her cold coffee went all over the rug as Anna knocked the cup on to the floor. She started to ineffectually mop it up with a tissue, and then gave in and went to dampen a sponge. Anything to take her mind off finishing that letter.

But, she had no choice.

Today (Thursday), I killed a woman in Hartsholme Park. Of course, there may be something of me at the scene, and so, to protect you, the other letter spells out in minute detail everything I have done, and completely exonerates you and everyone else in the family. However, I have no connection at all to the lady I have killed (and, unfortunately, her little dog), so I think this murder will be completely detached from me.

This was a dreadful thing I had to do. Ray will die, but I need to be with Mark, Grace, and Adam, so my plan has to work. You now need to choose whether to read the details in the other letter, or not. If you read them and decide you have to go to the police, please give me warning. Ray will die. If, for all our sakes, you remain quiet, then please seal the letter and put it somewhere very secure, just in case you need to produce it at some point in the future. There will be two more letters; one detailing Ray's death, and one detailing the third death, which is necessary to promote the theory of a serial murderer. When you have all three letters, please make sure they are all sealed, put them in the large brown envelope, and seal that. Then, I will stop, and hopefully, live a happy life.

Anna, I know this is a lot to take in but I have to do this. Ray Carbrook is an evil man, who cares nothing for anyone. You deserve happiness, and on the day you finally came to your senses and left him, you made that achievable. I waited for that day.

I love you very much, Anna. Please destroy this letter immediately, but keep the other one. The decision now is yours as to what happens next.

Jenny

Anna ran to the toilet. She really didn't think she had that much in her stomach. She finally slumped on the floor, her head resting on the toilet bowl, and tried to dry her tears.

She was all too aware she hadn't read the second letter, and she didn't think she could. But, of one thing she was sure. She would never go to the police. She loved her daughter-in-law so much more than she had ever loved Ray.

Jenny had been quite smart. If she had discussed her plan with her, Anna thought she could probably have talked her out of it – or at least talked her out of the serial murder bit! Why on Earth did someone else have to die first, someone with no connection to Ray at all?

Anna scrambled to her feet and switched on the television. She frantically tried to find the news channels, but only national news was airing, not local. There was nothing on any of them about a body having been found in Hartsholme Park, but it was a well-used place, and Anna knew it was a matter of a very short time before the death hit the headlines.

She couldn't open the other letter. Not yet. She hid it in the oven, along with the rest of the stuff from the parcel. She didn't destroy the first letter, but she knew she would have to. She couldn't burn it, so a trip to W H Smith's was called for to get a shredder. She also felt she needed the walk.

It was quite cool outside, so Anna walked quickly. She bought several things in Smith's, including some thin latex gloves, paying cash for everything. It was only when Anna got outside the shop did she realise how criminal her thoughts had become. She paid cash, so there was no proof, and she had bought a shredder – a perfectly normal thing to do for anyone! Although, normal people didn't buy them to destroy murder confessions.

A cup of coffee helped her feel a little more normal, but only marginally. The letter had left her reeling, and she needed to see Jenny.

Anna returned home at the same pace. The day hadn't warmed at all, and she was relieved to get through her own door. She cranked up the heating and went through to the lounge. Sorting out the bits and pieces she had bought took her no time, and she set up the shredder in the small bedroom. It was doubling as office space at the moment, and she sat at her laptop, now with its own desk, and clicked on to the internet.

Anna surfed through various news outlets and still found nothing. She once more cleared her history and reflected how habits change when it becomes necessary. She had never cleared her search history in all her years of using the computer for the business, and now she was clearing it immediately once she had finished on the laptop.

Anna quickly made a sandwich and a glass of water, and tried to eat lunch, but all she could think about was the other letter. She pulled on the latex gloves, picked it up, and held it for a moment. It was unsealed, so Jenny obviously wanted her to read it, but actually taking that step of removing the letter from the envelope was another matter altogether. On the front, Jenny had handwritten *Murder Number One.*

Anna took out the sheet of paper and opened it. It was typed.

To Whom It May Concern:

My name is Jennifer Carbrook, née March, and I was born on 10 October 1982 in Peterborough, Cambs.

On Thursday, 26 March 2015, I killed a lady. The death occurred in Hartsholme Park, Lincoln.

The victim has no connection to me; she is the first part of the plan I have formulated to kill Raymond Carbrook. My wish is this murder will be linked to his murder (and to a third murder), with the obvious decision being reached that it is a serial killer committing the acts. All three victims will be completely unconnected, other than by the manner of their deaths. After these three deaths, there will be no more.

My main concern is to steer suspicion away from Carbrook's immediate family, and I must stress I am doing this alone. Here are my reasons for committing these crimes, leading to the murder of Raymond Carbrook:

He violently raped me on Friday, 16 January 2004.
He is my father-in-law, and he showed no remorse.
He fathered my son, Adam Carbrook.

He has never spoken of it.
He has caused me to live in constant fear.
He has affected my marital relationship.
He beats his wife, Anna Carbrook, regularly.
I fear for Anna's life.

I intend leaving this sealed letter with Anna Carbrook, along with two further letters detailing the second and third murders. They will all be in a large envelope, so she will have no sight of anything. She will believe they are letters for my children, should I die whilst they are still young. If the seal is broken, it means she will have read it, and is therefore in full knowledge of the plan. If it remains sealed, she knows nothing. The police must act accordingly, and I pray she does not open the seal. I will use Anna as an alibi when I kill Carbrook, but she will not know this.

Now, to the details which will prove I killed the lady in Hartsholme Park...

Anna stopped reading at this point, unable to go on. She went out on to the balcony and stared down at the city she was growing to love. She had absolutely no idea what to do.

Nothing could be done to change anything; Jenny had murdered someone already and talking to her wouldn't help at all. She had committed the crime, and whatever happened from now on was already pre-ordained..

Anna swallowed several times, trying to fight the repeat bout of nausea, and slowly her stomach settled. She knew she had to finish the letter and seal it, but then what? Jenny would definitely be waiting for her phone call, but how could she speak to her now? How could she still love her?

She went back inside and pulled the letter onto her knee.

My plan was formulated around leaving my car clearly visible on my drive. I walked down to the station, after leaving home at 10am, wearing a beige woolly bobble hat, jeans, and a long beige coat bought in a charity shop in Leicester earlier in the week.

I bought a return ticket to Lincoln, and my train left at 11.26. I paid cash for the ticket. I arrived in Lincoln at 13.20 approximately. I walked to Hartsholme Park and went into the wooded area where you have found the body.

I took with me a large brown leather bag, and inside I carried a realistic stuffed dog, a knife, a plastic bag, duct tape and plant ties. I also took a thin pair of gloves and a short jacket.

Once I was in the wooded area, I half buried the dog and waited for someone to pass by on the path, which was approximately twenty metres away. I held the knife loosely inside my coat pocket, and the first person I saw was a lady. I shouted her and asked for her help with my dog. She also had a small dog with her. It was a Yorkshire terrier.

She made her way across to me, and I pointed to the dog I had buried. She bent down to help, and I stabbed her in the back of the neck. She fell to the floor and was struggling to breathe. I then stabbed her dog as he was barking loudly. The dog died instantly. I secured her hands behind her back with the plant ties – black ones – after securing her legs. She was barely moving at this point. I put the plastic bag over her head, sealed the bottom of it around her neck with duct tape and walked away. I believe she was dead before I put the duct tape around the base of the plastic bag. I took everything with me.

I walked further into the woods and changed my coat. I then put the long coat and gloves in the bag and walked back down into Lincoln. I washed in Lincoln Railway Station and caught the 18.35 back to Leicester. It was almost 20.30 when I arrived, and I walked back home. I arrived there at 22.00.

At no time have I had assistance with this plan. I deeply regret the loss of this lady and know her family will not be able to forgive, or forget, but it was necessary for setting the scene for the next murder.

I will send all three letters to Anna Carbrook, sealed inside the large brown envelope. I trust her not to break the seal. If the main envelope ever is opened, it will be obvious the letters are not for Adam and Grace.

Jennifer Carbrook
27 March 2015

Anna sat for a full hour, staring at nothing. The letters lay on the coffee table, and she felt lost. She needed to see Jenny. She didn't know what she could say to her; she didn't even think at that point that she would ever speak again.

And then Anna started to cry. Deep, deep gulps that actually hurt; she didn't know how to stop. Eventually, the tears faded, and she re-gloved her hands before picking up both letters. The first one she took into the bedroom and put it through the shredder. The assistant in Smith's had explained it was an extremely good one, because it cross cut rather than straight cut – *did he know what she would need to shred*, she wondered.

It was really strange; she felt better for getting rid of that letter.

Anna went back into the lounge and picked up the second letter; she hesitated. It struck her she could shred that one as well. However, she would gain nothing from that. If the truth came out about what Jenny had done, it might not be her they looked at, it might be Mark. This letter was proof it was just Jenny.

Anna put it back into the envelope marked "Murder Number One" and sealed the flap. She then used her candle lighter to melt some wax on to it and pressed the seal in place. She slipped it into the larger brown envelope and left it unsealed, as per the instructions from her daughter-in-law, then took it into the smaller bedroom and slid it under the mattress. Further decisions would wait for another day. For now, it was out of her sight.

Chapter 18
Sunday, 29 March 2015
Day Twenty-One

Anna didn't sleep much. She hadn't contacted Jenny, and there had been no call or text from her. She finally gave in and got up at five o'clock, made herself a cup of tea, and sat out on the balcony wrapped in a blanket. She closed her eyes for a moment, and when she opened them it was just after eight o'clock, and both her and her tea were cold.

She unwrapped herself and went back into the lounge, planning on making a cup of tea she would actually drink this time.

The new phone beeped once, and she picked it up. The text said, *Found*.

Anna stared at it and then moved with some speed across to the television. She put on the 24-hour news channel from the BBC and waited. She didn't wait for long. Within five minutes, the news' anchor was telling the world a body had been found in Hartsholme Park, a woman. Details were sketchy.

Anna could have told them a lot more.

*****

Anna deleted the text and sat and stared at the phone. Should she ring? Should she go to Leicester? She felt completely lost.

Realisation hit her; despite everything, she hadn't believed the contents of the letter were true. Anna had to speak with Jenny, had to stop her taking the next step. Sunday was clearly the wrong time to ring her. Mark would be there, even if the children weren't, and she obviously wouldn't be able to even acknowledge it was her mother-in-law.

Anna stood up and popped two headache pills from the blisters, washing them down with water. One of them stuck in her throat, and that simple action brought on another spell of tears. She couldn't even take a tablet properly. If she could go back and not walk away that morning...

Would she do it any differently?

No.

Again, the tears.

Anna lay down on the bed and took her book off the bedside table. She needed to stop thinking for a short while, and this was the sort of book which would guarantee that. She fell asleep almost immediately, and didn't surface for three hours. She could hear the television and realised it was still on the news channel she had put it on earlier.

Anna staggered to her feet, feeling a little worse for wear, but relieved the headache had disappeared. She walked into the lounge, and the television screen was full of pictures of a cordoned off area in Hartsholme Park.

Anna stood transfixed. The woman had been identified as a Mrs. Joan Jackson and her husband, looking lost and horrified at the same time, said she always took their little dog out in the early afternoon, every day.

'Oh, Jenny,' she breathed. 'What have you done?'

The police were asking for witnesses to come forward if they had seen Mrs. Jackson on any part of her walk, and in particular, they were interested in speaking to a man in his early twenties who had been seen riding a bike erratically through that area of Hartsholme.

She wanted to switch off the television, but she couldn't. She wanted to rant at Jenny, but she couldn't.

In the end, Anna did shut down the news programme – she didn't want to know any further details.

She moved to the kitchen area and dropped a slice of bread into the toaster, made a pot of tea, and took it all into the lounge on a tray. Tea. It occurred to her she seemed to be drinking it in preference to coffee these days; something else different in her new life.

The worst part about Anna's evening was she had no one to talk to, and her head was bubbling with things to say. What made it harder was she couldn't ring Jenny on a Sunday. She would have to wait until Monday. By then, she figured her head might have exploded anyway.

Of course, Anna didn't sleep when she went to bed. Her three hour "nap" had refreshed her, and she read until about two in the morning, finally dropping into an uneasy sleep for the second night running.

Chapter 19
Monday, 30 March 2015
Day Twenty-Two

Monday morning arrived, and Anna didn't get up until ten o'clock. Depression was settling over her like nimbus cumulus, and she curled up under the duvet and stayed there. She eventually gave in to the need for a wee and a cup of tea (in that order), and with those problems sorted, she opened the doors to her balcony. She saw Jenny's car pulling in through the car park gates. She was standing by the intercom when she buzzed.

'Come up,' Anna said harshly. She hoped Jenny caught the tone.

They looked at each other in the doorway, and Anna held out her arms. She could see the pain in Jenny's face, the drooping shoulders, and Anna was lost.

'I couldn't get here fast enough,' she sobbed. 'God, Anna. What have I done?'

'Come on. I've just made a pot of tea. Do you want something to eat?'

She sniffled. 'Just tea, thanks.'

'What have you told Mark?'

'I just said I was having a day shopping. He took Adam and Grace to school, and I set off as soon as he'd driven off the road. I must leave here by 12.30 at the latest to make sure I'm home for the children, but if there are issues with traffic or anything, I can always ring Katie to pick them up for me when she goes to get her two.'

They went out on the balcony, and Jenny shivered.

'Cold? Here.' Anna passed her the throw.

Jenny draped it across her shoulders and smiled for the first time. 'This feels so good, being here with you,' she said softly.

Anna handed her a mug of tea, and she sipped at it immediately. 'I left without having even a drink,' she said. 'I really needed to talk to you. It's been a long weekend.'

Anna looked at her for a long time, and she wriggled uncomfortably.

'You're a murderer.' Her tone was flat, her face emotionless.

'I know.' Her tone matched Anna's.

'You stop now, Jenny.'

'I can't. If I stop now, that lady died for nothing.'

'Mrs. Jackson, Jenny, not that lady. And you stop now. I can't begin to imagine how you're going to live the rest of your life, knowing what you've done, but you stopping now buys my silence.' Even as she spoke the threat she knew it was a useless phrase.

Jenny's stubbornness showed in her face. 'Ray will die.'

'No!' The anguish showed in Anna's voice.

She watched Jenny's face, and she knew without any shadow of a doubt she would kill Ray. She had lived with what he had done and the consequences for too long. If Ray had ever acknowledged his remorse to her, maybe she would have been able to put it behind her and just get on with her life, but that hadn't happened. Jenny's hatred had festered to such a point killing Ray was her only answer. And yet, Anna knew under this brittle exterior there still lurked the softer, kinder Jenny; the Jenny she had seen place a tiny dead bird in a cardboard shoe box and bury it in the back garden. That Jenny had to still be in there, surely?

'Anna,' she said calmly, 'if you think this is going to be easy, please think again. And I really can't think of that lady as Mrs. Jackson, because that personalises her, and while she's just a dog walker in a park, I can live with what I did. I am dreading the newspapers talking about her life, her family. But, I did it, and I have to live with it. Ray will be next, and it will be soon. And never forget that Ray's death is as much for me as it is for you.'

'Then I'm asking you not to do it, Jenny. Think of the children, think of Mark, Tim, and Caroline. They won't know why he's dead, just that he's been murdered.'

She laughed. 'Anna, they won't grieve for long. They know exactly what Ray is like. They know about the abuse you've taken over the years. The difference between them and me is I'm prepared to stop his evil ways, they can't. So, one night, I'm going to organise Adam and Grace to be at my parents' house for a sleepover, and then I'm coming to you. I'll go to Lincoln from here. It's good Mark works away during the week. I still have a key for Lindum Lodge, and I'm going to wait until the early hours before I go in. I know he'll be drunk and asleep, because that is apparently what he does every night now. I'm going to kill him in exactly the same way as I killed the lady.'

'But, why will the police think it's the same person doing the killing? This scenario with Ray is completely different to killing out in the open.'

'It's the same plastic bag, same ties, and same duct tape. Oh, they'll link it all right. Then the third one will be a different scenario again, but using the same stuff. And it will be very soon after Ray.'

Anna could feel her own will to live drifting away. 'Third one? There doesn't need to be a third one!'

'Yes, there does. And that's where it ends, Anna. After that, if I'm tracked down, I'll confess to the lot. If I'm not, then I keep quiet. You'll have the only evidence which can incriminate me, because you'll have three letters with details of each murder. There's nothing they can do to you, as long as you keep silent.'

'But...'

'Or to Mark.'

Jenny knew that would stop Anna in her tracks.

'Mark?'

'If they suspect it's me, they're going to look at Mark as well. Those letters make it clear nobody else is involved. Keep them safe, Anna, for God's sake, keep them safe.'

Anna gaped at Jenny, completely unable to speak. For a start, she didn't know what to say, and secondly, she didn't know her any more.

That realisation completely took the wind out of her sails, and just for a moment, Anna felt panicked. She actually physically shook her head as though that would bring her some relief, but, of course, it didn't.

'Jenny...'

'Leave it, Anna. I know you've a lot to think about. I'm going to go now. I just had to see you; I needed the comfort of seeing you. We will get through this, you know. I will get rid of him for both of us.'

There was so much strength in her words.

'Jenny – all this seems so extreme...'

Jenny shook her head. 'Listen to all my reasons, Anna, listen carefully. I was naïve when that monster raped me. Maybe if I had been ten years older, I would have been able to go to the police, tell Mark, tell you, but I wasn't. That man ruined my wedding day, my honeymoon, my life. I was so badly torn when he raped me I had to pretend to Mark I was having a period at the start of our honeymoon, because I knew he would be able to tell I was in pain if we made love. And then, after the birth of my first child, I find out he's fathered him. I can't love Adam in the same way I love Grace, I just can't, Anna. He's ruined the relationship I have with my only son. I hold myself back from Mark. I love him so much, but when he touches me or when we make love, I feel cold. And then, there's you. I know about the beatings; Tim once told me. I know if he could get hold of you now, you probably wouldn't survive it. At the very least, you would be seriously hurt. And I am 100% sure when it comes to a divorce, he would take everything. The man is pure evil, Anna. And you know it. I made myself a promise, a promise I locked into my heart. I said if ever you saw sense and left him, he would die.' Jenny's face was ashen.

Anna held out her arms, and Jenny came to her. She gave a small whimper as she put her head on Anna's shoulder, and Anna heard her whisper, 'We'll be free soon, I promise.'

She picked up her bag and walked to the door.

'I'll see you next week. It's Spring Bank holiday, the children are on holiday from school, and it means I can be away overnight. I'm going to tell Mark we've spoken, because I'm coming to stay the night. Invite your new friend over to meet me. We'll discuss details later.'

'We can't involve Lissy!'

'We're not. I just want her to see me, here. And she needs to see me the next morning. Don't come down with me, it upsets me to leave you. Take care, Anna. One day, we'll be happy.'

Chapter 20
Tuesday, 7 April 2015
Day Thirty

The apartment became unbelievably clean and tidy. Anna had spent a lot of money online, buying things she didn't really need but really wanted. All the time, it felt like she was giving Ray a good old smack in the face, because he always queried everything she bought, and in many cases, he mocked her purchases. She supposed it would take a long time to forget his total dominance and influence over her, but she knew she would get there.

And really, Anna knew it was Jenny who was getting to her. She didn't know what to do. She was dreading the phone call, saying, *I'm coming to see you.*

And the phone call arrived on Tuesday morning.

They had spoken on Anna's iPhone the day before, just a general conversation Anna had assumed was laying the groundwork for telling Mark she was in touch with his mother.

The call came on her new phone.

'It's me.'

It's me. It sounded so theatrical Anna wanted to giggle.

'I know.'

Jenny sighed. 'I'm sorry. My head is buzzing. I'm coming over to see you Thursday. And staying the night...'

Anna felt chilled all through my body.

'And...?'

'Thursday. Thursday night. I'm going to tell Mark today when he calls we have been in touch, and you've agreed to meet me. It has to be this week, Anna, because Mum and Dad are collecting Adam and Grace today and taking them to the coast for the rest of the week.'

Anna was trembling. 'Ring me when you know what time you're arriving. I have to go, I feel sick.'

She disconnected and ran for the bathroom.

Chapter 21
Thursday, 9 April 2015
Days Thirty-Two to Thirty-Three

Jenny was with her by 11am. Anna found it difficult to talk to her, to look at her, until Jenny took her by the shoulders, looked her in the eyes, and said, 'It will be fine. We will be fine.'

They sat on the settee, and she held Anna's hand. 'This is what is going to happen. We will invite Lissy over for a chat tonight. You've told me she's a night bird, so she will stay up late. Out of politeness, and because she thinks I'm not very well, she will hopefully go home around eleven, and I will immediately set off for Lincoln. I'll be there before midnight. The next part is improvisation, because I don't know if Ray will be home or not, but in any case, I should be back on my way here by 1.30 tomorrow morning, at the latest. And Ray will be dead.'

Anna shook her head. 'This is mental, Jenny. He's a big man, and you're a slight woman.'

'He'll be drunk.' She grinned.

'And where does Lissy come into this?'

'As soon as I get back here, I need you to go and knock at Lissy's door and ask her for some of the cough medication or honey you told me she had last week when she was ill. I'm going to be very sniffly, and cough all night just to convince her I'm really feeling quite poorly.'

'And Lissy being Lissy will call around tomorrow morning to check you're okay because she's that type of person. And you'll make sure she sees you still coughing and spluttering.'

'That's right. Now, I need to get out of these flats without going through the front foyer, because there are CCTV cameras there. Is there another way out?'

Anna nodded. 'Yes. Take the lift down to the -1 level. It's where we take our rubbish. The door to the outside is locked to keep strangers out, but you can get out of it by turning the Yale lock. The bin men have a key for when they need to get in from the outside, but the tenants don't, so I suggest if you want to get back in the same way, you ring me as you arrive, and I'll go down there and let you in.'

And that made Anna complicit. Those final words had implicated her, just as much as Jenny, and she comprehended that fact as soon as she spoke the words.

'And your car? How will you get around that?'

'That's the weak link. I will park it in the back and hope it's not caught on camera. But, to be honest, Anna, why would they suspect me? I have very little to do with Ray, we don't live close by to him, I'm here with you, Mark is in Derby, the children, along with my parents, are in Withernsea – there is no real connection.'

Anna knew she was right, but was so wound up by the whole thing she just wanted to go to bed and sleep for a week. The ostrich syndrome again. Instead, she made another pot of tea, and they sat and ate buns and biscuits.

During the afternoon, she knocked at Lissy's door and invited her round for drinks and desserts later that evening. Lissy checked with Jon to see he hadn't anything planned and then grinned.

'Sounds lovely. I'd like to meet your daughter-in-law. What time?'

'About seven? And bring some of your work. I want to order a dress for Grace, but I need Jenny to say which style and colour.'

Anna went back to her apartment and held up her thumb to Jenny. She smiled and nodded in acknowledgment.

'I'll go and move my car.' She stood and brushed past her. Anna touched her on the arm, and she stopped.

'Think about it, Jenny,' she pleaded.

'I have,' she said, and walked out of the door.

*****

Lissy came to Anna's just before seven. Anna had bought several types of buns, cakes, and desserts, and they looked impressive on the coffee table.

'Oh, wow,' she said, her eyes lighting up. She turned to Jenny. 'And you must be Jenny with the lovely Grace?'

Jenny sneezed and held her tissue to her nose. 'Oh, sorry. Head cold. Yes, I am. And we need to talk dresses, I understand.'

'You're not very well?' Lissy looked concerned. 'I should go...'

'Not on your life,' Anna said with a laugh. 'For heaven's sake, don't leave us to eat this lot. Come around here, park yourself, and take Jenny through what you do. I'll make some drinks.'

Jenny's voice had become really nasal, and Anna just hoped she would remember to keep it up all night. She put on the kettle and the percolator and busied herself in the kitchen. She could hear them talking, and Jenny's exclamations of delight followed by sneezing and coughing. She merited an Oscar.

They settled on a grey and lemon dress for Grace, very floaty, very girly, and definitely one of a kind. Jenny said she would love it, and then had a dreadful coughing attack which seemed to go on forever.

At just before eleven o'clock, Lissy said she was going.

'I can't watch you suffer any longer, Jenny,' she said with a laugh. 'Go to bed and get some sleep, if you can. If it's any consolation, it only lasts for about two days when it reaches this stage, but there's only sleep that helps. I'll go home and draw

94

up the design for the dress – I'll show it to you tomorrow before you leave.'

Within two minutes of Lissy leaving, Jenny left. She had checked out the bin area earlier so she knew exactly what she was doing, and Anna sat on her own and prayed for her.

Chapter 22
Friday, 10 April 2015
Day Thirty-Three

Jenny chose to go by the slightly more circuitous route to Lincoln, taking the A46 out of Newark. She needed to avoid the toll bridge at Dunham; she suspected there would be cameras on the bridge.

She parked about half a mile away from Lindum Lodge in a car park at the back of a play area. She had dressed entirely in black, and had pulled the knitted black hat down over her forehead to conceal any trace of her blonde hair. Everything she needed she carried in a drawstring, black sports bag on her back, leaving her hands free.

Jenny ran the short distance back to Anna and Ray's home, trusting if anyone saw her, they would assume she was a runner out for a late night jog. She paused at the gates of the large detached house and looked around. It was deserted. She slipped through into the garden and knelt down behind the laurel hedge surrounding the front garden. She stayed immobile for fifteen minutes and then assumed she was safe. If anyone had rung the police to say they had seen someone entering through the gates, the police would have been there pretty fast, especially in this prestigious neighbourhood. Shearwater boasted many upper class homes like Lindum Lodge; she had no doubt the cavalry, in the form of a police car, would gallop to the rescue at the mere whiff of a burglar.

Jenny began to stand from her crouched position and then froze, before dropping back to her original position. She had heard a car engine. She considered trying to move further around the garden, but then decided to flatten herself, sliding under the base of the hedge.

Jenny was shocked to the core to hear Ray's voice. It was now 12.30am, and she had presumed she would have to enter the house to kill him.

She could hear his words were slurred. 'Keep the change,' he said, and Jenny knew he must have arrived home in a taxi.

'Thank you, pal,' the taxi driver responded. 'You need any help getting in?'

'Nah, I'm bloody great. I can manage.'

She heard the driver laugh, and the car door slam; the taxi pulled away, and Ray came through the gate. She remained perfectly still, watching. He walked a few feet up the long path leading to the front door, and then tried to negotiate the step; one of three he would have to go up before reaching his home. Ray managed the first one, walked another twenty feet or so, and stumbled. His balance gone, he catapulted on to the grass at the side of the path, and lay there, without moving, face down.

Jenny waited. He stayed where he was for about three minutes, and then she heard an intake of breath from him; she knew he was falling asleep, too drunk to get up.

She moved smoothly, holding the knife in her right hand, the bag in her left. The night was deathly quiet and she felt as though the very air was wrapping itself around her. Soundlessly, she approached his inert figure and then brought the knife down into the back of his neck without any hesitation. There was a small sound from him, almost like a cough and sneeze combined. She twisted the knife and then pulled it out.

Jenny felt anger, frustration, loathing; it engulfed her, and she heard herself give a small cry. All the years of waiting for this moment were now as nothing; it was her time to take the revenge she had promised herself that afternoon as she lay broken and bloodied on the floor of the lounge. She wanted to take the knife again, and slash and slash and slash, rip him to pieces; she couldn't do that. This murder had to seem like the other murders. This one couldn't stand out because it was more ferocious with multiple stab wounds. One had to suffice.

Her hands were shaking as she took out the plastic bag and duct tape, followed by the plant ties. She secured his hands first and then his legs. There was absolutely no movement from him at all, but there was a lot of blood. The stench, that biting coppery smell of spilt blood, permeated the air around her and she gagged. The plastic bag slipped around as she pulled it over his head and once more she knew the duct tape was a formality; Ray was dead.

Jenny sobbed as she knelt back under the hedge. She put her bag on her back once more and stood by the gate, listening. She could hear nothing, and so slipped out of the gate and turned left, heading back in the direction she had travelled earlier. She had only been running for about a hundred yards when she saw a man walking some distance in front of her, using a stick to help him walk.

She stifled a sob, and increased her pace to catch him up. As she ran past him, Jenny shoved with her elbow and he staggered on to a border of flowers; a stone wall separated them from the garden. His head hit the stone wall and the crack made her wince. He turned over with a groan. He looked up at her, his tired old eyes not really comprehending what was happening to him, and she brought down the knife, her own eyes closing as she did so. She heard the gurgle, and then felt his hand grasp her wrist. Her eyes opened in shock, and she twisted the knife. His hand relaxed instantly and fell to the ground. Jenny was sobbing openly as she completed her tasks. Again the coppery smell was there; why hadn't she noticed it in Hartsholme Park? She left him in the flower bed with his hands and feet secured, and the plastic bag taped around his neck.

Jenny picked up her bag and ran, keeping to a jogger's pace until she was in sight of her car. She stripped off her blood spattered sweatshirt and put on a fresh black one. She packed everything in a bin liner and stored it under the passenger seat; if she did happen to be stopped for a police check, she figured they would check the boot. Any stray blood on her would be concealed by the fresh sweatshirt; she had to hope she could get away with it.

In the end, Jenny's precautions were irrelevant. She took the same route back to Sheffield; there was very little traffic about, and she was back behind Anna's apartment building by 1.45am. She rang Anna when she was five minutes away who went down, opened the basement door, and left it slightly ajar before returning to her apartment.

It had been a long three hours.

Chapter 23
Late Friday, 10 April 2015
Days Thirty-Three to Thirty-Four

'He's dead, Anna.'

Jenny said the words Anna had been dreading as she came through the door, just before two o'clock.

'Now go to Lissy, and see if she's still awake. I'll put my dressing gown on, in case she comes back with you. Quickly, go.' Jenny ran into the smaller bedroom, carrying the black bin liner with her.

Anna tapped quietly on Lissy's door and waited. She heard the slight squeak of her wheels on the wood flooring and whispered, 'Lissy, it's me.'

She quickly opened the door and said, 'Is she worse?'

Anna nodded. 'Her cough is draining her. Do you still have any medication left, or even some honey?'

'I'm sure I have. You go back to her; I'll bring it across in two minutes.'

Anna returned to her own apartment. Jenny had on her dressing gown, and was struggling out of her leggings. She quickly slipped on her pyjama trousers, and was just sitting on the settee, when Lissy knocked on the door.

Anna let Lissy in and they both looked at a desperately ill Jenny —that woman could act.

She started to cough, and Anna held on to her to give her support.

Lissy wheeled herself into the kitchen area and placed a bottle of medication on the side, along with a jar of honey.

'Thank you,' Anna whispered. 'Now go back home and go to bed! Stop designing! And please, apologise to Jon if we've woken him.'

'He's still awake. Been working on some difficult issues tonight, and it's wound him up a bit. He said to give him a shout, if we needed him.'

So now they had two witnesses providing alibis.

Anna went back to Lissy's door with her, kissed her cheek, and thanked her.

She locked the door and turned to Jenny.

She looked dreadful. This wasn't acting.

'He's dead.' The words came out as a whisper. 'I can't talk about it. I need to put it in a letter anyway, so can the details wait? The less you know, the better, because tomorrow the police will be here to tell you he's been murdered. I'm guessing it will be Mark they contact, because they can't contact you on a silenced phone. This all depends on when he is found. Do you have any missed calls from a strange number?' Anna looked at her phone and then looked at Jenny.

'There's nothing yet. Maybe I should take it off silent.'

'No!' Jenny was adamant. 'No, don't do anything out of the ordinary. Keep it on silent. They will probably try to contact you first, but then they'll try Mark. He will then ring me. Let's follow that order, and assume I'm right.'

Jenny had tucked her hands into the sleeves of her dressing gown while Lissy was with them; Anna had presumed it was to keep up the appearance of illness. She now slowly removed them. They were covered in blood.

Anna took over. 'I'll run you a bath. Have a shower first, and hand me your clothes. We need to wash them.'

Jenny trembled as she slowly took everything off. Anna handed her a towel, and she shook her head.

'Wait until I've washed it all off. Then, I'll use the towel. Just wash everything, including this.' She held up the dressing gown.

Totally naked, she walked towards the bathroom, and Anna put all her clothes on a hot wash.

It was twenty minutes later when Jenny called for the towel. She was raw from scrubbing at herself; she took the towel and folded herself into it.

'Come on,' Anna said gently and led her to the settee. 'Do you want a drink?'

She nodded. 'Brandy, a very large one.'

Anna opened the new bottle and poured her a hefty measure. She took a couple of sips and placed the glass on the coffee table. 'Sit down, Anna. I've thought about this all the way back, and I'm not going to give you any details until you see them in my letter. There's a chance you could slip up when the police come calling, and believe me, that wouldn't be good.'

Anna nodded. She was so relieved to see her back that details were almost irrelevant. Ostrich syndrome again.

They talked about anything, and everything, for a good half hour, avoiding all mention of Jenny's actions; Anna treated her as a child and tucked her up in bed, kissing her on the forehead before going to her own room.

She didn't sleep, but she did hear Jenny's phone ring just after four o'clock. The ringtone stopped immediately, and she knew Jenny was just as awake as she was. She heard her muted voice, and then the bedroom door opened.

'Anna, it's Mark. He has to have your address. He has to, Anna, and he has to come to see you. It's something serious, he says. Will you speak to him?'

The horror must have shown on her face, because Jenny crossed the room and hugged her.

'Be strong,' she whispered and passed the phone to Anna.

'Mark? What's wrong?' Anna felt the quiver in her voice and hoped Mark didn't sense it.

'I need to see you, Mum. Now. I need your address. Thank goodness Jenny has made contact with you.'

'I can't give you my address, Mark. Your father...'

'Mum!' There was anguish in his tone. 'Your address! Now!'

'I need a promise...'

'You don't. Just tell me the address, and I'll be with you as soon as I can. And make sure Jenny stays with you.'

Anna paused and then gave him the address.

'But...'

'No buts, Mum. I'm in Lincoln; I'll be with you in about an hour. I'll be on my own,' he added. 'Or at least, Dad won't be with me.'

She disconnected and stared at Jenny.

'Don't tell me anything at all,' she said shakily. 'I can't act as well as you. And don't forget to continue to be ill. The alibi is useless if you're not ill.'

Jenny reached across to Anna and held her hand. 'Look at your phone. Have you got missed calls?'

Anna opened her phone case and said, 'Two. And a voicemail.'

'Don't open it. Leave everything just as it is at the moment. That way, you know nothing. We can just pretend you were too wound up by Mark's call to bother with looking at your own phone.'

Anna nodded and looked at her daughter-in-law. 'I'm so scared, Jenny. So scared.'

'Anna, you're free. I'm free. Don't be frightened any more. Now, remember, Mark won't be on his own. The police will be with him. We were here all night; I was too ill to go out, so we stayed in with Lissy until about eleven o'clock. No need to mention we asked Lissy for medication about two o'clock unless it crops up. That's our back-up alibi. We went to bed as soon as Lissy went home. Have you got that?'

Anna nodded miserably, and Jenny tried to smile as she stood to leave her side.

'I'll put some coffee on. We need to freshen ourselves up. Did you sleep?'

'No. You?'

'Not a wink. I expected the call earlier than this, and I was on edge waiting for it. The drive back from Lincoln was pretty worrying as well, because I had to be so careful. It wouldn't have done to be stopped at any point of the journey by the police. I was so wound up when I went to bed; I knew sleep wasn't going to happen.'

Anna slid her legs out of bed. 'I'll shower while you're making the coffee. We'll get through this. Somehow.' She heard the bitterness in her last word and Jenny looked at her.

'Yes, we will. And I think the next few hours are going to be the hardest. Anna, just in case everything does go pear-shaped very quickly, I will tell them I went out within five minutes of our going to bed, I faked the illness, and you had no idea I had gone anywhere. I came back and switched on the cough and flu symptoms so you would go and ask Lissy for help. You will not be implicated in any way. I will need you free to look after Adam and Grace – and Mark. If I am arrested, all of the truth about Ray will have to come out, and Mark, above all the others, will need you. Go get your shower, and keep the worried look.'

Jenny moved into the kitchen and began taking the now dry clothes out of the tumble dryer, while Anna went to the bathroom. Anna leaned her head against the glass shower surround and sobbed. She sobbed for herself. She wanted to turn back time, to go back to being that scared, battered wife who had learnt to live with it.

And now, she wasn't a wife, she was a widow. A widow who didn't officially know she was a widow. Still a grey widow, not a black widow for about another hour. Anna had just lived through thirty-four days of turmoil; she remembered the feeling of happiness as she had driven away from Lindum Lodge for the last time that bright March morning.

A mere thirty-four days later, Anna's life had imploded in so many ways, and she knew worse could follow.

Anita Waller

Chapter 24

Mark arrived just after five, along with a Detective Inspector and a WPC, who asked them to call her Helen.

Mark pulled his mother into his arms and kissed the top of her head. 'Mum,' he said quietly and sighed. 'It's Dad.'

'Dad?'

'I'm sorry, Mum, he's dead.'

She didn't need to act. She felt horror-struck at hearing the news she had known for about three hours. 'What...?' The tremble in her voice was all too apparent, and Jenny moved to her side. She coughed, and Anna held on to her until the bout had stopped.

'Come over here, Anna. Come and sit down. Mark?' She looked at her husband, and he moved to Anna's other side and supported her as they moved to the settee.

Mark looked concerned. 'Jenny, you okay?'

She shook her head. 'No, I'm quite poorly, but I'll live. Anna's the important one, so just ignore me if that happens again. I've been like it all night.'

The DI, whose name Anna couldn't remember at all, sat in one of the chairs and leaned towards her.

'Are you ok, Mrs. Carbrook? Can we get you anything?'

Helen interrupted, and said she would make them all some tea.

'Why is he dead? He's only in his early fifties, and there's nothing wrong with him.' The last words came out almost as a wail. Mark hugged her again.

'There's more, Mum.'

'Mrs. Carbrook, your husband's body was found in his front garden. A taxi driver who had taken him home half an hour earlier found his wallet in the back of the taxi and took it

106

back to him, because he was in the area with another passenger drop off. He found him.'

'But, how...?'

Mark took hold of her hand, and Anna looked directly across at the DI.

'He had been stabbed in the neck, and then a plastic bag had been placed over his head. His hands and feet were tied with plastic plant ties. I'm sorry to be so brutal, Mrs. Carbrook, but this appears to have all the hallmarks of an escalating crime. Ten minutes away from where your husband was found, another body was discovered, an elderly man killed in an identical manner. We have very strong reasons to believe we have a serial killer in Lincoln, and your husband was either the second or third victim. We'll know more after the post-mortems.' The DI now took hold of her other hand. 'I'm so sorry, Mrs. Carbrook, I know it sounds very harsh and clinical, but we have to move fast. There may be other bodies as yet undiscovered. Did your husband have any enemies, or have any threats made against him you are aware of?'

Only Jenny.

Anna stared at him, shock plain to see on her face. 'No,' she said, 'not that I know of. He got on well with his workforce, was really good company to have around. I'm sorry; I'm not being very helpful, am I?'

'You're doing fine,' he said. 'I understand you don't live with your husband...'

'It's just a break.' Anna looked down at her hands; she didn't want her face to reveal any lies. 'I just needed a couple more weeks of personal time, and I would have gone home. When I left Lincoln – and Ray – it was a forever kind of decision, but I changed, he changed. He wanted me home, and I was on the point of telling him that was going to happen. Now, he'll never know..."

Helen placed a tray of teas and coffees on the low table, and they all began to drink. Anna was grateful for the distraction.

The DI turned to Jenny. 'I understand this is the first meeting with anyone from the family?'

She nodded. 'Yes, Anna needed space, and we all respected that. I spoke to my mother-in-law last week, and arranged I would come up and see her this week. She wanted to talk, but her own children are too close to her. And Anna and I are very close, so I suppose I'm the logical one to listen. We had a long chat, and she made the decision to go home to Lindum Lodge, but with some ground rules in place. Ray could be a bit controlling, and that really was why she left.'

Jenny turned to Anna. She sneezed quite violently, and everyone waited while she finished coughing. 'I'm sorry, Anna, I shouldn't really be saying all this. This was a private conversation between the two of us...'

Anna vaguely waved her hand around. 'It doesn't matter, Jenny. Truth always surfaces, and I would prefer to be upfront about the relationship between Ray and me. I just had a bit of a midlife crisis, felt unloved and unwanted, so I walked away. But, I missed him, because when all is said and done, we had been together nearly forty years. I wanted to walk back. And now I can't.' For the first time, she broke down in tears. She wasn't acting. The tears were genuine; she just wasn't sure what they were for.

Helen knelt down in front of her. She was a very pretty girl, and Anna felt really sorry for her – it couldn't be easy telling people their loved ones were dead.

'Anna, we need you to come to Lincoln. Shall we go and pack a bag?'

'Just a minute,' she sobbed. 'I need to clear my head. You said three victims, didn't you? All in the same area? Is it safe for me to go back there? I don't want anyone close to me to be victim number four.'

'We have reason to believe there was an earlier victim, but we're saying nothing until forensics have finished.' The DI spoke gently and followed up by telling her there would be police outside Lindum Lodge for the foreseeable future anyway, and they wouldn't be able to stay there until the forensic team gave them the all clear.

'Anna,' Jenny took her hand again. 'We'll stay with you until you're ready to be on your own again. Mum and Dad will look after Adam and Grace for us, so don't worry.' Once again she was racked by the cough, and Mark held her.

'You've really picked up a bad one with this,' he said softly and smiled down at her.

'I've been so ill,' she said. 'Up and down all night. Thank goodness for Lissy across the hall. She brought me medication at some god-awful hour, but I haven't really slept.'

She turned to her mother-in-law. 'Anna, you really should tell Lissy what's happened, because she'll worry about you if she doesn't see you. It wouldn't be good to come back here and find the door boarded up because someone had broken in looking for you!'

Anna nodded. 'I will. I'll ask her to feed Eric for me.'

Mark looked puzzled. 'Eric?'

She pointed to the tank in the corner of the room he obviously hadn't noticed. 'That's Eric,' she said.

He nodded then turned and looked at her. Inscrutably.

She felt uncomfortable and walked towards the door of her bedroom. 'I'll just pack a bag,' she said.

'Mum...'

She turned to look at Mark, and he said, 'I'll ring Tim and Caro. They'll be here soon.' His tone was quite flat, and then suddenly he moved towards her and held her tightly.

'I love you,' he whispered.

'I know,' she whispered back.

Helen accompanied her and suggested things she might want to take – after all, she implied, she didn't know when she would be back.

Anna went to Lissy's door, once more followed by Helen. There was a long delay while they waited for either Lissy or Jon to answer; Anna heard the soft sound of the wheels and knew it would be Lissy.

'Is Jenny... oh?' Lissy stopped talking when she saw Helen.

'No, Jenny's still as poorly as ever, but there's been a development overnight, and I have to go to Lincoln. My son is here as well...'

'Anna, what's wrong? Can I help?'

'Ray... my husband... dead,' she gulped.

'No!'

She nodded. 'We have to go.' She handed her a key. 'Can you feed Eric for me, please? I'll ring you tomorrow when I know more. I'm sorry to burden you Lissy, but I don't know what to do.'

'Just go,' she said. 'Of course we'll take care of the fish. And I hope Jenny soon starts to feel better. Take the medication with you; you might need it for her. You don't want another night like last night.'

*****

They booked into a bed and breakfast place about two miles away from Lindum Lodge, and, after hearing their explanation of why they were there, the owner, Kathy Williams, offered to make their evening meals for the duration of their stay.

Once again, Anna burst into tears, and Mark stood by helplessly while Jenny hugged her. She breathed the word *cough* into her ear, and she obliged with a very nasty spell. Mrs. Williams offered to make them a drink, and they sat in the

110

resident's lounge for about half an hour. Anna's tears had been genuine; she was crying because Ray had gone, not because she was going to miss him. She was crying due to his manner of dying and Jenny's involvement in it. That involvement was not clear to her yet, other than she had killed him.

*****

Once again, Anna couldn't sleep. Her mind wouldn't close down and it occurred to her that not knowing the details was possibly worse than if she had known them. Now she could only imagine the horror. She tossed and turned all night, drank endless cups of tea, and tried to cope with the crushing feeling inside her. She desperately needed to speak with Jenny on her own, but she knew that wasn't going to happen anytime in the near future. She hoped she was remembering to cough and sniffle; she feared Jenny's cold was the only thing keeping her from thirty years in prison.

The next morning, they made the decision to stay put, after leaving most of the excellent breakfast cooked by Kathy. None of them felt like eating, and they played around with the eggs and bacon until she came, smiled at them, and took away their plates. She knew exactly why they hadn't eaten it.

The DI, who she now knew to be called Gainsborough, arrived at eleven o'clock with information that shocked only one out of the three of them. There were three murders, which they were linking together as having been done by one person; the lady in Hartsholme Park, Ray, and an elderly man, who lived within walking distance of Lindum Lodge. As yet, they didn't know whether Ray or the other man had been killed first last night, but they were guessing Ray, because there were two blood types on the elderly man. Thankfully, they didn't name him; it was really difficult for Anna hearing Mrs. Jackson's name that first time, as it made everything all too real. She didn't want to know the third victim's name.

All the police personnel were really good to them, and assured them they would be back in Lindum Lodge very quickly – Ray had been killed in the garden and not the house, so the garden was really the main crime scene.

When they asked one of them to go with them to identify Ray's body, Anna visibly shook and Mark said he would go. She had been so afraid she wouldn't be able to carry out this charade, but she found she didn't need to act any of it – she was traumatised by events. Jenny was still sniffling, coughing and barking, and Helen, who had been named as their designated liaison officer, was clearly sympathetic towards her, and completely left her to get on with having the flu.

Mark left to go to the morgue, and Anna hoped to have a few minutes with Jenny, but that wasn't to be. Helen stayed with them, and they just couldn't talk of anything which needed to be discussed; platitudes were the order of the day.

Mark returned within the hour, and just nodded as Anna turned towards him.

'Will you two be okay?' he asked. 'I have to pick Tim and Steve up later today, and Caroline should be here by two o'clock. She lands just after twelve, but her car is at the airport.'

'Airport?'

'She's in Amsterdam, flying back now, and landing at Humberside. I've spoken to Kathy, and she has a single room for her and a double for Tim and Steve. I've booked them in; they'll want us all to be together.'

'Thank you,' Anna said. 'I need my family as close as possible.'

'No, Mum, that's not what I meant. The police will want us all to be together. Thank goodness none of us were in Lincoln last night and can all prove it.'

'Where are Tim and Steve landing?'

'Manchester. They got the first flight they could.' He kissed the top of her head. 'You'll have us all here soon enough, so stop worrying. We're here to look after you, now. All of us.'

Helen sat quietly in the corner and watched their interaction. She smiled at her. 'Anna, do you need anything?'

'Sleep,' she said. 'And all my children.'

Chapter 25

Caroline entered the room like a tornado. Her beautiful brown eyes now reflected the horror she felt, and she had clearly been crying since getting the news.

'Come here, sweetheart,' Anna said and pulled her close. She sobbed and sobbed uncontrollably, and Anna continued to hold her until the tears subsided. If she had known of her father's violence towards her mother, and Anna now believed she did, she had loved him despite that knowledge. And that love had been steadfast all her life.

Finally, Caroline took a deep breath and sat down on the sofa, pulling a cushion towards her and holding it across her stomach. Her comfort action, there since childhood. She reached into her bag and fiddled around inside until she located a hair bobble. She pulled the long brown hair up into a ponytail, giving her face a more elfin look. Her eyes were red from crying, and she looked at her mother for support.

'Can I see Dad?'

Anna shook her head. 'Not yet. They still have tests to do...' Her voice trailed away. She didn't know what to say to her, her Caroline.

'We need to wait for everything until Mark gets back. He's at Manchester Airport waiting for Tim's flight to come in.'

Kathy came into the lounge and looked at Caro. She smiled. 'You must be Caroline. Let me know when you want to go to your room. Would anyone like a cup of tea?'

A chorus of affirmations made her smile again, and she said, 'I only have one room left now, and while you're here I won't be letting it. You need time to grieve and recover, and I can at least give you some peace.'

She left to go to the kitchen, and soon returned with a tray of teapots, cups and biscuits. 'Shout if you need more,' she said and walked out of the room.

Helen stood to pour out the tea, and they sat around making small talk. It felt so strange. Surreal. Anna's husband was dead, her daughter-in-law was a murderer, she herself was a liar and an accomplice, Caro was an innocent, and they were all behaving as if nothing had happened.

Caro asked a few questions, but Anna felt she didn't really want answers. It was still too raw for her. They saw nobody from the police, other than Helen, who actually went around 3.00pm, saying she would be back later.

Anna went up to her room just after she left and finally dozed off. The knock on the door woke her from quite a deep sleep, and for a moment she was startled, not sure where she was.

'Mum, you awake?'

She flew to the door and into Tim's arms. Finally, they were all together. He held her tightly and continually kissed the top of her head.

'I'm here now,' he whispered.

They stood for a long time just holding on to each other, taking comfort from the closeness, and then he led her downstairs. Steve was in the lounge with Mark, Jenny and a newly returned Helen, all of them drinking yet more tea. Tim moved to stand by Mark, and Anna was hit afresh by how alike they were – dark blonde hair, vivid blue eyes, a slight dimple in the chin; how had she not realised how unlike Ray they actually were? She tried to imagine how Michael would look now and failed. She could remember how he looked at Tim and Mark's age though; exactly as they looked now.

Jenny was discussing with Helen the possibility of a flying visit back to Leicester to pick up some clothes, and she saw Helen take out her phone. She spoke briefly into it and then nodded.

'That should be fine, Jenny,' she said. 'Can you make it there and back today?'

'Yes. That's no problem. You can come with me, if that makes it easier for your bosses.' She coughed spectacularly, and the WPC moved away from her.

Helen shook her head. 'No, I'd rather stay with Anna. And I can do without catching whatever it is that you've got! Just take care, you're all still in shock, you know. We don't want any accidents through lack of concentration.'

Anna saw the brief flicker of relief pass across Jenny's face, and she picked up Mark's car keys. He had driven down from Derby in his Toyota before transferring to a police car for the journey over to Sheffield. Jenny and Anna's cars had remained in Sheffield.

'I'll be careful,' she said. 'This car drives itself, to be honest. Mark will worry about it all the time I'm away,' she said with a laugh. They heard her coughing in the hallway as she put on her coat.

She left soon after, and everyone else remained in the lounge, talking quietly and trying to make sense of what had happened. Anna listened to the banter between Steve and Tim, and gradually began to relax, although she remained silent for most of the chat; she knew too much.

They speculated on the who, the why, and the wherefore; they had no answers. Everybody seemed to agree that Ray was a good man to his workforce, that he had been a good father and a good provider, and he had been supportive of his many friends. Anna caught Tim's eyes flickering towards her several times; each sentence of praise for Ray was followed by a small smile from Tim directed towards her. He clearly knew his father much better than his siblings did.

Helen just let them talk, and when Jenny returned, looking quite drawn and tired, Anna suggested they all make moves to their rooms, and sleep. Thankfully, everybody agreed with her, and her first full day as a grieving widow was over.

Anna walked along the small landing to her room, and she could hear Tim and Steve quietly talking in their room, but as she paused outside her door, she heard Caro crying. She hesitated, not knowing whether to go and hold her or just let her grieve in her own way. Anna decided to leave her to her tears, and she entered her own room. She showered and changed into her nightie, before sliding into the coolness of the white sheets. Anna wasn't sure if she heard a knock or not, and she said, 'Yes?'

'It's me. Just checking if you're ok,' Jenny spoke quietly.

'Just got into bed. I'm fine. Sleep tight, Jenny love. You looked exhausted.'

'Night God bless,' she said, and a moment later Anna saw two envelopes slide under the door.

She flew to the door and opened it, but Jenny had disappeared, having returned to their room, Anna assumed.

She grabbed a towel and picked up the letters. She could feel herself shaking as she carried the envelopes across to the tiny desk in the corner of her room. Jenny hadn't been to Leicester solely to pick up clothes; she had been to use the computer. She had clearly felt it was urgent to get the facts down on paper, in order to protect the rest of them.

Anna couldn't face seeing their contents; she placed them into the zipped compartment on the outside of the small suitcase she had packed to bring to Lincoln, still handling them with the towel and feeling like a master criminal. Letter number one was still under her double mattress. Helen's presence in her bedroom while she was packing left her no chance of retrieving it from its hiding place in the other bedroom. For many reasons, Anna needed to get back to Sheffield. If the police had any suspicions at all about their involvement in these three horrific murders, they would search their homes.

And as the large envelope was still unsealed and contained an envelope which had "Murder Number One" written on it, both she and Jenny would spend the rest of their lives in prison.

Anna climbed back into bed and tried to get the letters out of her mind. It was only as she was on the verge of sleep she realised she hadn't called Lissy, or Charlie. Both these women had a calming effect on her life, she needed them.

Anna had to make the calls. She drifted into sleep with that thought, and woke next day to the same thought and beautiful sunshine.

Chapter 26

The call to Charlie was hard. She gave her the facts as they had been given them by the police, and Charlie's immediate reaction was she would drive straight to Lincoln to be with her. Anna talked her down from this by saying it was all a bit chaotic, and she was being well looked after by everyone. The worst part of the conversation, apart from Anna lying to her, was Charlie couldn't grieve with her. She knew Ray, knew how he had been with her, and Anna thought she actually felt it was a case of good riddance to bad rubbish.

'Call me if you need me,' she said. 'You know I'm always here for you.'

'I will. The police will probably talk to you at some point. I've told them about our separation, and how he turned up at yours looking for me.'

'So, can I tell them what he was really like?' Anna could hear the anger in Charlie's tone.

'Just tell them the truth. It's all we can do now. He's gone, and I won't deny I feel almost a sense of relief, but it was a horrible way to go. That's the part I can't handle.'

Charlie sighed. 'You're right. Look, take care, sweetheart, and ring if you need anything. Anything at all. What happens next?'

It was Anna's turn to sigh. 'I really don't know. I think they're coming to take statements from us, but that won't help them much. Jenny and I were in Sheffield, Mark was in Derby, Tim was in Florida, and Caro was in Holland. From what little I've gleaned from them, Ray's death is linked to two others, so it's looking as though he was in the wrong place at the wrong time.'

They ended their conversation, and Anna moved restlessly around the room. She wanted to go home to

Sheffield, wanted her life back on an even keel. Even at this stage, she knew she wouldn't move back to Lindum Lodge; she didn't even want to visit the place.

Anna waited until lunchtime before ringing Lissy, and they had a very brief conversation. She confirmed Eric was still swimming happily around his tank, and she said the new dress for Grace was progressing well. Anna promised to let her know as soon as she knew she could return, and she disconnected with a tear in her eye.

It was almost as if Ray's death was a sudden hammer blow. Yes, she had hated him after Jenny's revelations, but she hadn't wanted him dead. He was only in his mid-fifties, and should have lived for another twenty years or so; that had been taken away from him in a truly barbaric fashion.

Anna knew she had to read the damn letters, but she also knew she had to be on her own when she did. She couldn't risk anyone else even seeing the envelopes, let alone their contents.

They spent the afternoon with the police, all of them describing where they were at the time of Ray's death. Anna went into more detail about their relationship, stressing she was on the point of returning home. She hoped Mark's statement would back her up on that point, as he had been the one to tell Ray she was just taking a break. Both Jenny and Anna spoke of her illness that night, but neither of them mentioned Lissy's involvement in any sort of detail at that stage. That fact might be needed later. Jenny also confirmed Anna was going back to Ray.

Anna did admit to herself that the police, without exception, were amazing with them. Solicitous, they explained as much as they could, confirming the second blood type found on the elderly man was Ray's blood, clearly indicating Ray had died before the third victim.

They also said they had very little to go on at this stage. The cyclist in Hartsholme Park had been completely cleared, and was actually enjoying a holiday in Benidorm at the moment, so was not even in the running as a suspect.

What they did confirm was all three killings were done by the same person. They didn't say a man, they said a person. The bags over the heads of the victims were identical, as were the plant ties around their hands and ankles. They hadn't found the knife which had incapacitated the victims, but it was the same knife used on each victim.

And although nobody said it out loud, they were waiting for the next death with a degree of trepidation.

Two days later, they were allowed back to Lindum Lodge. Tim never left Anna's side throughout the visit, and she just wandered from room to room, her mind in shut down mode. She was aware things had been moved, but wasn't sure if by police or Ray. The computer had gone, taken away by the police for examination, and it suddenly dawned on her the lads wouldn't be paid if she didn't do something.

'Mark,' she said, and he jumped, clearly lost in his own thoughts. 'I have to do something about wages.'

He laughed, a bitter edge to the laughter. 'Shall we see if we've got a workforce to pay?'

'What do you mean?'

'Dad took his anger out on them. I think Gary's still with you, so perhaps that's where we start.'

Gary was the foreman and she rang him with little hope of his answering.

He did.

They talked for a long time, and the result of the conversation was work would continue, she would pay set wages until they got the computer back, and everything could be returned to an even keel, and he had, as usual, power of hire and fire. They made temporary arrangements for wages to be paid in cash, as she had no account details, and he assured her the workers would be more than happy to stay with her. It was only at the end of the conversation he said he was sorry to hear of Ray's death, almost an afterthought really.

Anna really began to see what monumental damage had been done the day she had swept those bloody anniversary cards off the window sill. That simple action had touched so many lives, and, mostly, not for the better.

She sat down in the office and held her head in her hands. It felt too heavy to support. She didn't know what to do next.

Anna sensed someone approaching from behind her, and Tim's arms encircled her shoulders.

'Okay?' he said and kissed the top of her head.

She nodded. 'As okay as I can be. At least we've saved the business and the jobs. It's just too much.' She cracked, sobbing into her son's arms. Other people came in to see what was wrong, and Anna heard Tim shoo them away; all the time he held her. And yet, she didn't know what the tears were for. They were tears which needed to be released, but were they for Ray? Everybody assumed they were, including Tim, because he kept patting her and comforting her, saying, "Let it all out, Mum, let it all out."

Anna heard the front door open and close, and just that little bit of normality caused her to give a massive hiccup and the tears to finally cease.

'Mark's gone to get a pint of milk,' Jenny said. 'I think we all need a drink.'

They sat around the dining table, staring at their mugs. Nobody had used Ray's Sheffield Wednesday mug.

'So, what next?'

She turned to look at Mark. 'What do you mean?'

122

'I mean, what's next? What do you want us to do? Jenny and I need to see Adam and Grace; we need to explain their grandfather is dead, even though they didn't really know him.'

It took all of her strength and willpower not to look at Jenny.

'Of course you must go to them! Do we need to ask permission or anything?'

'I don't think so, but we'll tell Helen where we're going. We'll stay with them tonight and be back tomorrow. Where will you be?'

'Not here,' she said, just a shade too quickly.

Tim intervened. 'We'll go back to the B & B. We'll look after Mum, Mark, you see to the kids. And give them my love.'

They locked up the house, and went back to the comfort of Kathy Williams' place. Anna stayed downstairs for a short while, and then excused herself, saying she was going for a nap. Seeing the spot where Ray had died had been traumatic enough for today. The front garden had still had crime scene tape around it, and it had wiped her out.

Anna collapsed on to the bed and buried her head into the pillow until she felt she was suffocating. She rolled over and stared at the suitcase containing the letters.

She had to know. Jenny's words would tell her the facts, and then those facts had to be buried. Safely.

Chapter 27

Anna waited until everyone had gone to bed for the night before removing the envelopes from the front pocket of the suitcase, again using the towel to prevent her fingerprints showing on them. Jenny had rung to say they had told the children, and Adam had taken it particularly badly. He felt he hadn't really known his grandfather, and he now knew that wouldn't happen. She confirmed they were only staying overnight, and her last words were: *Be strong, my Kyra.*

Anna looked at the envelopes – one said, "Murder Number Two" and the other, "Murder Number Three," both handwritten. She moved to remove the letter from the first envelope and then remembered Jenny's instructions – *Do not touch the letter without gloves on!* The gloves and sealing wax were under the mattress back in Sheffield.

She sat for a moment, reluctant to put the letters back, now she had actually found some courage, but realised the towel was too risky to use.

Kathy had told them to help themselves if they wanted extra milks or sugars during the night, and she had showed where she kept them in her kitchen. Anna suspected she might find some gloves there as well, so she crept quietly down stairs. It took her only seconds to spot them under the sink unit, and hallelujah! They were disposable ones. She helped herself to a pair, and went back upstairs, clutching some extra milk tubs with the gloves stuffed up her sleeve. She now seemed to permanently be thinking like a criminal.

Anna made a drink to calm herself and then pulled on the gloves. The letter was typed.

To Whom It May Concern:

My name is Jennifer Carbrook, née March, and I was born on 10 October 1982 in Peterborough, Cambs.

On Friday, 10 April 2015, I killed Ray Carbrook. There are many reasons for my killing him, but none of this would have happened if he hadn't raped me.

The facts of the murder follow:

I stayed the night with Anna Carbrook at her new apartment in Sheffield. We went to bed at 11.00pm after a night with her neighbour, Lissy. During that evening, I pretended to be really ill to help with my alibi. Neither Lissy nor Anna suspected I was faking the heavy cold and cough. Both Anna and I went to our rooms as soon as Lissy had gone, and five minutes later I left the apartment. I had parked my car at the back of the apartment block, and hoped this would be enough to avoid detection by CCTV footage.

I drove to Lincoln and parked the car some distance away from Lindum Lodge, in a car park at the rear of a play area. I had dressed completely in black and heavy cloud cover hid the moon. It was very dark.

I waited in the garden of Lindum Lodge for a few minutes. I thought Carbrook would be home in bed, as it was now getting on for 12.30am, and I planned to wait another half hour and then enter the house to kill him.

I was kneeling in the bushes surrounding the front lawn when I heard a car approaching. It stopped, and Carbrook got out. He was very loud and very chatty with the driver. I heard him tell him to keep the change, and he staggered through the front gates. He closed them in a much exaggerated way, and was clearly very drunk.

He turned away from the gates, and his legs seemed to buckle. He negotiated the first step on the path, but staggered on the second step, and fell on to the grass by the side of the path, falling full length. I waited a couple of minutes before moving.

He never moved. I believe he was too drunk to get up.

I stabbed him in the neck just once. He didn't fight back. I placed a plastic bag over his head and secured it with duct tape, although I believe he was already dead by this time.

I secured his hands and feet with plant ties and left him.

I then exited the garden and headed towards my car. There are absolutely no regrets for what I have done to Ray Carbrook. This man was so evil to both Anna and I – and probably other women – and he deserved to die.

Jennifer Carbrook
11 April 2015

Such a short letter, such a massive act. And Anna still had the third letter to read. She put the Ray letter back in the envelope and slid it back into the suitcase. She couldn't face the third letter yet, so she slipped on her dressing gown and went to sit downstairs in the resident's lounge. She put Classic FM on, and let the music quietly wash over her and soothe her.

'Mom?' The whisper startled her, and she turned to see Tim looking around the door. 'You ok?'

'I'm fine.' Anna smiled at him. 'Go back to bed.' Her smile felt false. It was false. She was starting to think she would never smile again spontaneously.

Tim came over and sat by her side. He slipped his arm around her shoulders and pulled her close.

'Mom, we have to go back for a few days. We'll come over again as soon as we can, but leaving so hurriedly left a few things in the air we have to take care of.' The American twang in his voice touched her heart, and she squeezed his hand.

'Go,' she said. 'You're only a phone call away, and either Mark or I will keep you informed.'

They went back upstairs together, and she left him at the door of the room he was sharing with Steve.

'Sleep well,' he whispered, and Anna just smiled at him. She had a letter to read first.

Anna used the kettle in her room and made yet another cup of tea. She didn't really want it, but she was delaying the inevitability of opening that third envelope. She sipped at the tea, and a vivid picture of Charlie flashed across her mind. Charlie knew so much about her, about her marriage, about the abusive nature of that marriage, and yet something as massive as this she couldn't share with her. Charlie quite simply would not be able to turn a blind eye to it, and yet Anna needed to talk to someone. Someone she could trust.

Not Lissy; she hadn't known her long enough to burden her with it, and yet, Anna felt she could talk to her about most things. They had discussed Ray, and why she was now living across the hall from her, but telling her she was pissed off with her husband was a bit different to disclosing her daughter-in-law had killed him.

The sigh seemed to come from the soles of her feet, and Anna reached into the suitcase pocket for the third letter.

There were two pieces of paper, one handwritten and the other typed. She unfolded the handwritten one and felt tears come into her eyes.

Lovely Anna,

It is over. He is dead. I acknowledge what I have done is wrong, but I can now begin to live my life properly, and I hope what I have done enables the same in you. Killing the last victim was the hardest. He briefly fought back, and that almost became my undoing. I managed to twist the knife, and it was enough, eventually. You now have full descriptions of my actions, so please keep them safe. You may need them one day, but I hope not.

I suggest we never speak of this again, and we try to rebuild our own relationship. I will understand if you never want to see me again, but it will make me deeply unhappy.

We must act our way through the funeral and support Mark, Tim, and Caro. After that, we will help you move back to Lindum Lodge, if that is what you want.

The large brown envelope I gave you with the first letter is for you to now put all three letters in. Seal it with the sealing wax in the same way you have sealed the three white envelopes and hide it away. In twenty years' time, you can burn it!

I think, one day, you will see this all had to happen. That man could not be allowed to live. I love you, my Anna, now read my final letter, and get them locked away, hopefully forever.

With love,

Jenny

P.S. Don't forget to destroy this letter!!! xxx

Jenny seemed to have thought of everything, and Anna shook her head, trying to clear her thoughts, before spreading out the second sheet of paper on her bed. She really knew nothing of this third murder, because Jenny hadn't even mentioned anything of it the night she had returned to her apartment from Lincoln. There had been no chance of talking since then; Anna's entire family surrounded her with love and no time for herself. Maybe that was a good thing, she didn't know.

The letter started in exactly the same way as the other two, and it was with a small hysterical giggle Anna hoped Jenny hadn't set up some sort of template for murder confessions on her laptop! Then she stopped giggling and began to read.

To Whom It May Concern

My name is Jennifer Carbrook, née March, and I was born on 10 October 1982 in Peterborough, Cambs.

On Friday, 10 April 2015, I killed a man, who I now know to be James Oswoski, on Shenfield Drive in Lincoln at approximately 12.45am. He was simply walking along the road, leaning on a walking stick.

I elbowed him as I went past and he fell on to the stone wall at the back of the flower bed, cracking his head. It was a twist of the knife in his neck which ultimately disabled him. He died on the flower bed, and I was able to place the bag over his head, seal it with duct tape, and secure his hands and feet with plant ties.

This is my final murder. There will be no more. I killed Mrs. Jackson and Mr. Oswoski to perpetuate the theory of a serial killer, but they were incidental murders. The only person I wanted dead was Ray Carbrook, and his was the easiest of all. He was virtually in an alcoholic coma when I stabbed him.

I deeply regret the two murders that had to be; I do not regret the death of Ray Carbrook. I have no way of knowing if these letters will ever come to light. I suspect one day, if my death is an early one, they will, because I am telling Anna the envelope contains letters for Adam and Grace, and the envelope can be opened after my death. Hopefully, I will have been able to destroy the letters before that, so that my children never find out the truth, particularly Adam who shares the same genes as Carbrook. I will wait twenty years, and if the letters will no longer be required, I will ask Anna for them back, saying they are no longer relevant.

I have to stress Anna is the unwitting pawn in all of this. She knows nothing, and I intend that it should stay that way.

I acted entirely alone, the planning was all of my doing, and it happened because Anna walked away from an abusive marriage. I would not have done it if I had thought the Carbrooks were happily married.

Anita Waller

The world is now a better place.
Jenny Carbrook
11 April 2015

The world is now a better place. Anna folded the piece of paper carefully, aware it needed to be kept as pristine as possible, and put it back in the "Murder Number Three" envelope. She then made sure that everything, including the letter she needed to shred, was safely back in the pocket of the suitcase.

Then she sat and cried.

Chapter 28

Anna didn't sleep much, and the morning arrived with a decision made. She needed to return to Sheffield.

Breakfast was a quiet time; Tim and Steve were returning to Florida, and they would all miss them. She decided to break the news of her return to her apartment, but it didn't go down too well.

Everyone took out phones or notebooks as she filled them in on her address, and Caro asked if she could come back with her. She said of course she could, and they confirmed with Helen that it was indeed okay for them all to go their assorted separate ways. Helen gave them what information she could about the investigation, but it seemed to Anna they actually had no leads at all, and in a strange sort of way, they were almost waiting for the next murder in the hope it would yield more clues.

'They will be releasing your husband's body within the next couple of days,' Helen informed her, and gently touched Anna's arm. 'I really am so sorry this has happened to all of you. You're a lovely family, and it just seems to be some random killing, no rhyme or reason to it.'

'You'll keep us informed?' Anna asked.

'Of course.'

'Then we'll all be on our way, as soon as we've said goodbye to Mrs. Williams. Thank you, Helen.'

They packed what little they had with them and went back downstairs. Mark was settling the bill with Kathy, and Anna tried to intervene.

'It's okay, Mum,' he said, without looking at her. 'I've got it.'

There was coldness in his tone that bothered her, and she looked at him.

'Mark?'

'What?'

'Don't speak to me like that.' It was her turn to be frosty. 'I'm your mother. Show respect, please.'

'Why? You're lying.'

'What?' Her stomach turned somersaults.

The others moved away, aware that something was happening between the two of them.

'I'm not lying,' she said and tried to hide the quiver in her voice. What did he know?

'I asked you about returning to Dad, and you said you would. You just needed a little more space, and you would go back to Lincoln. You said that quite clearly, Mum. And you meant me to pass that message on to Dad.'

'And it was true.'

'No, it wasn't. I knew it wasn't true the moment I saw Eric the bloody goldfish. There's no way you could have gone back to Dad with a goldfish in tow! He would have killed it, just like he killed the last one! You had no intentions of ever returning home.' His voice was getting louder and louder, and the others began to move back to them, led by Jenny.

'Hey,' Jenny said soothingly. She leaned her head against her husband's chest. 'You're right. That's why we were having Eric. When Anna bought him, it was in a mad moment, when she had no ideas about going back to your Dad, but that day we spent together in Sheffield she talked a lot about the return, and she asked me to take the fish. It's no big issue, sweetheart, not at all.'

'An apology will do nicely, Mark,' Anna said icily; guiltily. Eric the Fish had a lot to answer for. She looked towards Jenny, and Jenny gave her a small smile.

'I'm sorry,' Mark said, and extended his left arm to pull her towards him. 'That's been on my mind since that awful night.'

'No problem,' she said. 'Any more issues just ask, for crying out loud.'

Kathy hugged them all, and said they would be welcome back any time. They left her to all the work involved with such a mass exodus of all of them.

They didn't go back to Lindum Lodge; Mark drove Jenny off to pick up their children, and then Caro drove the two of them to Sheffield. In the end, it was Tim and Steve who were the last ones to leave, flying to Florida later that evening. Jenny said she would get to Sheffield for her car as soon as she could, and they parted with a hug.

*****

Lissy and Caro got on like a house on fire. Caro was very creative and loved to try anything crafty; all it took was a glimpse into Lissy's workspace for her to become immersed in a conversation which seemed to go on forever. Anna chatted with Jon, telling him about the investigation, their time in Lincoln, and the support she had been given by both her family and the police; he kept all of them fed and watered until Anna called time, saying they needed to go home.

She could see Caro wanted to argue, but she put on her stern face and said, 'Home.' Lissy laughed and escorted them to the door, but then insisted Caro return to continue with whatever they had planned for the following day.

Caro was impressed with her mother's apartment. She had bought a little two up, two down stone built terraced house in the heart of Lincoln, and had filled it with homemade items, just as Charlie had with her home. Anna's apartment was modern but was slowly becoming homelier, the more she added to it. Anna found it a little strange both she and Caro had lived with the perfection that was Lindum Lodge, and yet had changed completely the moment they were away from its restrictive influences.

They sat for an hour or so just chatting about things in general; they drank hot chocolate, ate far too many biscuits, and actually laughed.

As they switched off the lights and went to their separate bedrooms, Caro turned to Anna.

'I loved him, Mum, loved him very much, but I did understand why you left. And this,' She waved her arm expansively, 'This is so much more you than Lindum ever was. Lindum was Dad. Sell it; get it out of your life.'

Anna felt shocked, but tried not to show it. She had grossly underestimated her children; they knew their father.

*****

Anna slept much better for being home in Sheffield. She was awake before seven, and lay for a while just thinking things through. She felt quite frustrated she had nobody to talk to about the things troubling her. How could she say to Charlie, or Lissy – *Hey, my son's wife murdered my husband!*

Anna took Caroline around the corner to the little café for breakfast, and she began to see her in a new light. She had always thought of her as a confident young woman, but she seemed different. She was beautiful for a start. She had clearly passed through the scruffy era of duffel coats and heavy eyeliner, combined with her passion for heavy metal music, and had developed a maturity reflected in the way she spoke, stood, and interacted with people.

They enjoyed their meal, and then went shopping. They bought some summer clothes, but more importantly, they bought food. Caroline insisted they couldn't live on beans on toast forever, so they did a pretty grand food shop. The fridge looked amazing after they'd finished filling it.

'Right,' she said. 'Now I've done my chores, can I go see Lissy, please?'

Anna nodded. 'Of course you can.' She handed her some muffins. 'Take these with you; she likes them.'

It was quiet after Caro had gone visiting; Anna went into Caro's bedroom and lifted the mattress to get the first letter. She had emptied the main part of the suitcase just after they arrived home, but she had decided to leave the other two letters in the front pocket.

Once again she put on the gloves, took out the letters, and placed them with the first one. They were dynamite in the wrong hands.

Anna used the sealing wax to seal the two new envelopes, and then placed all three of them in the larger brown envelope. She then sealed that with wax, threw the wax and the seal into her kitchen waste bin, and put the envelope on the top shelf of the wardrobe in her own room so she wouldn't damage the sealing wax by sleeping on it.

It then occurred to Anna it was pretty stupid to leave something as unusual as sealing wax and a seal in the kitchen waste bin, so she took the half full bag down to the garbage room in the basement and breathed a sigh of relief when she got back to her own apartment without meeting anyone.

Anna's brain felt as though it was going to burst. She had been able to talk to the only person who really understood everything up to the final murder, and then she had lost Jenny. They couldn't really talk now, either; Caro was with her, and Mark was with Jenny.

Caro came home; they had a hot chocolate, and then went to bed. Anna heard Caroline's phone ring, and she said she was fine to whoever was on the other end, and then said goodnight very softly. She didn't know who the caller was, but she smiled. The tone of her daughter's voice told Anna quite a lot.

She slept. Not well but dreamlessly

When she surfaced next morning, Anna knew what she was going to do.

Chapter 29

Caroline went out early, promising to bring back something nice for lunch. She said she wanted a walk around the city centre, wanted to clear her head, because she hadn't had too good a night.

'I miss Dad,' she had said simply, and Anna had nodded. 'I know you do, sweetheart, and it's going to be difficult for quite some time. Are you sure you don't want me to come with you?'

'No thanks, Mum. I need to be on my own. I'm not good company anyway, at the moment. I'll be back before lunch, don't worry.'

Anna went out on to the balcony and watched her daughter walk along the river side and head towards the town centre. It was only when Caro was completely out of sight did Anna come back indoors.

Anna stared at her phone for a while; it occurred to her it had become a massive part of her life. In her pre-escape days, she had very rarely used it. Now it never seemed to be out of her hand.

She scrolled down her list of contacts and pressed a name. She felt calm. She had spent too long thinking through this action to be dithering about it. She waited for the call to connect.

When it did, it was answered almost immediately, and there was a couple of seconds before she heard, 'Hello?'

'I have a fish called Eric.' Anna held her breath as she said the words.

There was a further silence of around five seconds, a long time to wait. Then, she heard a gasp of breath and one word.

'Anna.'

Anita Waller

Chapter 30

They talked for an hour. Anna sobbed through the first five minutes and listened to the man she had given up all those years ago attempt to calm her, long distance.

'Let me come to you,' he repeatedly said, and she had to keep saying no. 'I dared to hope you would call me when details of the murder began to filter through.'

'I can't. I have my family to think of; how do you think they would react to you turning up on my doorstep?'

'Anna, I am a friend.'

'I know, but you're a friend they've never heard of, never mind met! I can't see you; I just needed to hear your voice.'

'And I've needed to hear yours since the day we agreed never to see each other again. I've always left my phone number out in the world, just in case... and thank God I did.'

They finally ended the telephone call with Anna promising to call him the following day. She didn't give a time; she had explained Caroline was staying with her, and she would have to wait until she wasn't in the apartment. It all felt very clandestine; that was the way of Anna's life at the moment.

*****

The funeral was arranged for 7 May, and Tim and Steve arrived three days earlier to make sure they were there to support Anna. She had opened up Lindum Lodge in the short term and knew decisions would have to be made about the place.

Caroline had moved back to her own home in Lincoln, but for the period of the funeral had joined her brother and his partner at Lindum Lodge. Anna had spoken very little with

Jenny; she knew they were coming over to Lincoln on the Wednesday to be available for the day after, but Anna was surprised when Mark said they would be staying with everyone else at Lindum Lodge. She couldn't imagine how Jenny would be feeling about that.

Anna had moved back into Lindum Lodge over the bank holiday weekend, and had spent one night on her own there. It hadn't been a good night, and she had slept very little. Too many ghosts.

She had spoken with Michael during the long evening, and had almost been tempted to ask him to come over, but resisted. She wanted no complications at this stage, needed to have Ray completely out of her life before the possibility of moving on could be anywhere in the picture.

*****

Tim and Steve arrived late the following day, and immediately, Anna's spirits lifted. She had put them in Tim's old room, and it felt good to have him back there. Mark and Jenny would take the master bedroom, Caroline her old room, and she, herself, was sleeping in the guest bedroom.

Deep down, Anna wondered if putting Jenny in the room which used to be the exclusive domain of the Ray/Anna partnership was some sort of punishment, torture even, but she knew she could never sleep in it again.

The day of the funeral was overcast; the previous night had been a sombre affair, with everyone lost in their own thoughts. Jenny looked different – she had cut her blonde hair much shorter, and she appeared so much more mature. Everyone else looked the same, and Anna realised life still had to go on; these children of hers would continue to live long after Ray had been despatched, and long after she had followed him.

They were all clearly dreading the day to come, and when the cortege pulled up outside the gates of Lindum Lodge, they moved outside to get in the sleek black cars. There was a crowd of people. Anna felt quite taken aback by it; she hadn't realised they knew so many. It was only later she came to realise it was because of the nature of the death, not the person who had died.

The funeral went smoothly, and they all returned to Lindum Lodge for drinks and food. The caterers had cleared up and gone by seven o'clock, and finally, the family could settle down and talk.

Anna began. 'We need to talk about your father's will. Although Simmonite's are coming tomorrow to talk you through it, unless your Dad changed it over the last few weeks, I know what's in it. He made the will after discussion with me, because he wanted to know what I wanted, should he die before me. What we decided was there would be immediate payments to all three of you of £50,000, and the rest will be mine. The business, at my request, will go to Mark, if he wants it. Your father was aware Tim and Caroline wouldn't want any part of it. Mark, you don't need to make any decisions now, you need to talk this through with Jenny and the children, because it will mean a move back to Lincoln.'

Anna paused for a moment to look at all their faces. Jenny was inscrutable. Mark looked pensive, and Tim grinned at her. Caroline had tears in her eyes.

'I have to make a decision about Lindum Lodge. If you decide to come back to Lincoln, Mark, you are very welcome to live here. You can do what you want with it, redecorate, add extensions, whatever, to make it your home for you four. If you don't want it, I am going to sell it. I won't be returning here. I live in Sheffield now. It will always be my property, if you decide to live here, and will have to be sold on my death so it is split equally between the three of you, but by the time that day arrives, you will probably be in a position to buy the other two out, and make it yours, in every sense of the word. It will be up to you to make sure the business thrives, and that needs to start now. If you decide it's not for you, I will be selling the business. I can't run it from Sheffield. All this, of course, depends upon Dad not having changed anything because I walked away. We won't know until tomorrow, but I wanted to give you all a heads up tonight so you can sleep on it. Anybody want to say anything?'

'Whoosh!' Mark said. 'That's a pretty big decision you've landed on our doorstep, Mum.'

'It certainly is, 'Jenny added. 'I've never thought about returning to Lincoln...'

'Well, the decision needs to be made sooner, rather than later. If you want to look at the accounts, Mark, I can show you them. We have the computer back from the police now, and I've sorted all the wages out for the workforce so everything is up to date. And it's a good workforce and a good business. You would be mad not to take advantage of it, but I am aware of all the other issues. If Dad had died of natural causes, I don't think you would have hesitated, but he died here, in the front garden, and that has to have an effect. You could, of course, buy another house in Lincoln and run the business from there, but this is set up for it. The choice is yours; it makes no difference to me. I can sell Lindum Lodge now, or you can sell it or buy it when I die.'

'Well, I don't know if this helps, but I think Dad made exactly the right decision, if this is what his will still states.' Caroline's voice was a little weak, but she felt she had to say something. 'Tim? How do you feel? Would you have wanted to share this with Mark?'

Tim laughed. 'You're joking. I don't even live in the country now, and nothing would make me want to work here. I say go for it, Mark. Make it even bigger and better than Dad did, and give Adam and Grace a future.'

They chatted for another hour, and then, one by one, drifted off to bed, leaving Jenny downstairs with Anna.

'I don't know what to say, Anna.'

'I know. Will you be able to live here? I really would like you two to take the business on; I can show you the admin side, and Mark will be a natural in Ray's role. It makes sense.'

Jenny still looked troubled. 'Ray's death freed us. I'm just a bit worried it's going to ensnare us here now. The first thing I would have to do is completely change that front garden, so I don't see him every time I walk up that path.'

'Then do it. We all need to move on, in whatever way we can, from this. You and I will find it so much harder, but that's our penalty, isn't it? The others will eventually accept he's gone, and life will return to normal. Not for me and you.'

'I'll talk to Mark after the official will reading. He may have changed it anyway. This was never about profiting from his death financially; it was about profiting from it mentally. For both of us.'

She stood and moved towards the door. 'I'll see you in the morning, Anna. I suspect I have a conversation waiting for me upstairs.'

'Night, Jenny. Love you.'

'Love you too, my Kyra.'

Chapter 31

Jeff Simmonite arrived just after 10.00am the next morning, and by midday, he had gone. He confirmed the will was still as Anna remembered it.

Mark and Jenny had talked long into the night, and he asked for a couple more days to think things through and talk to the children before finalising their decision to move back to Lincoln.

Jenny stood by Anna's side in the kitchen, making lunch for them all, before their departures at various times for their own homes.

'Who decided yes?' Anna asked her.

'Mark, really. I'm going along with it because it will give stability in our lives, a good start for the children, and it takes us a bit nearer to you. The only drawback is living with what I did, and the fact I did it here.' She held up a finger as Anna opened her mouth to speak. 'No, Anna, I don't regret anything. On a personal level, I feel liberated, and that has to be good for my family. Ray had to die. Eventually, everyone will start to feel less grief stricken, and life will go on. We will move in here, and I've made it a condition of living here that we turn the front garden into a parking area for our cars and change the double garage into accommodation for when you visit. That means you can come stay with us, without having to go upstairs where there are so many bad memories for you, and it will change things downstairs as well. Mark's agreed to everything I want, so really the agreement to take over the business is more or less a formality. It will only be if the kids really kick off and come up with valid arguments against the move that things could change.'

'Well, I'm glad. I would hate to see the business I built up, just as much as Ray did, go to somebody new. Let me know your final decision as soon as possible, we'll bring Simmonite's back in and get it made official, and I'll take you through the administration side of it. It will certainly make things easier for you with childcare, because you'll be working from home, and the salary is pretty good. I saved every single penny of my earnings for the fifteen years or so I was doing the job. Time for me to retire on my hard-earned wealth now.'

Jenny smiled. 'Mine won't be anywhere near as hard-earned as yours was.' She reached across and kissed Anna on the cheek.

They took the sandwiches and drinks through to the lounge, placing them on the coffee table. Mark's face looked slightly less drawn than it had done since the night he had turned up in Sheffield to bring the news about his father.

'Have the police said anything?' he asked.

'Not a thing. They seem to be a bit in limbo from what I can gather. I noticed a police presence at the funeral yesterday, and Gainsborough came up to me to offer condolences on behalf of the department. But, there's nothing on the investigation. No weapon for a start. They never close down a murder case so, I suppose, one day something will surface, but for now, there doesn't seem to be anything.'

'Mom, you coming over to us?' Tim tried to steer the conversation on to lighter areas.

'Not yet, Tim. I want to see about buying something in Sheffield and getting myself properly settled, and I need to be available for a while until Mark and Jenny are happy they can continue to run the business without me. As it stands at the moment, I'm the only one who knows anything,' she said with a laugh. 'But, I promise I'll come over for a holiday soon. I'll give you advance warning so you two can maybe arrange some time off to show me round.'

They started to drift away shortly after lunch; Tim and Steve were the first to leave. Their flight was scheduled to leave Manchester at 6.00pm, and after the longest hug ever, Anna watched their hire car disappear down the drive and turn on to the road. Tim's head didn't turn towards the spot where his father had died.

Mark and Jenny followed shortly after, with Jenny promising to ring her that night. Caroline was the last to go; she couldn't hide her tears.

'I miss him, Mum. So much.'

'I know, sweetheart. We all do in our very different ways, but you have always been his special one. Just remember him with love.'

Caro got into her car and drove away, stopping for a couple of seconds on the drive to look across the garden to where her Dad had died. Anna turned her back on the garden and walked into the house.

Anna waited ten minutes or so, and then rang Michael.

'It's over,' she said simply. 'Everyone has gone home.'

'Can I see you?'

'Yes. But not here. People still look at this place; it's become a bit of a tourist attraction. I'm heading back to Sheffield tonight, but we could meet up in Newark?'

'In our cafe?' She could hear the smile in his voice.

'Yes, our cafe. Is it still there?'

'It certainly is. What time are you leaving?'

'I just need to pack the car, and then I'm ready. I can be there for two.'

'A coffee will be waiting.'

Anna checked every room and carried her small suitcase downstairs. It occurred to her she would have to put furniture into storage, because Jenny and Mark would want their own, and it would have to be done quickly. She would have to arrange to meet Jenny at Lindum in a couple of days and go through

145

everything; the business needed someone at the helm pretty quickly.

Anna loaded the car with a few items from the kitchen, and was just getting into the driving seat, when Gainsborough pulled into the driveway. She waited while he walked across to her.

'Do you need to go inside, DI Gainsborough?'

'No. You heading off out?'

'I'm going back to Sheffield. I don't want to be here on my own. Everyone's gone...'

He nodded sympathetically.

'I do understand how difficult it can be. I just popped by to check you're all okay, and to tell you we're putting all this on Crimewatch. Maybe it will jog someone's memory, give us something to go on, however small. You should be here; it would add something to it, if they can interview you. And possibly Mark?'

'When?'

'11 May. Next Monday. Is that okay with you? Can you be here?'

She nodded. 'Of course I can. I'll contact Mark. He works away during the week, so it's not a certainty he can be here, but I definitely can.'

'Thank you. I don't mind admitting there's not much to go on. We can't find any connection at all between the three victims, other than they're all from Lincoln. Somebody knows something, must have seen blood on clothing, that sort of thing.'

Anna had a brief flashback to a naked Jenny walking across to the bathroom while she herself held the bloodied clothing.

'I'll be here. It won't be easy, but I can do it.'

He smiled. 'We don't give up, you know. We'll get him.'

'I hope so. We need closure.'

He turned and walked back to his car. He folded his tall frame into the passenger seat and rolled down the window. 'See you Monday, Anna. Nine o'clock?'

She nodded and held up a hand in agreement. The car reversed down the drive, and she sank slowly into her own driving seat. Crimewatch always brought results. How many times had she watched the programme, and thought how good it was that all those people had rung in, because their memories had been triggered about that crime?

Anna drove to Newark with mixed feelings. This could be a difficult weekend in front of her.

She walked into the café, which had been 'their' cafe all those years ago, and saw him immediately. Tall, grey hair now replacing the dark blonde of their early years, but still the bright blue eyes she remembered so well. Anna would remember them anywhere, of course; both her sons had the same eyes. He wore a pale grey suit, and the sight of him stopped her breath.

He stood as soon as he saw her and walked towards her. He opened his arms, and she walked into them. They stood for an indeterminable amount of time, and only moved when the waitress stopped what she was doing to watch them. He led her to the table, held the chair out for her, and she sat down. She hadn't said a word. Neither had he.

And then they both spoke at once.

'Michael...'

'Anna...'

And they laughed.

And all was right between them.

They talked about inconsequential things while consuming three coffees and a scone. Afterwards they walked through a park, as they had done before; the day they had decided to split up they had said the awful words in that park. It would now hold good memories for them, instead of bad.

Anna spoke of her returning to Lincoln on Monday for the Crimewatch programme and her handing over of the house to Mark and Jenny.

'I consider Sheffield to be my home now,' she said. 'I absolutely love where I am living, it's the right size for me, and if one of the apartments comes on the market, I'm going to look at buying it. If I can get one the size that my friends have bought, that will be even better. Their home has three bedrooms, mine only has two.'

'Can I see it?'

Anna nodded. 'Of course. Let's get all this Crimewatch and business transfer out of the way and back to a normal sort of living, and you can come over. But not until then. It would be wrong. I've only just lost Ray.'

'Did you love him?'

She shook her head. 'No. Not in any way. I was scared of him. I didn't want him dead, and I do wonder if I'd been there, would he still be alive? I'm sure he would. He didn't go out drinking at night; that only started after I left.'

She didn't add that other factors had conspired in Ray's death. Some secrets were just that, secret.

They parted soon after; Anna needed to get home, needed time to think. Michael didn't start his own car until he had seen her drive safely out of the car park and head in the direction of Sheffield.

He now knew the love he had held on to for so many years hadn't just been imaginary; it was real, and life could have been so different for both of them. He hated the thought she had been scared of Ray; she hadn't said why, but he knew she would, one day.

Michael drove home with his heart singing. For now it felt like an affair, but he had hopes one day they could be open and enjoying each other's company.

Chapter 32

The people at Crimewatch were very gentle with her. Mark was there in support – as he said, what could they do, sack him? He was leaving anyway. They spoke of the emptiness within the family, the loss felt by the men he employed at Carbrooks, and the changes they were now being forced to make. Mark ended his short speech by asking anyone who knew anything at all, who may have seen something out of the ordinary on that dark night, to come forward with it.

Jenny had arrived with Mark, and after the cameras had disappeared to film the other two locations, all three of them sat down with a coffee to discuss what would happen next.

'Well,' Anna began, 'I thought I would crack on with some packing today. There are some things I'm going to take to Sheffield with me, and if there's anything you three want that belonged to your Dad, then just take it. The bigger stuff, the furniture, needs to be put into storage or sold, or whatever. I don't really care. I've set myself up in Sheffield, so there's nothing here that will be of use. Do you two want anything? This house is much bigger than yours, so you might want to hang on to some things.'

'We'll keep the office as it is; you've set that up well. And maybe the furniture in the guest room can stay, because we won't have anything to put in there.' Mark smiled at his mother. 'Is that okay with you?'

'It's absolutely fine. Jenny?'

Jenny looked grey. 'Yes, it's good. Mark's right. This all seems very... sudden.'

'I know,' Anna said gently. 'And if there wasn't the business to consider, we wouldn't have to rush. In fact, if there wasn't the business, I would simply be selling the house. Look,

I believe this is what we have to do. Let's clear the bedrooms. Then, bring Chris and John, our two best decorators in and get yours, Grace, and Adam's rooms done. Have them re-carpeted, or whatever you want on the floors, and then it will feel like your home and not ours. No ghosts.'

Jenny nodded. 'Okay. Shall we make a start? Mum and Dad are at ours packing for us so we can stay latish.'

They concentrated on the three bedrooms, and managed to dismantle and move all three beds down into the garage. Anna sorted things and blessed the day she'd agreed – been told – a double garage was a good idea.

She had an area for charity shop furniture, an area for general charity shop stuff, and an area for bits she was going to take with her. As Mark and Jenny came across items they wanted, they moved them into the guest room for sorting at a later date.

They stood back and surveyed the empty rooms. 'Okay, I want colour.' Jenny was adamant. 'These carpets are going nowhere, they're what I would buy anyway, and they're cream, so we'll use colour on the walls. We'll have new curtains, new bedding, and our bed is new anyway. It will be ours.'

'Right.' Anna looked around the room she had shared with Ray for so many years, and felt nothing. Had she hated him that much? Wasn't she supposed to be grieving?

'If you want to be moving quickly, we have to speak with the lads tonight. They have to be starting by next week at the latest.'

Anna went to the office to find out where Chris was likely to be and realised he was working fairly close by. She rang him, and he said he could be there in ten minutes.

Chris was a little bit overwhelmed when he arrived. The bedrooms had been decorated some six months earlier, and he hadn't thought he would be back so soon.

He made notes of everything Jenny wanted, including a wallpapered feature wall in the master bedroom. She would provide that, if he would tell her how much she needed. They moved into the office, and Chris gave Jenny shopping lists for all three rooms. Anna checked and confirmed he could start the following Monday, although John was tied up until Wednesday.

Chris left, and the three of them sat down and ordered a pizza. Nobody had the strength, or inclination, to cook.

Mark loaded up Anna's Audi before leaving to head back to Leicester. He pulled his mother close and held her. 'You've changed,' he whispered. 'A different person.'

Anna smiled at him. 'Good. But, I'd changed the day I left here. It's not your father's death that has changed me, it's more his life. It wasn't a life I wanted any longer. Nearly forty years was long enough.'

She felt him stiffen and then relax. He knew what she meant. Deep down he'd always known. He'd obviously inherited her ostrich syndrome.

Anna headed back to the sanctuary of Sheffield, and wheeled the suitcase with the items she'd brought back with her across to the lifts. The doors opened, and Jon stepped out.

'Hey, stranger,' he said with a grin. 'How are you?'

'Tired,' she admitted. 'I've been at Lindum Lodge all day. We filmed for Crimewatch this morning, and we've been sorting bedrooms the rest of the time. You can imagine...'

He nodded sympathetically. 'Call, if you need us. We're always available.'

'Thank you, Jon,' she sighed. 'I think a full night's sleep will solve most of life's ills at the moment though. I intend on going in, making a pot of tea, and heading to bed with a good book.'

He smiled once more and kissed her cheek. 'Take care, Anna. Enjoy your book.'

She manoeuvred the large suitcase into the lift, and the doors closed. She leaned her head back on the wall and closed her eyes, exhaustion seeping into her body. So tired.

Anna's apartment felt chilled, and she switched on the heating. Feeding Eric was a priority and then the promised cup of tea was placed on the coffee table. She made a sandwich, went into the bedroom to get her book, and opened it at the bookmarked page. She was reading Harper Lee for the first time in her life and was enjoying it. Anna managed to get through two paragraphs, before laying her head on the back of the chair. She woke up three hours later to a cup of cold tea, a toasty warm apartment, and an inviting bed. Harper Lee had the bookmark replaced in the same spot, and Anna walked to the bedroom, clicking off the heating as she did so.

Chapter 33

Michael's first visit to her apartment had Anna fraught with worry. She had only met up with him that one time in the café, and they had been surrounded by other people. This would be a face-to-face meeting, with nobody else there.

The transfer of the business had gone through smoothly, and Anna had spent two days with Jenny taking her through the administrative side. They were now living in Lindum Lodge, and Anna had changed her will to specify what was to happen to the house on her death.

She stood on the balcony and watched Michael's car pull into the car park. He then disappeared from view, and she crossed swiftly to the intercom ready to release the lock downstairs. She whispered, "Come up," and then he was there.

Michael enfolded her into his arms and kissed her soundly. 'So many years...' he said softly and kissed her again.

Anna led him by the hand into the lounge area, telling him to sit down, and she would get coffee. They talked and talked; the years rolled by, as they filled each other in on where their lives had led.

Michael spoke at length about Patricia, about the difficulties she had faced as the degenerative disease progressed. He also spoke of Erin; as she had grown older, she had been his rock, taking over when he simply hadn't been able to get out of a meeting, or he needed to see a client with their completed accounts.

'In the end,' he confessed, 'her death was a blessed release for her. She was ready, even though Erin and I weren't. She's been gone three years now. I can't say I've been lonely, because for the last two years of her life she wasn't really part of the family. I've learnt to live without company. And I have Erin whenever she has time to pop in. I retired from business ten years ago, but I still retain a controlling interest in it.'

'And now? Do you have any plans now you've got over the initial phase of being alone?'

'I don't want to be without you again,' he said, pulling her closer. Anna let her head rest on his shoulder. 'That's my first plan.'

'Michael, we can't be open, not yet.'

'I know. Your family would never accept me at this early stage; they'd think you arranged it. I promise there'll be no surprise visits; we'll be discreet, careful. Is that what you want?'

She nodded. 'Yes, it is. I gave up so much...'

'We gave up so much. It was always you, Anna. Always. Believe me, I've learned how to wait for you. I can wait a bit longer to make everything right.'

Michael made no further references to their future, and they spent a pleasant morning in conversation. She found out he didn't care for football, and she smiled to herself. If he wanted to see more of her, she would have to educate him.

They went out into Derbyshire for lunch, after heading for the car park separately before meeting up again at Michael's car. It was just a precaution; Anna really only knew Lissy and Jon, and their apartment didn't overlook the car park. She was aware she might bump into them in the lift, and didn't want to have to lie about who Michael was.

It was a wonderful afternoon; the sun shone, and they walked and talked and laughed. Heading back to Sheffield later, they discussed getting back into the building, and decided Anna would be dropped off first, and Michael would arrive ten minutes later.

It worked; she saw no-one. And Anna had about five minutes of private thinking time. It wasn't long enough to

34 Days

analyse all her feelings, but the over-riding one was of happiness. She blessed the day she had found the courage to ring him.

Anna put background music on – a bit of Rod Stewart never hurt anyone, she reckoned – and she pressed the door release as soon as the intercom buzzed.

It felt so natural; they talked even more, and then around nine o'clock, Michael stood.

'Okay,' he said. 'I'm going to go now. What arrangements do we need to make for tomorrow? Shall I meet you somewhere away from here?'

She laughed. 'I hadn't thought that far. You're booked into the Hilton?'

He nodded. 'I knew I would want to see you tomorrow. There's no point tripping backwards and forwards between here and Lincoln.'

'Shall I meet you at the Hilton for breakfast? I'd like that.'

'That would be wonderful. Eight-thirty ok? And then we can decide what we're doing over coffee.'

Michael picked up his jacket, and she followed him to the door. He pulled her into his arms and kissed her. The kiss lengthened and deepened, and she folded herself into him.

They separated, and he smiled down at her. 'So long. So long I've waited for this.'

Anna leaned her head on his chest and relaxed. 'I have bacon in the fridge,' she said.

'You do?'

'I do.'

'Better than Hilton bacon?'

'Much better than Hilton bacon.'

'So shall I cancel the Hilton?'

'I think so,' she said. 'I think so.'

Chapter 34

Jenny switched on the computer and waited for it to power up. It was wages day, and for the first time she was doing it on her own. She hoped Anna was going to be available on the other end of the phone...

The office overlooked the front garden, and plans had been put in place to change it. Jenny had slightly re-arranged the room so she sat with her back to the window; she couldn't stand to look out at the place where she had stabbed Him. Him. She couldn't even give Him a name. Even though He was dead, Jenny didn't feel the release from stress she had expected.

It had given her the freedom to see Anna, but had left her with many more issues. The funerals of all three of her victims were now over and done, the police appeared to have no idea who the murderer might be, and it all seemed to be dying down. The newspaper reports had dried up completely, having been overtaken by the Royal birth of Princess Charlotte and the election of David Cameron to a second term of office.

What concerned Jenny the most was her lack of guilt. In her mind, the bookend murders, as she chose to call them, were merited in order to get rid of Him. Jenny had deliberately avoided watching television in order to miss the media coverage; it had only been marginal anyway because of good news days in the rest of the country.

Financially, they had benefited, of course they had, but that hadn't been part of the plan at any stage. She hadn't envisaged having to leave their home in Leicester, especially not to move to Lindum Lodge. It already looked nothing like the home Anna had shared with Him; the bedrooms were completely revamped, and she could go into their master bedroom quite happily, without feeling or seeing ghosts from the past.

The front garden was the main issue. Always the front garden. The ghosts were definitely there. She was the only one who had seen Him, lying there stoned out of his mind with alcohol, blood pulsing out of a gaping hole in the back of his neck. Jenny could still feel the slippery movement of the plastic bag as she tried to get it over His head, made difficult to handle by the blood on the inside of the bag. The sight of Him trussed like a turkey, a dead turkey, made her shiver. Karma. What goes around comes around. She tried to think of other clichés in a vague attempt at dissipating her thoughts, but couldn't.

Jenny forced herself back to the wages, and began to input the data dropped off by Gary Vanner the previous night. Somehow, between the three of them, they had managed to hold together and rebuild the workforce. She didn't have to ring Anna; in the end, it was straightforward. She saved her work and then logged in to invoices. Once they were done, Jenny began to relax.

She swung the chair around, and saw the garden yet again. The crime scene tape had been removed, and it looked perfectly normal. Next week, the digger would be here, and the lawn turned into a smart parking lot for four cars. Then He would be gone.

She hoped.

The children had taken very well to the move. Their new school had been very welcoming, and Mark had slipped into his new role like a duck to water. He and Gary had bonded really well, and Gary, without saying the specific words, had hinted that the workforce was happier with Mark than they had ever been with his father.

So everything in the garden was rosy, except it wasn't. The garden was the problem. With a huge sigh, Jenny swung her chair around once more, faced the desk, and closed down the computer.

She picked up her now empty coffee cup, heading for the kitchen. Maybe tomorrow she would nip over and see Anna – she missed her and knew they had lost a lot of what they had built up recently. She needed the relationship. Anna, after all, was the only one who knew the truth.

The telephone call was short; no, Anna wouldn't be in. She had booked to go away for a couple of days, and was travelling that afternoon. They had spoken for a couple of minutes and then Jenny disconnected. It was only later she realised Anna hadn't actually said where she was going.

*****

Michael pulled Anna close as she returned to the sofa.

'Come here, I've missed you.'

'I've only been gone two minutes.'

'I know. It was a long two minutes.'

She smiled up into his face. 'It was Jenny. She wanted to come over for a couple of hours tomorrow, but, as you heard, she now thinks I've gone away for a few days. Maybe if I'd been thinking on my feet...'

He laughed. 'Anna, I could have gone for a walk around the city centre while she was here; it's ages since I've been to Sheffield. I would have enjoyed it. Don't close out your family for me.'

'I know. She just put me on the spot. And now I can't ring her back and say I'm no longer going away, because then she'll think I'm ill or something and come hot-footing it over here. Tangled webs and such like going on here,' she finished with a laugh.

'Shall we?'

'Shall we what?'

'Tangle a web? Let's book ourselves into a Peak District hotel, and have a few days getting to know one another, without the possibility of bumping into your friends.'

'I'll have to ask Lissy to feed Eric...'

'Anna, Eric seems to grow hourly. The poor fish might have exploded before you pack your suitcase anyway. Maybe he'll enjoy being on a break and a normal diet for a few days. Shall I book us in somewhere?'

'Let me go and check Lissy and Jon aren't going away before we do that.'

Anna stood and moved towards the door. The intercom buzzed, and she froze for a second. She pressed the answer button and heard Caroline's voice. 'Let me in, Mum.'

'Okay, sweetheart.'

She turned to Michael who was already moving towards her.

'Go down in the lift. I'll text you when I know why she's here. You have about twenty seconds,' she said with a mildly hysterical giggle.

He kissed her briefly and went out of the door.

She pressed the release button and waited at the door. She saw Michael give a brief wave and head for the stairs.

In a panic, Anna noted the cups and plates on the coffee table, so she let the door swing closed and cleared the mess. She dumped them unceremoniously in the dishwasher and went back to the door to wait for the lift.

Caroline was wheeling a small suitcase, and as she kissed Anna, she said, 'Can I stay the night, please?'

'Of course,' Anna answered with a smile. 'Take off your coat and sit down. Do you want a drink?'

'Wine?'

Anna went into the fridge and took out a bottle of Chablis. 'This ok?'

'Is it wet?'

'Yes.'

'Then it's ok.'

'You here for a reason?'

'Work. I was actually booked into some hotel in Leeds, but I'm heading south anyway tomorrow, so I carried on for a bit so I could see you.'

'You're very welcome.'

Anna poured the drinks and placed the glasses on the table. Caro drank deeply and then smiled. 'That was good.'

'Then put your feet up. I'll just go check the bedroom is tidy; I've been using the computer and had some files out. Won't be a minute.'

She picked up her phone as she went through to the bedroom and sent Michael a text telling him of Caroline's plans. His return was immediate.

Will head back to Lincoln for tonight. Will wait for your call tomorrow. Love you. Mx

Love you.

Anna held the phone against her and felt tears prick her eyes. It had been so long since a man had said, "love you" to her.

The bed needed nothing doing to it, so she just folded the top down and went back into the lounge.

Caro was leafing through a magazine and looked up as her mother came back to her. 'I heard a ping. Is it your phone?'

'Yes. It was a text. I'm owed £5472.26 for the accident I had two years ago. All I have to do to get it is to contact them and give them my bank details,' she said with a laugh. 'Your bed's ready. Is it an early start tomorrow?'

'Not now I've travelled down to Sheffield. I'll leave about ten, I think.'

'You like the job?'

'Love it. I've been offered a promotion, but I'm still thinking about it. It would mean me moving to France. We have an office in Paris.'

'Lucky you. I'm going to say nothing until you've made your decision, because I don't want to influence you. Only you can know if this is right for you. We'll talk when that decision is made.'

Caro nodded. 'And there's nothing to keep me in Lincoln now. I don't see anything of Mark and Jenny, because I'm always travelling, you're here, and Tim is in Florida. And I've met someone...'

'Oh?'

'Yes. He's called Luc and works at the Paris office. That's the only thing stopping me from saying I'll take the job. If it doesn't work out between us, then it would affect one or both of our jobs, potentially.'

'Deep thinking to do then. Take your time, Caro, don't jump into it. But, I know you won't.'

They chatted until around ten o'clock, and then Caro said she needed to sleep. She kissed Anna, and went to the smaller bedroom where Anna heard her speaking on her phone, presumably to Luc. She smiled to herself and hoped Caro would make the right decision.

Anna texted Michael, explaining she couldn't talk because Caroline was still there, but she would ring him after ten the next morning. They continued to text each other after Anna had gone to bed, a bed which seemed surprisingly empty now.

It was raining heavily next morning when Anna accompanied Caroline downstairs to the car park. She waved goodbye and ran back inside the building, shaking her umbrella as she did so. The lift opened, and both Lissy and Jon came out. Jon manoeuvred the wheelchair with practised ease, and Anna stepped back to speak with them.

Anita Waller

'Off out?'

Lissy nodded. 'I have a hospital appointment, just an annual check-up. And wouldn't you just know it, the weather's bloody awful. On the plus side though, Jon is taking me out for lunch after the appointment, and then we're nipping to Meadowhall for a few bits. Making a bit of a day of it, really.'

'Here, take this. You'll need it.' Anna handed her umbrella to Lissy.

'Thank you, you're a star. Mine's in the car,' Lissy laughed. Jon wheeled her out and set off for the car at a run.

Anna stepped into the recently vacated lift, and was dialling Michael as she walked through her own door.

They chatted briefly, and Michael confirmed he would be back in Sheffield within the next couple of hours.

'Lissy and Jon have gone out so you should be okay; you'll not bump into them.'

'I'll still take care,' he said with a laugh. 'See you soon, my love.'

162

Chapter 35

Apart from a couple of updates from the police, Anna heard nothing concrete about the investigation. She rarely spoke to Jenny; discussions seemed trite and unnecessary, because they couldn't talk about the really big issues that were between them. The Crimewatch programme hadn't brought anything new to the surface, and everyone in the family expressed concerns about it, all for different reasons.

It was with some trepidation Anna returned to Lindum Lodge. It was a hot day, and she drove with the window down, Michael following in his own car until the point he left her as he returned to his own home.

She had two last pieces of paperwork to sign for the transfer of the business, and it would be over. Ray would be out of her life permanently. The house and front garden looked very different.

She pulled her car on to the new parking area and wondered why Ray hadn't thought of doing this. It looked very white and clean in the bright sunlight, and she paused to look around when she got out of the car.

Adam and Grace ran out of the front door, waving excitedly.

'Nan! We thought you'd never get here!'

She smiled at them and opened her arms to hug them before planting kisses on their heads.

'I've missed you two guys,' she said, and buried her nose in their hair to drink in their smell.

'Mum says come through to the kitchen,' Adam said. 'She's put coffee on, and we've made you some cupcakes.'

Anna laughed. All this had been denied to her for far too long. Now she could really get to know these two precious grandchildren. She followed them through to the kitchen, listen to their excited chatter about the baking they had done.

Jenny turned to her with a smile. 'Hello, mother-in-law. I've missed you.'

'Hello, daughter-in-law. I've missed you, too.'

They moved together and held each other tightly for some time. Anna felt tears prick her eyes, and she moved to sit at the large kitchen table.

'This is nice,' she said, running her hands along the surface.

'We've splashed out a bit. We decided to go for a big table, because the children can do their homework here. We eat at night in the dining room, but all other meals are in here. The house has changed a bit.'

Adam put a cake stand on the table and turned it around so that an extra-large cupcake was facing his Nan.

'We made that one especially for you, Nan,' he said. 'Mum said you like strawberries.'

Grace placed four small plates by the side of the cake stand and then handed one to Anna.

Anna reached across and took the cake. It was spectacular. Frosted icing decorated the top in swirls of calories, and it was all crowned with sliced pieces of strawberry.

She put it on her plate and admired it. 'I don't quite know what to say. It's huge.'

Grace solemnly handed her a fork. 'You might need that.'

'I might need a spade,' she laughed.

Once the children had watched her successfully eat it, they asked if they could go in the garden.

'Yes,' Jenny said. 'Try not to get as scruffy as you did yesterday.'

Anna raised an eyebrow in query. 'We've given a part of the garden to them, a plot each. You wouldn't believe the competition that's created. Grace is turning hers into a fairy garden; it's costing me a fortune. I have to keep buying fairies and little bridges and suchlike for her. Adam is growing vegetables and a rose bush. Just one rose bush. It's for his granddad, he says...' Her voice trailed away.

'He's growing up so fast. He's almost as tall as me.' Anna smiled. 'And let him remember Ray. Every child needs grandparents. That's part of the price we have to pay for what happened.'

'And you still have my letters?'

'Of course. That's something I want to talk about. I am going to be moving shortly. The apartment next door to Lissy and Jon has come on the market. It's the same as their apartment, with the opposite configuration. I've put in an offer before I left this morning, and I'm waiting to hear back from them. I might have to increase it a bit, because I offered £5,000 less than the asking price, but that was just testing the waters really. Even if I have to pay the full amount, I want it. It's so spacious, newly decorated, it's lovely.'

'Wow! I'm so pleased for you. A proper new start then.'

'It also has a built-in wall safe, so your letters will go in there. I will be giving you a key to the apartment and the safe combination, as soon as I've set it up. If anything happens to me, you get there as soon as possible and get your hands on those letters.'

Jenny looked stunned.

'You're not ill?'

'No, not at all. It's just I'm now likely to be travelling more than I've ever done. It would only take one bad road accident, and it would all be over. In fact, it wouldn't necessarily have to be my death; I could have a stroke, or a heart attack. I just need to make sure you can get those letters before anyone else does. I'm quite settled in my mind to being the custodian, but anything can go wrong.'

Anita Waller

The kitchen door burst open, and Grace appeared, her face glowing. 'Look at the size of this, Mummy!' She held out her hand and deposited a huge earthworm on the kitchen table.

Jenny stared at it in horror and looked at Anna, who was grinning.

'Shall I see to this?' Anna said, picking up the earthworm and carefully carrying it back outside, followed by Grace.

'I don't think Mummy likes worms on her kitchen table,' Anna confided in a hushed tone to Grace.

'Not like worms? Why?' The tone of her voice suggested it was an outrageous thought someone wouldn't like worms.

'Maybe it's because you eat at that table, and she doesn't want germs on it,' Anna said. 'Perhaps worms should stay where they're happiest, in your fairy garden. Shall we put it back there?'

Grace nodded. 'Yes, ok. Come and see the fairies, Nan.'

And that's where Anna was when the estate agent rang to say if she upped her offer by £3,000, the apartment was hers. She did.

Mark came home for lunch, and they formalised the transfer at the solicitor's office. Anna returned to Lindum Lodge, said her goodbyes after promising to visit every week until the children returned to school after the summer holidays, and set off with a wave.

Ray really was gone now.

*****

Anna pulled up around the corner and entered Michael's postcode into her satnav. She had never been to his home before, and was feeling quite nervous about it. She was there within ten minutes, and he came out with a welcoming smile on his face.

166

'Is everything settled?'

She nodded. 'It is. And I've got the other apartment as well, so it's been a good day.'

'Then we must celebrate.' Michael led her into his home, and the feeling of comfort overwhelmed her. He clearly loved old furniture, and his huge sofa and chairs beckoned enticingly. The furniture surrounding her was obviously antique, and it gleamed in various corners of the large room. She wanted to run her hands along it, take in the ambience the beautiful items created.

Anna sank into the sofa, and he disappeared for a few seconds to return with a bottle of champagne and two glasses.

She smiled up at him. 'It's a good job I'm staying over, isn't it?'

*****

Jenny rang Anna's landline, keen to check that she had got home safely following her cautionary words of earlier. It wasn't like Anna to think like that, and it had gnawed at Jenny until she gave in and rang to check. There was no answer so she rang her mobile.

Anna answered almost immediately. 'Jenny?'

'Hi, Anna. Just wanted to check you'd got home safely and to thank you for coming. The children have loved having you here. I tried your landline, but...'

There was a moment's pause. 'Oh, sorry, I didn't quite manage to get to it.'

'Are you at home then?'

'Yes, of course. Feeling a little silly with the mobile phone in one hand and the landline phone in the other,' she said with a laugh. 'I'm fine, Jenny, really. Nice easy journey home.'

'You didn't have problems at the bridge then, with the accident?'

'Er...no. Soon got around it.'

'Okay, as long as you're safe. See you next week?'

'Definitely. I need to get to know Adam and Grace much better.'

'Bye, Anna.'

'Bye, Jenny.'

Jenny disconnected, and immediately rang Anna's landline. There was no answer despite letting it ring for a while.

She tapped her forehead with her phone and wondered just where her mother-in-law was, because she sure as hell wasn't at home in Sheffield.

Anna rolled over and snuggled into the welcoming arms of Michael. 'Sorry about that. It was Jenny, just checking I got home safely. She doesn't suspect I'm not in Sheffield.'

Chapter 36

That same night, Caroline made her decision. She would take her chances, and she agreed to the transfer to France. Luc had been part of her life since just before Ray's death and hadn't walked away, unable to cope with her grief. He'd been there for her.

They had talked constantly about whether she should commit; to the job and to him. In the end, Caroline committed to both and immediately felt better. The stress had gone, and her decision was welcomed by everyone it touched.

She tried ringing Anna, but couldn't get her on the landline, so she rang her mobile phone instead. She couldn't reach her on that either. She smiled as she thought it was just like that after Anna had walked out on Ray; no communication. She left a voicemail saying, 'Mum, I'm bringing Luc to meet you on Saturday,' and rang off.

Caroline knew that would throw her mother into a minor panic and sat back and waited for the phone call to be returned. Anna had put her phone on silent, and knew nothing of this second call of the night until the following morning.

She rang Caroline as soon as she realised she had missed her call, but this time, it was Caro who didn't reply. She was in a meeting, ironing out her responsibilities and other details for the new job, due to start the following week, in Paris.

Saturday arrived, and so did Caroline and Luc. He was tall; his dark curly hair just a trifle too fashionably long, combined with sparkling blue eyes, told Anna exactly why Caroline had been attracted to him.

However, he clearly cared for her, those same sparkling eyes following her every movement with love, or something very close to it. It put Anna's mind at ease; she could trust this man with her daughter in a country where the language would always be her second one.

They went out for lunch, and during the afternoon, Anna took her leave of them. Caro promised to be in constant touch; she was moving to France the following day, although not to live with Luc. Initially, she would be in an hotel until she found her permanent residency.

Anna waved them off and returned to her apartment. Her phone rang as she was going through the door, and she hurried to answer it. It was rare for the landline to be in use, and she picked it up expecting it to be a sales call. It was DI Gainsborough.

After the initial polite chat, he said he merely wanted to fill her in on the investigation so far, and he would like to see her in person.

'I'm in Lincoln on Wednesday,' Anna said, 'if that's of any use to you?' She felt cold. She had heard nothing for weeks, so why now?

'That will be fine. Are you going to Lindum Lodge?'

'Yes. While the children are on school holidays, I go over once a week to see them. Will it take long?'

'No. What time do you get there?'

'I can be there for nine.'

'Nine o'clock it is, then. That will leave you a full day with the children. See you Wednesday, Anna.'

Shivering, she replaced the receiver and went out on to the balcony. There was a gentle breeze, a warm breeze, but it didn't help the chill Anna felt running through her body. *What did they know? Why did he want to see her now?*

She went into the bedroom and opened the wardrobe. The envelope was still there, as she had known it would be; she simply needed the reassurance of seeing it. It would be the first thing to be removed when the new apartment was officially hers. The safe would be a godsend.

She phoned Jenny later and explained she would be arriving early on Wednesday morning, as Gainsborough wanted to speak with her. There was a moment of silence.

'Did he say why?'

'No, nothing other than he wanted to give me an update.'

'Do you need me there?'

'Yes, if you want to be there, no, if you don't. Your decision, Jenny.'

'I'll be there. The children can either go in the garden or up to their rooms. I need to know what they know.'

'Okay. And I'm going to get rid of the mobile phone now. I'd forgotten about it until I went into the wardrobe just now.'

'Oh. I should have said. I got rid of mine as soon as I had...finished.'

'Finished? That's a strange way of describing what you did. See you Wednesday, Jenny.' She replaced the receiver, and tried to calm the anger inside her. The small mobile phone was on the work surface, so Anna placed it on the floor and hit it with the small hammer she kept in the kitchen. She dropped the destroyed instrument into the waste bin and carried the sealed bag down to the bin room underneath the apartment block.

Michael arrived later and stayed until she returned to Lincoln on Wednesday morning. They both left at 7.30am, and Anna arrived at Lindum Lodge with ten minutes to spare. The days and nights spent with Michael were having a calming effect on her, and she hoped Gainsborough's visit wasn't going to upset the equilibrium.

It was a lovely sunny morning, and the children were both out in the garden. Jenny had explained to them that the police were coming over, and had to stay in the garden unless an emergency cropped up. They nodded solemnly and went outside where she could hear them actually getting on with each other, chatting happily about football.

Gainsborough arrived promptly, and they sat around the kitchen table, drinking the coffee Jenny had waiting for his arrival.

'Okay,' he said. 'I just want you to hear of any developments from the Crimewatch broadcast and see if you have any questions I can answer. I won't be able to answer everything, obviously, but if I can tell you something, I will.'

They both nodded. Anna couldn't help but notice the pallor on Jenny's face.

'The only lead we picked up from the programme was one report of someone walking up to a car into the car park by the children's playground, and the driver changing their clothing before getting into the car. There is no proof this person is connected to the crimes, and we're probably clutching at straws, but it is one tiny snippet of information. A lady up at the time feeding her baby was getting him back to sleep, and happened to look out of her window and saw it. She didn't know if it was a woman or a small man. She had no idea what car it was, couldn't even tell the colour because it was under orange lights. She did show us where she saw it, but a fingertip search has revealed nothing.'

Anna felt a tear roll down her face. She couldn't imagine how Jenny must be feeling; Anna herself felt dreadful.

'And that was it. Nobody saw anything, heard anything, remembered any sounds out of the ordinary; we are no further on than we were back in May. It seems the perpetrator has given up, which makes me think...'

'Think what?'

'Well...' He looked uncomfortable. 'This is just me talking. I just wonder if one of these three was the real target and the other two were incidental.'

Anna let out a small cry, and Gainsborough leaned across and touched her hand. 'I'm sorry, Anna, that's me talking out of turn. There could be all sorts of reasons why the murders have stopped – he could be in prison, ill, out of the country; and I need to stop saying "he." It could just as easily be a woman.'

Anna looked horrified. 'A woman? Would a woman have the strength to kill two men on the same night?'

'Definitely. One was absolutely dead to the world anyway with alcohol, and the other was an old man without the physical strength to fight back. Just because this type of random crime is normally committed by a man doesn't mean it was in this case.'

Jenny said nothing. She stood and moved around the table to stand behind Anna, placing her hands on Anna's shoulders, bending down to kiss the top of her head. She couldn't speak.

Gainsborough stood and drained the last of his coffee.

'And that's it for the moment. We're scaling down the investigation slightly, but trust me, it's not being shelved. We have three grieving families all wanting answers we can't give them yet, but we will one day. I have given the other families the same information I have passed on to you. If anything else crops up, I'll be in touch.'

Jenny walked him to the front door and watched as he drove out of the new parking area. He had parked directly over the spot where she had killed Ray.

```
```

Chapter 37

Anna stayed overnight at Michael's again, after leaving Jenny's. She didn't want to go without seeing Mark, so had agreed to eat dinner with them before heading off back to Sheffield. A quick text to Michael let him know of her plans, and he was opening his front door as she pulled on to his driveway.

The journey over to Michael's home had been uneventful, and Anna had gone over again the assorted conversations she had had during the day with Jenny. They had been interspersed with helping with the fairy garden and a game of football with Adam, but it was becoming clear Jenny was fragile.

Anna had suggested they take a holiday; she would come over and run the business for them for a couple of weeks. Jenny declined.

'I don't want to inflict this house on you,' she said. 'And the conversion of the garage we're having done, to give you your own space so you can come visit us, is nowhere near ready. I can't do it to you, Anna.'

'Then go to the doctor. Explain you're feeling on edge. He'll be able to prescribe something.'

'I already have. Please don't tell Mark. I've been taking the pills for a week now, but the doctor said it would be at least a fortnight before I felt any sort of difference. I'll be fine, Anna. Stop worrying.'

Anna was worried. She also knew there was nothing she could do. As soon as the granny flat was finished, she would insist they go away; there would be no excuses then.

Michael led her into the lounge and handed her a glass of wine. He kissed her gently. 'It's been a long day without you.' He smiled into her upturned face.

She leaned against him. 'I know. And it will be a long time before we can be open about whatever is happening between us.'

'Come on, sit down. We've a football match to watch. All our problems will pale into insignificance if England loses tonight.' Anna smiled to herself; although he was ambivalent towards football, Michael was the one insisting they watch it.

Anna switched her phone on silent, sent a text message to Jenny saying she was home, and settled down to watch television.

Jenny received the text, replied, *Okay, love you,* and rang Anna's landline. There was no response. She would have been surprised if Anna had answered.

*****

The next morning Anna checked her phone, and saw that she had a text from Charlie. *Hey you,* it said, *you still alive? Not spoken for ages. RING ME!!!*

She had two missed calls from Charlie and one from Lissy. She decided to wait until she got back to Sheffield before contacting them.

They had lunch in Newark and then headed off for Sheffield, Michael never more than a car length away from her. They parked on opposite sides of the car park, and Michael gave her ten minutes to get into her apartment before leaving his car. He sat with his mobile phone in his hand just in case she had to send a quick text to warn him about anyone being around; they were getting very good at having a clandestine affair.

Michael eventually locked his car and walked across to the lift. He laughed as he entered the apartment and took his holdall into the bedroom. 'This is like being back at the beginning, isn't it? All these years, and we're still creeping around like teenagers. You'd think at our age we could be open about our relationship, but no! Not us... we were never going to be easy, were we?'

'We can't be easy.' Anna sounded serious. 'I'm a murder suspect, don't forget.'

Again, he laughed. 'Murder suspect indeed! Pretty long arms with you in Sheffield and the bodies in Lincoln. I'll put the kettle on. You go and sit down.'

'Actually, I need to ring Charlie. She sent me a stroppy text last night to ring her, and I have been neglecting her. She's been so good with me throughout all this...'

'Then let me make you a drink, and I'll go read in the bedroom until you've finished. She'll not hear any background noises then.'

Anna smiled up at him. 'Thank you.' At times, his thoughtfulness overwhelmed her. Used to a lifetime of selfishness and indifference from the man she had married, Anna was learning to appreciate what a relationship should be like.

'Thank you. That makes sense.'

Charlie answered her call straight away. 'Hi you! You okay?'

'I'm fine, Charlie. I didn't get back from Lincoln until late last night so thought I'd wait till today to ring. And are you all okay?'

'Of course. Dan's on a diet, so there is tension in this happy household, but apart from that, we're good.'

'On a diet? Is he ill? I simply cannot imagine a slim line Dan.'

'He's been diagnosed with diabetes, so I've banned everything he likes. It's quite funny really. But, it's the rich tea fingers, instead of the chocolate digestives, hitting him the hardest. However, he's lost a stone in four weeks, and the plus side is, so have I! You'll not know us next time you see us.'

They chatted for half an hour about mainly inconsequential things, and then Anna filled her in on what DI Gainsborough had passed on the day before.

'They seem to be up against a brick wall, then?'

'Seems so.' Anna paused slightly. 'I haven't grieved, Charlie. I know I stopped loving him a long time ago, but even so, I was married to him for thirty-five years. I feel absolutely nothing now he has gone.'

Charlie sighed. 'The children will be grieving; they loved him. Take comfort from that and move on. And on that note, I'm going to have to love and leave you. I have someone coming to collect two quilts I've made for her, and her car's just pulled up outside. I can't let Dan answer the door, because he appears to be dripping blood on my kitchen floor.'

She heard Dan shout, 'Hi, Anna,' in the background, and she laughed.

'Go and deal with your assorted crises, Charlie. We'll speak soon.'

'And make sure we do,' Charlie responded. 'Love you.'

'And love you, too.'

Anna disconnected with a smile, and Michael came through from the bedroom. 'Everything okay?'

'It's fine. Dan's dripping blood on the kitchen floor, and he's on a diet, but everything's okay with Charlie.'

He walked across to the huge window and looked down. 'It will be a different view for you soon. How long before you can move?'

'Oh, not long. About another four weeks. I can probably get a key, if you'd like to see it?'

'That would be good, but it's right next door to Lissy and Jon. They might hear and come to investigate, so, no. Let's leave it. We are going to have to think about the future, though.' He sounded serious.

177

'Not yet,' she was quick to reply. 'Can you imagine the reaction of Mark and Jenny, Tim, Caro, if they found out I had met up with you? I'm not even sure Charlie would understand, although out of everybody, she would be the one most likely to accept the situation. We can't think of any sort of future together for at least a year.'

Michael pulled her to him, and they looked at the view together. He kissed the top of her head. 'Whatever you say, Anna, but one day, we'll be seen. I just want you to know right now I'm going nowhere. I love you; I've waited for you for too long.'

They stood for a while looking out across the part of the city visible to them, and then Anna moved to the kitchen area to see what she could prepare for their evening meal. She opened the fridge, rifled quickly through its contents, and closed the door with a sigh.

He laughed at her disgruntled expression. 'Let's have a pizza on the balcony, with a bottle of wine.'

'You sure?'

'Of course I'm sure. Shopping tomorrow, then?'

'I'll do an online shop now, and they'll deliver tomorrow.' She came and sat by him. 'We're turning into a couple, aren't we?'

'Hope so,' he said with a grin.

*****

Anna went across to Lissy's flat later and stayed for just over an hour. Michael had said he fancied a bath, and she had left him to it, telling him to take his time; she'd be at least an hour, going on past experience, as they had some catching up to do.

Jon and Lissy were delighted to see her. Jon made the drinks, provided a plate of cakes, and disappeared to his computer area, leaving the two women to chat.

Lissy wanted to know all about the changes at Lindum Lodge, the children, and if Jenny and Mark were okay. Anna filled her in on everything, including the visit from Gainsborough. Lissy looked troubled. 'You're never going to get closure on this, are you?'

Anna shook her head. 'It's starting to feel like that. I know it's a strange thing to say, but it's almost as though they're waiting for another murder to see if they can get any further clues from that, because they got nothing from the first three! He went to great pains to tell me they never close a murder enquiry, and most murders are solved at some point; it was almost as if he was saying don't hold your breath on this one.'

Lissy could see Anna was looking troubled. 'Let's change the subject.' She held up the garment she had put to one side when Anna walked through the door. 'What do you think of this?'

It was a dress for a little girl of around five years, and it was almost cobweb like. The fabric was so delicate in a very pale shade of grey, with a white lining bringing out the ethereal quality of the top layer. The tiniest of blue flowers were scattered in a pattern meant to be random, but Anna knew was carefully triangulated by Lissy.

'Oh my God, Lissy. How beautiful.' Her tone was reverential. 'I'd never let any child wear it.'

Lissy laughed. 'You would this particular child. She, like me, spends her life in a wheelchair, and is one of the sweetest kids I know. I've taken extra care on this one.'

She laid it down gently, and, with the subject away from Ray's death, they continued to talk about insignificant things, until Anna rose to leave.

'It's been lovely,' she said, as she bent to kiss Lissy. 'And it's not going to be too long before we're proper neighbours.

We'll be able to go out on our balconies and talk like little old ladies over the garden fence.'

'Less of the little old ladies,' Jon said, as he re-joined them. 'Lissy, you need anything? I'll walk Anna to her door, then I'm nipping down to the car. Won't be a minute.'

Lissy shook her head, and Jon and Anna left her picking up the dress once more.

Jon looked troubled. Anna sensed he wanted to speak and waited at her door. 'Everything okay?'

'Not really. She's not very well. Her pain has increased, and she's sleeping more. Your visit today has been a godsend. She's actually been quite animated. Thank you.'

'And what do the doctor's say?'

'She hasn't told them. She keeps saying it's just a phase. It's more than that. I just wanted you to be aware of my concerns so you can watch for any changes when you're with her. I can't force her to see a doctor...'

Anna squeezed his hand. 'I'll watch out for her. And I'll report back. It may just be a medication imbalance, but if it is, her doctor does need to know. You may just have to send for him. Or go and talk to him.'

'Thank you, Anna. I feel better for two of us being aware.'

Jon turned towards the lift. 'And now, I've got to go and rummage in the car for something to bring back up, or she'll know it was just an excuse,' he laughed.

She entered her own apartment, and Michael was in the bedroom. He was hanging up a couple of shirts in her wardrobe, and she froze. He had lived out of his holdall every other time he had stayed for longer than a day.

'I hope you don't mind,' he said, 'but these shirts crease so much if I don't hang them. I didn't want them to go into the other room, just in case anyone did a Caroline and turned up unexpectedly to stay. I've just eased your clothes up a bit and taken up three inches of room at this end. And as this wardrobe actually locks, it's the ideal place to put any bits I have. Are you ok?' He had suddenly noticed the shock on her face.

'No. I'm fine. It just suddenly hit me I should have organised something for you anyway.' Anna tried to talk her way out of it.

Michael nodded, not completely convinced. 'I've moved the shelf stuff over slightly to put my dressing gown up there, but it's still in a packet for the time being. I bought a new one so I can actually leave that here. I didn't want to damage that.' He pointed to the bed. 'So I'll put it back when I've done.'

Anna looked towards the bed and saw the envelope. The words on the front stood out – TO BE OPENED IN THE EVENT OF MY DEATH. Jenny had written them on to perpetuate the myth Anna thought the letters concealed inside were for her children and instructions for her funeral.

'Ray's death convinced me I should be prepared. They are letters for the children.'

Michael nodded. 'I guessed it was something like that. I'll put it back carefully, I promise. You'll be able to put it in the safe in the new place, keep it secure. Just don't forget to tell them it's there.'

Anna knew instantly she had made an error; she should have told him they were Jenny's letters to her children. Now, she would have to remember both lies.

He picked up the envelope and slid it back on to the shelf. 'There, all done. I feel I'm properly part of your life now I have a dressing gown of my own,' he said with a grin.

She smiled at him, but the smile didn't reach her eyes. 'Shall I order the pizza?'

'Mmmm. I'm ready for a glass of wine, beautiful lady. We'll sit out on the balcony, shall we?'

Anna nodded, and walked out of the bedroom. She just needed five minutes to compose herself. She picked up the bottle of brandy. That would help.

Chapter 38

Five weeks later, Anna moved into her new apartment. She had booked a removals company, because, despite being just across the spacious communal vestibule, she had heavy furniture.

The two men who rang for admittance were delighted to be doing the job – an easy day for them. They arrived before 8.00am, and were finished within two hours. Anna sank back on to her sofa and stared around her. So many boxes to be unpacked – how could she have accumulated so much in such a short space of time?

Anna pulled her large handbag towards her and took out the brown envelope with Jenny's instructions on the front. Crossing to the wall safe, she opened it. Inside was a piece of paper with instructions on how to set the combination lock. It was a four digit one, and Anna decided to use her birthday and Jenny's birthday, entering 1-2-1-0, and closing it with a little prayer.

Anna entered it again, and it clicked open. She breathed a sigh of relief. She placed the envelope in it, along with her passport, and re-entered the numbers. The original owners had opted to have a mirror covering it, rather than a picture, and she swung it over to conceal the safe completely.

Now, she could unpack.

Lissy arrived at lunchtime with a picnic basket and a large bunch of flowers.

'Welcome to your new home,' she said with a smile. 'I've brought lunch.'

Anna promptly stopped the organisation of her kitchen, and they sat and giggled through the impromptu meal and wine. It was all finger food and paper plates, with wine drunk from plastic wineglasses, and Anna couldn't remember ever enjoying a picnic more. By 2.00pm, she could see the strain on Lissy's face, and she packed everything away into the picnic basket and wheeled her back next door.

'Have a sleep,' she said firmly, kissing her on the cheek. 'Thank you for lunch, thank you for my flowers, and I don't want to see you again today. Rest, Lissy. That's an instruction, not a request.'

Lissy smiled. 'Bully,' she muttered good-naturedly, and wheeled herself inside. Anna watched her move towards her bedroom and quietly closed the door.

She texted Jon. *Lissy hopefully gone to bed. She looks tired.*

Anna then rang Michael; they had agreed not to meet for a few days so if her family arrived unexpectedly, they wouldn't bump into him. They chatted for half an hour, and then she went back to the unpacking. One wall of the large bedroom was filled entirely with wardrobes. The end one, nearest the window, was a small one, and she allocated that to Michael. She would discuss it with him, but she thought they had better fix a lock to it.

At 4.00pm, the intercom buzzed. Anna could hear the excited chatter of the children, and Mark's voice said, 'It's us.'

She released the entrance door and then went to stand by the lift. The children barrelled out, excited to be seeing Nan's new home. How they had changed now they were getting to know her; another black mark against Ray.

She led them to her apartment and showed them round. She was thankful there was nothing in the wardrobe she had earmarked for Michael; she had put his toiletries bag and dressing gown into a drawer. She wanted nothing in it until it could be locked.

'We're taking you out for a meal tonight. As long as we're heading back by about eight o'clock, we'll be fine. Grace won't be too late in bed. You know Sheffield better than we do, so you choose where we go.'

'There are some lovely restaurants up by the Winter Gardens; we can have a walk up there, if you like. We'll get in one of them, I'm sure. And thank you, that will be lovely.'

Mark looked around. 'What can we do?'

'Set up the computer room? The small bedroom is going to be for my craft storage, and my computer desk is already in there. I'm going to get a small sofa bed for in there. It can be used as an extra bedroom, if I need it.'

Mark nodded. 'Okay. We're here to help.'

'Have you set up the middle bedroom?' Jenny asked.

'No, I was just getting my room done so I can sleep comfortably tonight. If you'd like to put the new bedding on,' she pointed to the door to the bedroom in question, 'that would be a help. There's also a large box in there with towels, spare bedding and such like in it. I'm going to use that built-in cupboard thing in there for that, so you could empty it, if you don't mind, Jenny.'

The children were out on the balcony, enjoying the sunshine and chatting. Mark disappeared into the small room, and without speaking, Anna beckoned Jenny towards the mirror.

She swung it open and revealed the safe.

'It's already in there,' she said quietly. 'I'll text you the combination and the code to get in the entrance door.' She handed her a key. 'This is for my own door. Keep it safe. Having all these numbers won't help you, if you can't get in here.' .

Jenny nodded. 'Thank you, Anna.'

Anna swung the mirror back into place, and Jenny moved towards the middle bedroom. 'It's lovely,' she said. 'Your new home, it's lovely.'

By the time they walked up the High Street and then Fargate to get to the restaurants, it was just after six, and the apartment was clear of boxes, all beds made, and her office room was fully functional.

They had a barbecue meal and walked back down feeling extremely full. Mark and Jenny decided to head straight off for home, instead of going back up to Anna's place, and she waved them off with a smile. Jenny had been quiet, and Anna hoped it was because she was now on medication.

Anna spent her first night in her new home chatting with Michael on Skype before going to bed just after 10.00pm, with a mug of hot chocolate and a book. She read one page, and the hot chocolate slowly became cold chocolate through the night, but Anna had slept soundly and felt refreshed by the time she stirred next morning. It had been a good day.

Anna wandered around her new home, making notes of things she needed. The main item was the sofa bed; if Mark and Jenny wanted to come for a few days, she would need somewhere for the children to sleep. Adam could sleep on the sofa bed, and Grace could sleep in with her, leaving the middle bedroom for Jenny and Mark.

The time was definitely not right to bring Michael into the equation. She actually wondered if it would ever be right to bring him into it; he had a beautiful detached home in Lincoln, and she doubted he would want to move to Sheffield and leave that behind.

The weather was turning cooler now, and Anna put on a jacket before heading for John Lewis to look at sofa beds. She found one almost straight away, with deep blue upholstery; she would decorate the room around this colour. She paid for it and organised a delivery time, then walked back down towards home.

Her life was good.

Anna was an accomplice to murder. It was like a thud on the back of her head as the thought hit her. The sudden shock recurrence of the thought overwhelmed her, and she sat on one of the stone seats in Fargate. Her hands were trembling, and she felt hot, almost ill.

Anna stayed where she was for ten minutes and then stood. She went to a nearby coffee shop and ordered a black coffee. Drinking it calmed her down somewhat, and when her mobile phone rang out, she answered it quickly. Caroline was reporting in, checking that everything was okay in Sheffield, and to confirm her mum was happy.

'Are you happy?' was Anna's response.

'Very.'

'How is your little apartment?'

'Little. I love it. Luc stays over occasionally, but it's mine. And we're happy. The relationship with its set parameters works well for us. Maybe one day, it will grow into more, but for the moment, it's good as it is.'

'And the job?'

'Fab. I'm so glad I said yes to it.'

'Well, that's three of us settled into new homes! I just need your brother to return from foreign parts, and I'll be complete,' she said with a laugh.

'Huh. That's not going to happen is it? Would you leave Florida for England?'

'No, I wouldn't.'

They ended the conversation, and Anna felt better. She continued her walk back down to her new home, and after taking off her jacket, laid down on the sofa. She woke two hours later, and it was as if nothing had happened to upset her. But, she needed Michael.

Within ten minutes of Anna's phone call to him, Michael had packed a small holdall and set off for Sheffield. He was getting used to the journey now and found it to be quite a pleasant one. He sang along to the radio, and the journey time seemed shorter than normal. He needed to be with her.

That night, the talk turned to the future. Anna said that maybe in two years' time they could formalise their relationship, but until then, they couldn't. As she pointed out, the police didn't know she had walked out on Ray for good, and it would drag Michael into the equation as a possible suspect, if they revealed they were now together.

He looked serious. 'Anna, you know I've always loved you, don't you? Since the first day you arrived with your yellow Marigolds and your hair tied up in a ponytail, I've loved you. Give me hope.'

'Hope? What do you mean?'

'I want to marry you. I want to live out what remains of my life with you. Will you marry me, Anna?'

She laughed. 'You need to ask? Of course I'll marry you. In two and a half years.'

He groaned. 'So long. That's going to test my patience. Why can't we marry now and keep us hidden?'

'Because you know that wouldn't work. And why is it so important to be married? I love you, surely that's enough.'

'No, it's not enough. Body and soul I want you, Anna Carbrook. It's time you became Anna Groves.'

She stood. 'If you're going to make daft suggestions, Michael Groves, I'm going to make us a cup of tea.'

He grinned at her. 'I never make daft suggestions, Anna. I'm always deadly serious. Just think about it, that's all I ask.'

Chapter 39

Jenny felt worried. She was sure Anna was hiding something, and whatever it was could potentially bring the whole sorry mess collapsing around everyone's ears.

For the first time, she began to wonder if Anna had left Ray for a reason different to the one she had allowed to leak out of her. Had she had another man in the background? She had certainly been adamant she wouldn't return to Ray. Had she played right into Anna's hands by killing off the man she had just left?

There had been no indication of anyone else in her life, not at any point, until very recently. It just seemed strange her return to Sheffield after being in Lincoln never really happened on the same day.

Staring out of the window, Jenny tried to come up with answers. Only one seemed feasible. Next time Anna came over, she would give her two hours to get back home and then ring her landline. If there was no answer, she would ring her mobile and see if she said she was at home. The pattern so far had been Anna said she was home, so Jenny decided the following day she would go straight to Sheffield after dropping the children at their schools, on the pretext of a sudden whim for a shopping trip to Meadowhall. She could also take the photographs they had found in the office; photographs of an earlier time in Anna's life.

She now had the key and entry code to get in. She would first press the button for Anna's apartment, and if there was no response, she would let herself in. And wait.

*****

Jenny had no option but to park her car in the car park. She parked it beside a huge 4 x 4 vehicle, blessing the day she'd bought a small car. It was pretty much hidden by the behemoth beside it.

She walked quickly across to the door and pressed for Anna's apartment; there was no response. She pressed again and waited.

She keyed in the code sent her by her mother-in-law and heard the satisfying sound as the door clicked to allow her entry. She hefted the cardboard box of photographs she was carrying, so they were a little more comfortable, and moved into the vestibule.

The lift was already on the ground floor, and within seconds she was outside Anna's door. She double-checked in her mobile phone for the burglar alarm code and inserted her key.

Jenny's relief was palpable as she handled everything without difficulty; she put the cardboard box down by the side of the sofa, made herself a drink, and sat down to wait for Anna's return.

Thirty-five minutes later, Jenny heard a key in the door. Anna looked startled as she spotted Jenny stand to move towards her.

'Jenny? Is something wrong?'

'No, I fancied a day shopping, spur of the minute. I was going to go on my own, but then decided to come here first. I let myself in, hope you don't mind.'

'Not at all. Meadowhall?'

'That would be good.'

'Right, just give me five minutes to put flat shoes on and change into trousers, and I'll be with you. I've just been for breakfast.' Anna was thinking on her feet. She moved into her bedroom and called to Jenny to make her a quick cup of tea, and she pulled out her mobile phone. She texted the word, *Stop,* and sent it to Michael. She quickly pressed the silent switch and waited until he returned the text with, *OK*.

Anna exhaled slowly. Problem averted.

She changed her clothes and shoes quickly, then went back to Jenny. 'We'd better take both cars, then you can shoot straight off for the children whenever you need to. This is good. A surprise shopping trip!'

'That's what I thought,' Jenny agreed. 'The children commandeer you when you come over, so I thought it would be nice to spend time together, just us. I miss you, Anna.'

Anna took a sip of her tea and carried it to the kitchen area. 'Come on, I don't need this. We'll get a coffee when we get there. Let's go spend.'

They went to the lift, and as they were descending, Anna took out her purse.

'Damn,' she said. 'I've not got my credit card with me.'

The lift halted, and the doors opened. Jenny stepped out.

"You go to your car, Jenny. I'll nip back up and get it. I can't possibly go to Meadowhall without a credit card!' Anna laughed.

She pressed the button for her floor, and the doors began to close. She took out her phone and rapidly texted Michael to tell him to come to her apartment and let himself in; Jenny wouldn't be back. She would be back mid-afternoon, and Jenny would be on her way to Lincoln.

He texted back *Ok, have a good time,* and she released the lift doors she was holding back, pressing the button for the bottom floor.

Jenny sat in her car and watched for Anna coming out of the door. She stood on the step and looked around puzzled; Jenny got out of her car and waved. *So Anna hadn't known she was here...*

Anna acknowledged where she was and went to her own car. This day was proving to be a little bit different to the day she had planned, but she enjoyed a good shopping trip.

Jenny set off for Lincoln just after 1.30pm, none the wiser. They had enjoyed a lovely day, bought new clothes, new cushions, new curtains, and Jenny paid for lunch at one of the Italian restaurants in Meadowhall.

They talked about everything under the sun, but Anna spoke only of a solitary life. She said she was happy, happier than she had been for many years, but confessed she was struggling to come to terms with Ray's death.

'I'm not,' Jenny said. 'Did he care about me when he pushed me down on to that floor and dragged that towel off me? He was a brute, Anna, an absolute brute. And he knew I would do nothing about it. He was wrong about that, wasn't he?'

The waiter came over with their bill, and Anna reached across to touch Jenny's hand. 'Sssh, waiter approaching with a demand for money.'

'My treat,' Jenny said.

They walked back to their cars together, and Anna kissed Jenny. She watched as she pulled out of her parking space then waved before getting into her own car.

She then took out her mobile phone and rang Michael.

'Hi, I'm on my way home. It's been good, but I'm not sure why she came.'

'Maybe it was to drop this box of photographs off, Anna.' He sounded strange. 'Photographs. In a cardboard box, by the side of the sofa. Photos of you and your family.'

Anna went cold. 'I'll be home in about quarter of an hour,' she said. 'Love you.'

'Love you,' he replied and disconnected.

She drove home at some speed.

Chapter 40

There was a photograph frame on the middle of the coffee table. It held a picture of Mark and Tim on their eighteenth birthday. There was no denying they were twins.

There was also no denying their parentage.

Michael stood and walked across to her, pulling her towards him. He kissed her gently and then said, 'We need to talk.'

He led her to the sofa, and she sat down. She stared at the photograph and knew what he was seeing.

'They are my boys, aren't they?'

'I think so.'

'Anna! It doesn't need a bloody DNA test to prove it to me!'

'Until recently, I didn't know for sure...' Anna stopped talking, suddenly aware of where the conversation was leading. She couldn't tell him about the DNA test activated by Jenny; it wouldn't take a genius to put two and two together.

'And why do you know for sure now?'

She hesitated. Thin ground here. 'I walked into your arms in that cafe in Newark after all these years, and I saw how like you they are, and how totally unlike Ray they were.' She hoped she'd got away with it.

'Anna, I would have wanted to be part of their lives. You know I would.'

'You couldn't be, Michael. We both had responsibilities. And they can't know now, not when they've lost the man who brought them up, believing he was their father.'

'Anna, the first time they meet me, they'll know.'

'No! They won't. They don't need to know I've known you for all these years. I can tell them I met you in a café or something...' Her voice trailed miserably away.

'Anna,' he said gently. 'They're my boys. You seem to be forgetting I might want to get to know my sons better, to be part of their lives. Knowing this changes everything. Can't you see that?'

She nodded, defeated. 'I can, but I don't know how to handle it. What on Earth do we do about this? If we tell them, if I introduce you to them, they're going to think... oh, I don't know, I paid to have Ray bumped off so I could have you and have Ray's money. It would all make sense.'

He looked at her with one eyebrow raised. 'You didn't, did you?'

'See! That's exactly what I mean! And, no, I didn't. If I'd wanted him dead, I'd have done it myself.'

Michael pulled Anna into his arms; she was close to tears. 'Hey, come on, we'll work something out. I'm not sure what yet, but we will. Now, tell me about my sons.'

Anna began to talk, slowly at first, about their early years. Mark had been the studious one, Tim had been a devil-may-care child, who tolerated school because he had to, not because he enjoyed learning. Mark was the one for that.

She told him about the day Tim had told them he was gay, introducing Steve as his partner. She didn't mention the beating she had taken; Michael knew nothing of this side of her life, and she could see no reason why he should.

She spoke of Mark meeting Jenny, and talked of her love for Adam and Grace. Again, there were complications in that Grace was his granddaughter, but Adam was Ray's son. She wondered if she would ever be able to tell him the truth, this man she was learning to love. And to trust.

'Mark was with me on Crimewatch. Didn't you see the similarity there?'

He shook his head. 'I couldn't watch it. I couldn't bear to see you upset and not be there for you, so I deliberately didn't watch it. I wish now that I had; I would have seen what sort of young man he had become.'

Anna laughed. 'You don't need to worry about either of them. They're both happy, and I think Mark has really found his niche now he's taken over the business; I always felt he was like a fish out of water before, working for the sake of working, but he's now hands on, learning skills from the lads we employ, and hopefully increasing profits as well. Tim works in IT – don't ask me to tell you what he does, because I really don't know, but whatever it is, both he and Steve work together. I understand it's their own company, and they employ a fair number of people, but that's as much as I know. They live in Florida, unfortunately.'

'You'd rather he was here?'

She sighed. 'Yes, he was mine, and Mark was Ray's. I miss him so much. And he was on my side from the beginning of all of this...'

Michael looked puzzled. 'Why do I get the feeling you're not telling me everything, Anna? What don't I know?'

'If there's anything you don't know, it's only because I'm not ready to talk about it yet. Maybe one day – but it doesn't affect us in any way.' Anna felt sick inside. Being arrested as an accomplice to murder might affect them just a little bit.

Michael inclined his head. 'I'll have to accept that, I suppose. You will tell me before we marry, though? No secrets after that?'

She smiled. 'Yes. I'll tell you before we marry.'

'Good. We'll be married in, oh...four weeks?'

'It'll take Lissy longer than that to make my wedding dress. And what I'll tell her it's for, I have no idea. If we got married in four weeks, we'd have to live a life of lies, and you've just said you don't want that. I cannot tell my children I've remarried this quickly. I can't.'

'Then let's put our thinking caps on and work something out. I don't want to be without you, Anna. I'm sure Erin will welcome you with open arms.'

'Tell me about her. She's very attractive.' She had seen photographs of Erin all over his home.

'Well, she's grown up somewhat from when you last saw her. She's 39, was married so her surname is now Jameson, but she divorced him. He hit her, once. That was enough. She's a pretty strong-minded woman, and she wasn't going to give him the chance to do it again. She's never taken up with anyone else that I know of, but, hey, I'm just her father. She's a sales administrator in charge of a team, and loves it. She lives and works in Newark, so I see her fairly regularly when she's not travelling around the world to some convention or another. She looks very much like Patricia, nothing like me.'

'So, no grandchildren then?'

'Yes, I have two. Adam and Grace,' he answered with a smile.

Anna pulled the box of photographs towards her. 'Did you see their pictures in here?'

'No.' He looked puzzled. 'I didn't look. It's private to you.'

'Then how...?' She waved her hand at the frame still standing on the coffee table.

'It's an open box, and that was the top picture. I sat down and saw it. It was like looking at a picture of me in my younger days. It's the only one I've looked at.'

Anna delved further down and found her favourite one of the children. She showed it to him, and he smiled. 'Grace looks like you. Adam doesn't. Is he like Ray?'

'Yes.' Her reply was stilted.

He felt he'd touched on an open wound, so said nothing further. She would tell him one day. Her life, it seemed, had been complicated.

Her phone vibrated then rang, and she saw it was Jenny calling. She placed a finger on his lips and answered it.

'Hi, Jenny. You home safe?'

'Yes. And I was in plenty of time for the children. I just wanted to thank you for a lovely day. We must do it again. Next time, I'll give you advance warning,' she chuckled. 'Oh, and the kids are delighted with the stuff you've bought them. Grace thinks it's wonderful to have an adult colouring book.'

'They're very welcome. It's lovely to be able to spoil them. It's what Nans do, you know. See you soon, Jenny. Love you.' She disconnected. 'She's safe.'

'Good. Is she a good daughter-in-law, apart from the fact she wrecks our days out?'

'Yes, she is. She's had to put up with a lot I can't go into, because I gave my word, but she's a brilliant wife and mum.'

'And you will be.'

'What?'

'A brilliant wife. My brilliant wife.'

''Christmas 2017.'

'September 2015.'

She laughed.

'I wish.'

'But, why can't we? Why do we have to wait? I'm older than you, and I could die any minute.'

'Are you ill?'

'No, but...'

'You're not going to die any minute, unless I throw you over the balcony. Then you might.'

'You're a heartless woman, Anna Carbrook, soon to be Anna Groves.' Michael shook his head and pretended to wipe away tears. 'I don't ask for much; just a wife to love and care for me, a happy home, a readymade family I can get to know, steak and chips for dinner...'

Anna collapsed with laughter and stood up. 'Steak and chips I can manage.'

She moved to the kitchen area, and with a disgruntled look at her, he turned on the television.

'I'll watch Eggheads then, if you're not going to co-operate.'

She smiled and ignored him completely.

But, Anna did wonder just how long she could hold out for.

Chapter 41

Jenny still felt uneasy. Anna being secretive about something should never have crept into any equation. She switched on the computer and pulled the accounts towards her. She'd have a day paying bills and allow herself time to think.

She needed Anna to be focussed; she had murdered three people, and Anna held the proof. She really didn't want Anna having one glass too many one night and talking about anything she shouldn't be talking about.

The stress was beginning to show, not only in Jenny's face, but also in her attitude. She knew she was snappy with Mark and the children; Mark had taken her out of the kitchen, and had harsh words with her when Adam had caught a verbal tongue lashing from her.

But, still, Jenny knew it had been worth it. She remembered the last time they had seen Anna and Ray, around eighteen months ago. Adam had asked for a drink of water, and Ray had passed him one with the words, "Here you are, son." Oh yes, without a doubt, it had all been worth it. As Adam grew older, he looked more and more like Ray, and less and less like either her or Mark. She wondered what Mark's true father looked like, if Mark and Tim actually resembled him. She would never know. He was dead.

Jenny stared thoughtfully out of the window, the accounts paying morning put into abeyance as she wondered what to do next. She strongly suspected Anna had met someone else, but it must be a fairly new relationship, and originating in Sheffield.

Or was it? Because she definitely wasn't returning to her own place after leaving Lincoln on Wednesday nights. Even so, she could be going back to his place in Sheffield, and not her own.

Frustration was beginning to mount in her brain, and Jenny once more pulled the accounts towards her. She had to know. She needed to find any weaknesses; her freedom depended on it. This would probably mean another trip to Sheffield; possibly more than one trip, because she would just have to hide and watch.

One day, she would see the mystery man, and then decisions would have to be made.

*****

Jenny hit pay dirt the first trip over to Sheffield. She had hired a car for the day knowing that Anna would recognise hers; she couldn't guarantee a large 4 x 4 would be conveniently parked to hide her.

Jenny pulled into the car park and parked as close to the entrance to the block as she dared, sliding the black car into a spot by a van advertising a carpet cleaning business. She took out her book, not really taking in the words, because her eyes were constantly straying to the large entrance door.

A man walked out, and she held her breath. He walked across to a silver Lexus and sat in the driver's seat. The car didn't move. Slowly, Jenny exhaled. She had, just for a second, thought she knew him.

He continued to sit without starting the engine, not doing anything, just waiting. And then Anna came out, cast a glance around the car park, and walked towards the Lexus. She climbed into the passenger seat and turned her face towards the man.

Jenny raised her phone and took a photograph of the registration number of the car.

The lights on the car came on as the man started the engine; he reversed and then drove out of the car park.

Jenny placed her book on the passenger seat, started her own engine, and drove out of the car park in a vain attempt at following the Lexus. It had already disappeared.

She set off back to Lincoln, stopping in a layby for a welcome coffee and some thinking time. She had been right. Anna had met someone, and now it all boiled down to trust.

Did she trust Anna to keep her secret? The letters clearly exonerated Anna of all blame, so if anything did come out, only she would be punished. She would lose everything. Once again, Ray would have wrecked her life.

She needed to know who this mystery man was, where he lived; only then would she be able to decide what to do about him.

Jenny finished her coffee and got back in the car. Thirty minutes later, it had been returned to the car hire company, and she was once more back in her own car heading for Lindum Lodge. Both the children were at after school clubs, so she had time to formulate some sort of plan before heading out to collect them.

Jenny sat and stared at the computer screen. After going to the DVLA website, she had put in the registration number, but it told her nothing of any use at all. She hadn't really expected help from that quarter, but now, she could rule it out. She heard the front door open and quickly closed down the website.

Mark smiled at her from the office doorway. 'You're back then?'

'Er... yes.'

'I called home earlier for a spot of lunch, but it was like the *Mary Celeste*. Abandoned and deserted.'

'Oh, sorry. Needed some fresh air, so I went for a walk.'

'Not in Hartsholme Park, I hope.' His tone was sharp, concerned. 'They've not caught the bloke who killed that woman yet, and it's not safe for you to be going places like that on your own.'

Jenny forced a smile. 'No, I ended up 'round by the Cathedral. Don't worry. Went in a few shops, had a cup of coffee and came home. You should have rung; I would have come home and made us some lunch.'

'Didn't matter. I only had half an hour. I'm going up to have a shower, unless you want me to go and get the kids...'

'No, I'll get them.' She smiled at him, and he disappeared upstairs.

Her smile went as quickly as Mark did. Mention of Hartsholme Park had been difficult. Out of all three of the murders, Joan Jackson's had been the one that had affected her the most.

And now, following today's revelations, Jenny was considering a fourth one.

Chapter 42

Anna and Michael drove to Chatsworth House. The garden centre profited greatly by their visit, and then they went to the coffee shop, and they also profited by their visit.

They walked, talked, and enjoyed each other. Michael spoke several times of "when they were married," but Anna just smiled.

Michael was beginning to understand her, and slowly realising commitment to another man was not on the cards at the moment. She never spoke of Ray, other than when she had any police information to impart, and he did wonder what Ray had done to her to cause this reticence. He could only guess.

He could wait for her to open her heart to him completely; for now, it was enough to know she loved him.

The autumn days had brought cooler temperatures, and after sitting on a bench for a few minutes drinking in the views over the rolling grasslands of Chatsworth, they decided to head back to the car.

Michael turned on the engine and switched on the heater to warm them.

'I like this car,' she said. 'It's very comfortable. And warm.'

'You want one?'

Anna looked at him and laughed. 'No, thank you, I've got my Audi. I'll stick with that.'

'Are you sure? I'll be more than happy to get you one.'

'I'm sure. You need to drive my Audi and then you might consider getting one of those.'

'Is this our first disagreement?'

'Could be.'

'Then we'd better get married quickly, before all this bickering and arguing drives a wedge between us.'

'I'll not let it,' she said solemnly, holding back the laughter.

'Good. Now, about this wedding...'

*****

The hotel was a mere two minutes away from the Registry Office inside Sheffield's Town Hall. They had opted to spend the nights before and after the ceremony there, as neither of them wanted to be spotted by Lissy and Jon dressed up in their finery.

And they did look fine. Tall and elegant, Michael wore a dark suit, with a tie matching the flowers Anna carried in her small bridal posy of cream and lilac.

She had chosen a cream dress and jacket, and wore a cream and lilac fascinator in her blonde hair. They said their vows, thanked the two strangers who had agreed to be their witnesses, and became Mr. and Mrs. Groves almost without any fuss, on a warm and sunny mid-September day.

They had decided to continue exactly as they had been doing for the next two years, keeping their marriage from all their children. Anna had insisted on the conditions, or no marriage.

Michael desperately wanted to talk to Erin about it, but knew when Anna said nobody was to know, she meant exactly that.

Finally, he had his own way, and they were married. They stayed in the same hotel for their wedding night, and had their first meal together as a married couple in their room. The hotel had, following the groom's instructions, served the meal by candlelight and used beautiful silverware. It was a magical atmosphere, and halfway through the meal, Michael handed Anna a small, gift wrapped package.

She opened it with fingers that didn't seem connected to her brain; inside was an exquisite diamond bracelet, inscribed with the words, *My Forever Love.*

She wanted to cry. She had waited almost all of her life for this, and ironically, it was Jenny who had been the instrument to make it happen.

She stood and walked around the small table, kissing Michael; he knew a bridge had been crossed. The kiss was deep and full of longing. He pulled her towards him and held her tightly.

'I love you,' he whispered.

'And I love you too.'

Their lovemaking that night was intense; finally, they were in the right place.

*****

Jenny became immersed in her search for the mystery man. She was also starting to think Anna maybe wasn't quite so innocent – had she been having an affair when she walked out on Ray? Had she seen Jenny as a gift to get rid of Ray for her?

She slammed her hand down hard on the desk and muttered under her breath.

'Just who the fuck are you? And why do I think I've seen you before?'

The vehicle registration was of no use at all unless she happened to simply spot it on the road one day; and she couldn't really keep nipping over to Sheffield to stake out the apartment building.

Jenny walked through the house until she reached the garage. It was in the process of being converted into a small flat for Anna's use, and she needed to see how close it was to completion. It was very close.

There was just a carpet to choose, and then they could look at furnishing it for her. In theory, she could invite Anna over to stay for a few days in about a week's time, and then hope something cropped up to give her a clue as to the mystery man's identity.

*****

Anna was more than a little puzzled by Jenny's invitation, and Michael was ever so slightly disgruntled. Their married life had only just started, and she was leaving him!

She laughed at his expression, saying this was the agreement; carry on as normal.

'But, how long are you going for?'

'She's asked me to go Monday to Friday next week. I'll be able to slip out to see you. We won't be completely separated.'

Michael still looked unhappy, and she gave him a kiss.

'It's the price we have to pay, at the moment. And you need to go to Lincoln at some point anyway. Didn't you say you needed some work doing to the electrics? Take advantage and have them done next week. I can recommend a building firm...'

'I'm sure you can,' he said with a grin. 'Right, I'm going down to the newsagents, see what newspapers they've still got left at two o'clock on a Saturday afternoon. Won't be much, I expect.'

'We could have them delivered...'

'We could, but I quite enjoy the walk. I'm also going to go a bit further and pick up a lock to put on that small wardrobe, then I can move some more clothes in. Hiding my boxers under your panties doesn't really work.'

'Good idea. I'll go and have an hour with Lissy while you're out. It seems ages since we had a chat.'

He opened the door to go to the lift at the same time as Jon came out of their apartment.

They looked at each other for a moment, and Michael held out his hand.

'Are you Jon?'

'Yes, I am.'

'Michael, Anna's friend from her days in Lincoln.'

The two men shook hands and walked towards the lift.

'Is Anna ok?'

'She's fine. I'm in Sheffield for business, so I'm just popping out for a short meeting, then coming back to take Anna for a meal. I believe she said she was going in to see your wife this afternoon for an hour. She speaks highly of both of you.'

'Yes, we've become close friends. She's had quite a rough time since she left Lincoln to come here, but she's getting there now, I think.'

They reached the vestibule and went their separate ways, Michael breathing a sigh of relief he had managed to come up with a plausible explanation that would, one day, lead them to be open about their relationship.

He immediately rang Anna to explain what had happened and relayed the story he had given Jon. She went to Lissy's, fully prepared for confirming what Michael had said, and eventually went back to her own apartment satisfied that all was still well. If she was honest with herself, Anna was finding the whole situation amusing and exciting, but she knew she would come under unwelcome spotlights if DI Gainsborough were to find out.

The spotlights from her own family would be a different matter.

*****

Monday morning saw Anna open her door first – she really didn't want Jon bumping into Michael again, especially as it was only nine o'clock. That particular two and two would *definitely* make four.

Michael stepped past her and straight into the lift she had called for him. He waited in his car until Anna climbed into the Audi, and he followed her once more to Lincoln, turning off at his own exit.

He felt grumpy; it was all very well agreeing to Anna's conditions, but it didn't mean he had to enjoy them. They had decided Anna would put her mobile phone on silent so he could text at any time and not be heard. She would respond as soon as she was able.

The children had been absolutely delighted to hear Anna was to stay for five days. During the long telephone call, she had promised to take them to school every day, and she had been able to hear the excitement in Grace's voice. She was looking forward to seeing them.

Jenny led her into the converted garage. It was beautiful.

It had a small bedroom, a lounge, a small kitchenette, and a wet room. It was furnished with everything she could possibly need, and Anna just stood for a moment, taking it all in.

'This is wonderful,' she said finally. 'Absolutely wonderful. When you said a garage conversion, I had no idea it could possibly be like this.'

Jenny smiled. 'We don't like you being so far away. Now you can come and stay whenever you want, this is yours. No one else will stay in it; we have the guest room upstairs for any other visitors. If you want to bring anything else in, please do. We just want you to be comfortable.'

Anna kissed Jenny.

'It's perfect as it is. Stop fussing. I love what you've done for me.'

'Then don't feel awkward about leaving us, if you want time out. The kids can be a bit overwhelming.'

Jenny led Anna over to a cupboard in the corner of the room and showed her where towels and extra bedding were; she was clearly proud of what she had accomplished.

'I have everything I could possibly need,' Anna laughed. 'It will certainly be a pleasure to visit this house from now on!'

'Then I'll leave you to settle in. Come through to the kitchen when you're ready, and we'll have a drink.'

She closed the door carefully behind her and waited. A couple of moments later, she knocked and reopened the door. As she had expected, Anna was sitting on the sofa, her mobile phone in her hand, and obviously typing a text.

'Sorry, Anna, do you want tea or coffee?'

Anna put down the phone. 'Coffee, please.'

Jenny closed the door feeling troubled. She had no idea who Anna was texting, and it could be perfectly innocent, it just felt not quite innocent. She needed to see that phone. She needed to feel safe.

The letters detailing the murders had been very necessary; her concern was Anna would spill the beans about having the letters to someone who became close to her. Or had been close to her all along.

Jenny was starting to believe she had made the biggest mistake of her life placing her trust in Anna. At the time, she had felt she needed Anna to alibi her; now, she wished she had had the courage to just kill the damn man.

Anna went through her phone and cleared it of all texts from Michael – she didn't want anyone seeing anything accidentally. She stood and put her clothes away in the small wardrobe, and then went through to the kitchen.

Jenny handed her a coffee with a smile. 'Come and sit down,' she said. 'Let's catch up.'

'Nothing much to catch up on. Eric's turning into a whale, Lissy and Jon are fine, although Lissy looks a bit under the weather, and I'm finally getting my head around being answerable to nobody. Thirty-five years of bullying doesn't leave you overnight.'

Jenny reached across and squeezed her hand. Anna didn't usually mention Ray, or indeed, refer to her life with him. It was as if, with his death, she had metamorphosed into a different human being; something had changed in Anna to prompt that comment.

They sat at the large pine table, and Anna encircled her coffee mug with her hands.

'This is lovely. It's quiet without the children, though.'

Jenny laughed. 'Don't knock it, Anna. You watch what happens at four o'clock. For now, let's just enjoy it.'

'Okay. Do we have any plans for the rest of the week?'

'I thought we might have a day going around the shops in Lincoln. Would you like that?'

Anna nodded. 'Yes, very much. As long as you don't frown at me again when I want to get something for Adam and Grace. I've never been able to spoil them before; now, I can.'

'Right. Shall we just relax here today and hit the shops tomorrow? Is that ok with you?'

'That's fine. And Wednesday, I'll take off for a couple of hours, because I'd like to visit some friends who I never get to see now. I know you do wages on Wednesdays, so is that okay with you?'

Jenny froze. It felt as though Anna was being quite blasé about her trip out, almost as if she was acting.

'Of course it is,' she responded. 'I'll do us a nice meal for the evening.'

'And I'll make sure I'm back in time for the school run.'

They chatted for a while, both of them consciously keeping away from the subject of the three murders. Anna felt at times she needed to talk about it, but clearly Jenny had done what she needed to do, and now it was filed away, never to be mentioned again.

Jenny made a cake for when the children arrived home, and after lunch, Anna invited Jenny into her tiny apartment with a self-conscious laugh.

They sat on the sofa, enjoying yet another coffee, and finally, they began to relax in each other's company.

Anna picked up her phone to set an alarm for three o'clock; it wouldn't do to be late for the children on her first day of school run duties. She felt she might just forget the time. Jenny laughed at her.

'I would have reminded you.'

She put the phone back down beside her and noticed an incoming call. She answered it, and saw Jenny frown. It hadn't rung.

'DI Gainsborough?'

She listened, and Jenny saw her face blanch.

'Where? Another woman?'

There was another lengthy silence, and Jenny waited. She could hear the odd word and felt sick. The whole incredible period of time was starting to fade into the background, but it seemed it wasn't like that to the police.

'Well, thank you for letting me know before it hits the T.V. tonight. I'm actually in Lincoln at Lindum Lodge for a few days, if you need me for anything. You can reach me either on my mobile or on Mark and Jenny's landline.'

She said goodbye, disconnected, and turned to Jenny.

'There's another body,' she whispered. 'Jenny...'

'No!' There was a look of horror on Jenny's face. 'No, it's nothing to do with me! Where...?'

'In the centre. On one of the side roads near the Cathedral. They've found a woman's body. She's been stabbed in the neck, and her hands are fastened together with plant ties.

I don't know anything else, but the similarities are enough to make them think there's a link to the other three. And that's as much as I know.'

'Anna, I swear to you...'

'I know, Jenny, but it's going to stir it all up again, isn't it? We need to be prepared. We have to tell Mark, Caro, and Tim. I don't want them hearing it from some other source.'

Chapter 43

Adam and Grace sat at the kitchen table doing their homework, and the three adults, enjoying the comfort of the lounge, were watching the news. There hadn't been much discussion between them, because two of them knew it wasn't the same killer; the other one assumed it was.

Jenny appeared to Anna to be in a state of shock. Her face was ashen, and since the phone call from DI Gainsborough, she had hardly said a word. Anna had left a message on Caroline's voicemail, and had spoken to Tim. Mark had called home as she was speaking to Tim, so he got the gist of the issues as he caught the tail end of the conversation.

There were no new details, and when the presenter asked Gainsborough if he was linking the new death with the three earlier murders, he was very guarded in his response. He said they couldn't definitely link them; there were differences, and it would take much more work before they could state categorically they were all committed by the same person. The programme then showed pictures of the three people already killed, and Anna heard Jenny draw in her breath as the photographs flashed on to the screen.

Don't lose it, Jenny, she silently prayed. Mark glanced at his wife and put his arm around her.

'I know, sweetheart, it's bringing it all back. Stay strong. They'll catch this evil bastard one day. Trust Gainsborough. He knows what he's doing.'

Anna stood.

'I can't watch this. If you don't mind, I'm going to my room and read for a bit, and then I'll have an early night. This is all too much... too many bad memories resurfacing.'

Jenny smiled weakly at her mother-in-law. There were unshed tears in her eyes, and as she spoke, her voice became tremulous.

'Of course we don't mind, Anna. You have everything in there for you to make a drink, and there are some biscuits and other nibbly bits in the kitchenette part. I'll see you in the morning.'

Anna popped into the kitchen and kissed both her grandchildren, repeating her promise of the school run next morning. She went to her tiny apartment and showered, then slipped on her nightie and dressing gown. Curling up on the sofa, she pulled her book, and her phone towards her.

Using the phone first, she texted Michael.

I'm fine. Did you see the news about another body? May be the work of the man who killed Ray. I miss you. Going shopping tomorrow with Jenny, but told her I'm going to see a friend on Wednesday. I need to see you. Newark?

Michael, sitting on his own sofa with a book, smiled as he heard his phone beep. It would be either Anna or Erin, and both would be very welcome texts.

He read her words and wrote, *I will be in our cafe at 10am. Drive carefully. Don't worry if you can't make it for any reason. I can wait until Saturday, if I have to.*

Anna's mind kept drifting back to the news programme. Was it a copycat murder? There was absolutely no reason for it to be Jenny – she would have made sure it was an exact copy, perpetuating the serial killer idea. But, clearly, it must have been in Gainsborough's mind; he wouldn't have rung to pre-warn them, if he hadn't thought it was a possibility it was the same killer.

Tim had repeated his offer of a holiday for her during their conversation, but once more, Anna had declined. She said it wasn't the right time; the investigation was still ongoing, still very much a presence in her life. She had to be free in her mind before visiting Florida.

Anna had left a message for Caroline; she had deliberately made it sound a "not to worry" message. Caro must have believed it, because she hadn't returned the call.

She picked up her book once more and began to read. Two pages later, she put it down. She was uneasy; her life was different now, and she didn't like being apart from Michael.

Anna had an unsettled sleep. She knew it was because Michael wasn't with her, but now, with the new development in the case, she was more convinced than ever it would have to remain a secret.

She got up just after 3.00am and made a cup of tea. She was tempted to ring Michael, knowing he wouldn't mind, but decided against it. Just because she was awake didn't mean it would be fair to wake him.

She went back to bed, and finally dropped off, waking just before her alarm went off for the seven o'clock call.

Her phone rang while she was taking the children to school and glancing down she saw it was Gainsborough calling. She dropped them off and waved goodbye; she drove around the corner where she parked up.

She listened to his voicemail, asking her to call him, and she immediately rang.

'It's Anna Carbrook,' she said in response to his rather gruff 'Gainsborough.'

'Ah, yes. I just wanted to let you know that we're certain it's not the same killer. Whoever killed your husband and the other two people, it wasn't this chap. The other three were carefully staged using the exact same materials, none of which match up to this stuff used on this latest victim. I can't go into details, but we're pretty sure this latest one is drug related, and I suspect we'll have someone in custody by the end of the day.'

'Thank you,' she said. 'Thank you for keeping us informed. And you're no further on with finding Ray's killer? It's like living in a vacuum. None of us can move on.'

'There's nothing new,' he said. 'The person seen changing their clothes in that car park remains just that. Nobody else has come forward about it; we've not picked it up on any local CCTV pictures, so basically it's a lead that's fizzled out. I'm sorry, Anna; it must be so frustrating for you.'

'It never goes away,' she said slowly. 'Whatever I do, it's there. And it makes it worse because I know if I hadn't thrown a wobbly and walked away from him for a few weeks, he would be alive now. He wasn't the sort of man who went out at night, that wasn't his lifestyle. In fact, his evenings were usually spent working out the following day's jobs and contacting his work force. So I blame myself in some small part of my brain.' She stopped talking then; the grieving widow act had been played just enough, she felt.

'Did you stab him? Put the bag over his head? Anna, you're not to blame for any of this. Will you pass the information I've given you on to the rest of your family? Or do you want me to ring them?'

Anna felt slightly panicked. Jenny would go into meltdown if Gainsborough rang her direct. 'No, you're fine. Go and catch a killer, and I'll tell the family.'

They disconnected, and she sat a while, taking in what Gainsborough had said. Just for a brief moment, when they had first heard the news, she had thought Jenny had committed another murder to reinforce the serial killer theory.

But now Anna had different thoughts about Jenny. She was getting the impression Jenny was running scared. Perhaps she could reason with her during their shopping trip, let her see she had nothing to worry about. The police were no further forward.

She drove home and rang both Tim and Caro, leaving voicemails when neither of them answered her call. She told Jenny and left her to contact Mark.

Jenny was quiet on the drive into Lincoln, and when they parked her car, Anna asked if she could help. 'You're clearly worrying about something,' she said.

'It's just this with Gainsborough,' she lied. 'It's brought it all back. It wasn't easy for me, killing the other two people. It was very easy to kill the bastard, though. And I'll never regret it, Anna, no matter what happens. He destroyed my life. I took his. Job done.'

She got out of the car, and Anna followed. She didn't believe her; it was more than that.

They spent a lot of money. Despite her concerns about Jenny, Anna actually enjoyed her company, and as the day wore on, Jenny became more relaxed.

They picked the children up on the way home, and by the time Anna went to bed that night, she felt much easier in her mind.

Tomorrow, she would see Michael, sort out some sort of cover story for where she had been, and then settle down to being at Lindum Lodge until Saturday morning; she could then go home to Sheffield and Michael.

Chapter 44

Friday afternoon was quiet. Jenny had a doctor's appointment so Anna packed her small suitcase, ready for her return home the next morning. Despite missing Michael, she had enjoyed her stay at Lindum in the tiny 'nanny flat,' as the children had taken to calling it.

The couple of hours she had spent with Michael on the Wednesday had been lovely. It had been quite a cold day, and they had walked in the park after their first cup of coffee, but then had opted for a second cup to warm them before driving back to their separate dwellings.

They had discussed football. Anna had laughed at his horrified face. He tolerated her love of the game, and now she wanted him to go to a match.

'But,' she insisted, 'I'm not missing this one. They're playing Arsenal in the Capital One Cup. It's a Tuesday night match, and I'm pretty sure Mark won't be there, because evening matches finish too late. I will check before I bully you into going, but I really would like you to go with me.'

Michael sighed theatrically. 'Well... if I must.'

'I'll pay for the tickets,' she said with a laugh.

'Too damn right you will! I've agreed to go, wench, just don't expect me to pay as well! Are we going in a box, or something, with a bit of comfort to it?'

'We're going on the kop.'

'What???'

'You'll love it. I'll teach you the songs...'

He groaned. 'It'll be cold.'

'Chilly, not cold. And I'll buy you a scarf. You'll be fine.'

'Did it say anything in our wedding vows about this?'

'Yes. Don't you remember the bit about being Owls supporters until we die? I do.'

'I must have missed that bit. Okay, I give in. But, I point blank refuse to sing.'

Anna laughed. 'Oh, you'll sing. That's what we do on the kop. We bounce, and we sing.'

They finished their coffees and walked back to their cars, arms around each other. He kissed her and waited until she had set off before going to his own vehicle. God, how he loved her – but singing and bouncing on the kop?

Jenny arrived back from the doctors to an empty house. Anna had gone to collect the children for the final time that week. She hung her coat in the cloakroom and went through to the kitchen. She stared out of the window while automatically switching on the kettle, deep in thought. She knew no more now than she had done when Anna arrived.

Checking her watch, Jenny saw she had about fifteen minutes before Anna, Adam and Grace came hurtling through the door, so she moved swiftly across the house to Anna's sanctuary.

She looked around, but nothing was out of place, and Anna's suitcase was standing by the door ready for her journey back to Sheffield. She lifted it on to the bed and unzipped it. Rifling through everything took very little time, and she closed it once more.

Her mind was frantically going through other options; she lifted the pillows, checked the bedside drawers, flicked through Anna's book, and even checked the bathroom. There was nothing that gave her any idea of who the man in Anna's life was.

Jenny heard a car pull up outside, and she quickly left the flat, moving back to the kitchen with ten seconds to spare before Grace flung open the front door.

'Hi, kids,' she called. 'Orange or apple juice?'

Anna walked into the kitchen and smiled. 'And I'll have a coffee, please, Jenny. I need the caffeine. These two monkeys have never stopped talking all the way home.'

Jenny laughed. 'It's Friday. They're always like that on a Friday.'

'Well, I'll just go and get my cardigan. It's turning quite cool out there.'

Anna put her bag on the kitchen table, turned, and headed for the flat. She opened the suitcase in which she had already packed the cardigan and put it on, immediately feeling warmer. She closed the door behind her then opened it again, a small frown on her face. Something wasn't right; Anna saw the suitcase was on the bed and not standing by the door where she had left it.

Only one person could have moved it. She knew who the person was, she just didn't know why. Anna knew she didn't have the courage to query Jenny's actions; she wasn't a good enough liar.

Jenny was obviously looking for something, and Anna went quickly back towards the kitchen, aware her handbag, with her mobile phone in it, was there. The phone was still on silent, and there could be texts from Michael waiting for her that she knew nothing about.

The bag was where she had left it, and she breathed a sigh of relief. She reached into it and took out a tissue. Her phone was no longer in the small side pocket where she always placed it, but just in the main central section of the bag. Jenny had obviously checked it. She picked up her bag and headed towards her own room once more.

The phone showed no texts waiting for her, no missed calls, but she went into her messages anyway. There were two messages from Michael, both from the previous day, and she breathed a sigh of relief. Had Jenny had time to check the messages before she heard Anna coming back to the kitchen?

Michael was in her phone merely as MG but the content of the texts would say a lot more than the initials. Anna wiped both texts from the phone and went back to the kitchen, leaving her bag in her room. This time, she stood it on top of the suitcase, by the door. She took careful note of exactly how it was placed and headed back to Jenny and the children. It was her last night with them, and she intended enjoying it.

They played Monopoly, Mark bankrupting everyone very quickly. The children went up to their rooms around 8.00pm to read for a while before bed, and Anna excused herself, saying she was going to read as well, then have an early night.

She had been in her own flat about an hour when she heard the knock on the door. It slowly opened, and Jenny's head appeared. 'You okay?'

Anna smiled. 'Yes, of course. Come in.' She patted the seat at the side of her. 'Cup of tea?'

'That would be nice. Mark's moved on to the whisky, so I thought I'd come and check you've been okay in here for the week.'

'I've been really comfortable.' Anna switched on the kettle. 'The only thing that's spoilt it is the call from Gainsborough. Still, that appears to have blown over. Biscuit?'

Jenny nodded. 'Thanks. So, is there anything else you need in here that would improve it?'

'Good heavens, no. Honestly, Jenny, I think you've thought of everything. I've been so comfortable, and it's been lovely being with Adam and Grace for the week.'

'Maybe you'd like to have them for a couple of days to stay in Sheffield at some point?'

There was the briefest of hesitations, but Jenny noticed it.

'Of course. You know I would love that. There's so much to show them. If they want to come at some time in half term week, that would be good, but not until the Wednesday, because on the Tuesday night I'm going to the match. I know how Grace feels about football, so it would be better to have them from Wednesday onwards.'

Jenny shook her head. 'No, they can't do half term. We've decided to go to Florida for ten days, catch up with Tim and Steve, and do the whole Orlando thing. Believe me, it took a lot of persuading to get Mark to give up on an Owls/Arsenal match, but we've booked it. We've not talked about it with you, because we're keeping it from the kids. Grace will be an absolute wreck if she knows too early. We figured the day before would be soon enough to tell her.'

'Oh, that's wonderful for them. Let's leave it until a little nearer Christmas for them to come to me. Get the holiday over, and by the time you get back the shops will already be looking very festive. We all need a good Christmas this year.'

They chatted for a few minutes, and then Jenny took her cup to the small sink unit, washed it, and put it away. 'I'll leave you to sleep, Anna. I'm glad you've enjoyed it. Next time you come, will you bring me the letters, please?'

Anna's mouth opened in shock. 'What? But... why on Earth would you want them? They're securely locked in my safe, and nobody knows about them. And that's the way it has to stay. They're dynamite, Jenny. Pure dynamite.'

'I'm going to put them in a safety deposit box. They won't be in the house. I just think Sheffield is too far away. You said it yourself, anything could happen to you, and my first priority for everyone's sake would be to retrieve those letters. That might not be possible if they're in Sheffield.'

'But, they won't go away. There's only the two of us know the combination.'

'I've thought about it, Anna, and I'd rather they were in the bank, safely locked away.'

Anna was stunned. Jenny had obviously decided she didn't trust her any more, but she had no idea why the situation had changed so dramatically.

'If that's what you want...' Anna said slowly.

'Yes, it is. Next time you come?'

Anna nodded. 'Next time I come.'

Jenny smiled as she left the room. 'Night, Anna. See you in the morning.'

Anna didn't speak. Couldn't speak.

She washed her cup and the plate that had held the biscuits almost without registering what she was doing. This new development had thrown her. Something was clearly simmering in Jenny's mind, something that had set her so much against her mother-in-law she was now distancing herself from her.

Anna struggled to sleep that night, trying to make sense of the change in Jenny. She was aware it wasn't a sudden change; she couldn't pinpoint the turning point though.

Next morning she was packed and ready to go by half past nine. Grace was tearful.

'But, I like having you here, Nan.'

Anna laughed. 'I know, sweetheart, and I like being here. But I live in Sheffield now, and I have to go feed Eric!'

Adam kissed her, and she hugged him. 'See you soon, Adam.'

She climbed into her car, and Mark closed the boot lid. He leaned in the window and kissed her.

'Drive carefully, Mum. Let us know when you're home. Love you.'

'Love you, too, and I'll text when I pull in to the car park, I promise. Stop worrying. I know this run like the back of my hand now.'

He stepped back, and Jenny leaned in to kiss her.

'Take care. We wouldn't want anything to happen to you.' Her tone was cold. 'And give MG my regards.'

Anna's heart rate increased, and she turned on the ignition. She looked at Jenny and nodded. There was no smile on her face.

'And you take care as well, Jenny. I'll be fine.'

She pressed on the accelerator and the car slid away from the drive, on its way back to Sheffield and Michael.

She pulled up a mile further on and rang him.

'I'm on my way.'

'Good. I'm already here, fridge stocked up, Eric fed. You need to go tell Lissy you're home as soon as you get here, so she doesn't come in and overdose poor Eric. My God, I've missed you and this place. Drive carefully, and come back to me, Anna.'

She laughed. 'Give me an hour.'

'Well, don't speed. You've only got one piece of mail, and it's from DVLA. Do they do speeding fines?' he chuckled.

'I hope not. No, that'll be my new driving licence. I had to change my name and address on it. I'm legal now, it seems.'

They disconnected, and fifty-five minutes later Anna pulled into the car park. Worry had travelled back with her, and she didn't know what to do. There had been threat in Jenny's voice, and she was all too aware of what Jenny could do when someone crossed her.

She sent a brief text to Mark, saying she was safe, and was very quickly engulfed in Michael's arms. He held her for a long time and then released her, saying, 'Go tell Lissy you're home.'

Jon answered the door; Lissy still wasn't well, and he'd left her to have a lie in. Anna said she would pop around later to see how she was, and she returned to Michael.

Anna picked up her mail and opened the brown envelope. It was her driving licence, and she smiled with pleasure at the name Anna Groves. She put it in her purse and grinned at him.

'Just have to keep that from prying eyes.'

He looked serious for a moment. 'I wish we didn't, Anna.'

'So do I. But, the family have been through so much since I walked out on Ray...'

'I know, and it's only been six months,' he finished the thought for her.

Michael poured out two cups of coffee and they finally began to relax on the sofa. Uppermost in her mind was the Jenny situation, but she kept quiet. She didn't know what to say, how to say it; the issue was difficult when the subject was a serial killer.

Chapter 45

Anna and Michael parked the car in the car park of a nearby casino and began the trek up to Hillsborough. Blue and white shirts filled the pavements, and the fans were clearly in a good mood. They didn't see too much Premiership opposition at their ground; today was special.

Michael shivered and said he hoped it would be warmer inside the ground. Anna merely smiled. She went to one of the stalls and bought him a scarf, wrapping it around his neck with care.

'There, you look like one of us now.'

They passed through the turnstile, and Michael winced. She laughed at his expression.

'I said you would have to breathe in.'

'You didn't say anything about not breathing at all,' he grumbled.

They climbed the steps hand in hand, and then Michael knew exactly why she had wanted to come.

Hillsborough looked magnificent under the luminescence of the spotlights. The stands were already filling up and becoming a sea of blue and white; the pitch was immaculate, and he thought back to the pictures Anna had showed him of a few years earlier when that same pitch had been under six feet of water following the floods. It took his breath away, and he knew next time she said let's go to a match, he would simply say yes.

The Leppings Lane end of the pitch was filling up with Arsenal supporters, but it was clear the loudest voices would come from Sheffield.

They chatted about anything and everything, and when the players came out on to the pitch, Michael was as enthusiastic as the other twenty-five thousand Wednesday supporters. It briefly occurred to him the Arsenal players might well feel intimidated by the mighty fan base, and then they settled down to watch the football. The first goal came from Ross Wallace after only twenty-seven minutes, and Michael experienced the bouncing combined with hi-ho Sheffield Wednesday first hand.

By the end of the match, he was exhausted. Anna was glowing; a 3 – 0 win over Arsenal had certainly made her eyes shine. 36,000 fans from both sides had taught him exactly what his new wife loved about the game.

They walked back to the car, following a singing, laughing crowd of fans, and it was after eleven o'clock by the time they reached home. Anna plugged her mobile phone in to the charger and noticed a text had come through from Mark, now enjoying the sunshine of Florida with Jenny and the children.

Yes!!! It said, followed by, *and we saw you!*

Anna had set the recorder to record the televised match so that she could relive it; she knew Michael would enjoy the re-run as well. He had been impressed. She knew she had to watch it as soon as possible, hoping only Mark had seen her in the crowd.

She showed Michael the text, and he pulled her into his arms.

'Look, stop worrying. He can't know I'm with you. He'll just assume you're there on your own.'

And then she sobbed. 'Jenny knows.'

'Jenny knows what?'

'She knows somehow there is a man in my life. She's been checking my stuff, and saw two texts from you on my phone. I didn't want to worry you by telling you. No, I'm wrong. I wanted to pretend it hadn't happened. As I left on that Saturday morning, she whispered, "Give MG my regards."'

'Look, whatever happens, we'll be fine. We're married now, and there's nothing they can do about it. I love you, Anna.

And you love me. Do you want to come clean, or do we carry on hiding it until Jenny forces us to "fess up"?'

Anna was troubled, and it showed in her face.

'Let me think about the best way forward. I honestly don't know what to do. With the investigation...' her voice faded away.

'Anna, you do seem unduly worried about this investigation. What's wrong? Do you know something you've not told me?'

She shook her head. 'No, I've told you everything Gainsborough has passed on to us. I just didn't want to complicate matters by having people think I was seeing you before Ray was murdered – that would give me a damn good reason to want him dead. Especially as we've now got married. And no.' She held up her hand as she saw him about to interrupt. 'I don't regret that. I wouldn't change anything we have. We have time to decide what to do; they're not due back from Florida for another week.'

It was only when they watched the replay they realised they might have an issue. They were both on the screen after Wallace's goal had been shown several times; the camera had panned across the kop Wednesday supporters and captured Michael turning towards Anna with his arms held out. It was a fleeting vision, but clearly Anna.

It was also like looking at an older Mark; the new scarf around his neck was exactly the same as Mark's, and she knew if Jenny had also watched the match, she would have seen exactly what she was seeing now.

Anna turned to Michael, knowing she couldn't hide this from him. 'We have a problem.'

He laughed. 'Damn right we have a problem. It's so obvious we're together. We have to come clean, Anna, we have to.'

She shook her head. 'That part would be simple. If Mark watches a rerun of this, and I don't doubt he's left their recorder on for it, he's going to see the most obvious thing in the world; the man taking me into his arms is the older version of himself – and also Tim.'

'Oh, Anna.' He pulled her close. 'These are our kids, not our parents. They can't tell us what to do, how we must behave. You'll not lose them, they love you. And they support you. I know very little about your life with Ray, but I can put the pieces together, and I believe it wasn't a good life. And the kids knew, didn't they?'

She nodded, miserable.

He stood. 'Let's go to bed. We need to sleep on this. And I mean sleep. I don't want you to be awake half the night with worry. I'm here for you, and we'll sort it.'

'There's something else I need to sort tomorrow,' she said. 'And you're right. I can't do anything for a week anyway. So let's try and forget it.'

Anita Waller

Chapter 46

They were both quiet and ate very little for breakfast. Neither of them had slept particularly well, and after clearing away the scant breakfast detritus, Anna went across to the wall safe and keyed in the combination.

She took out the card, explaining how to reset the code just to make sure she didn't end up locking it permanently and keyed in the new code of 0112.

'Need help?' Michael looked puzzled.

'No, but I need you to keep this number safe. If anything should happen to me, you'll need to get in here to clear it out. I've changed the number to both of our birthdays, 01 for yours and 12 for mine. I've keyed it in as 0112. Remember it, Michael, will you?'

He took out his phone and tapped in his security number before entering the safe combination in his notes.

'Right,' he said. 'Nobody can get at that, unless they know my security number.'

'I need to do that on my phone,' she said thoughtfully. 'Put a security code on it. If I had done that already Jenny wouldn't have been able to see your texts. Sometimes, I'm so stupid.'

'Or trusting,' he said with a smile. 'You're definitely not stupid, Anna.'

She felt happier Jenny could no longer get at the letters. During the long sleepless night, Anna had decided that the letters would remain with her; she would not take them to Lincoln.

Having changed the entry code for the safe, she knew Jenny could no longer get at them. She would wait five years

230

and then give them to her. She could do what she wanted with them then, but for now, Anna felt she needed the security of hanging on to all three of the letters. The Jenny she had loved had changed again, and become someone she didn't know anymore.

The old Jenny wouldn't have gone through her suitcase, checked her phone; this new Jenny needed help, and giving back those letters had the potential to create all sorts of problems, would possibly give Jenny the means to blackmail her, make her give up Michael – and that was unthinkable.

Michael thought nothing of her changing the combination on the safe. He was aware of her three letters for her children that were to be given to them on her death but the only other thing in there was her passport. It crossed his mind she would need to change her name on that, but there was no rush.

'Pass me your phone, and I'll put a code on it. Do you want the same number as the safe? You'll remember it then,' Michael grinned.

'Well it does feel a bit like shutting the stable door,' she said, but handed him the phone anyway.

Before he could set it, the phone rang.

He looked at her. 'It's Tim.'

'No...' Her voice cracked.

He held out the phone, and she pressed to answer.

'Tim? This is an early call.' She tried to inject enthusiasm into her voice.

'I can't sleep.'

'Right. Well, it's lovely to hear from you. Are you okay?'

'Sort of. Are you?'

'I'm fine. Did you enjoy the match?'

'It was amazing. Did you watch it?'

'Yes. Mark, Jenny, and the kids are staying with us for a couple of days. Mark, Adam, Steve, and I watched it. Who is he, Mum?'

'Pardon?'

Who is the chap who looked as if he was going to eat you, the one in the next seat?'

'I have no idea. He said his name was Andy, but he was just a fan, like me. What exactly are you getting at, Tim?'

'That's not how it looked. Maybe I'm over-reacting, but I worry about you. You've never really felt any grief for Dad, and I was concerned...'

'Concerned?' Anna allowed her voice to rise a little. 'Concerned about what? I mean, I don't know who that chap was, he just disappeared straight after the final whistle, but even if I'd gone with him, can I just ask what concern it is of yours? Or Mark's?' All the time she was raising her voice, there was a little moment of happiness in the back of her mind Tim had said, "never really felt any grief" rather than "grieved." Tim had always understood what was happening.

'Look, you're vulnerable at the moment. I do worry about you. I'm a lot of miles away from you. Mark didn't seem concerned about it, but I couldn't sleep for thinking about it.'

'Didn't Jenny watch it?'

'No. She was sunbathing with Grace by the pool.'

'And didn't you get excited by the goals? Didn't you want to hug and kiss everyone in sight after each of the goals? Well, guess what, Tim, so did I. And so did every one of our 25,000 or so fans. Does Mark feel worried as well? For goodness sake, you two boys give me a lot of problems. Now, back off, or I'll snog Westwood in front of everybody next time.'

Tim's laughter echoed down the line. He knew of his mother's admiration for the goalkeeper.

'I'm sorry, Mum. I've watched that bit at least half a dozen times; each time more convinced than ever that you've married some stranger without telling us. I'm an idiot. Mark wants you.'

She drew in a breath while she waited for her firstborn twin to take the phone.

'Hiya, philanderer,' he said with a laugh. 'Has Tim been reading you the riot act? He was furious when he first saw it, so I knew he'd ring you. He just doesn't understand the passion of the game, does he? Was it good?'

'It was amazing. Jenny didn't watch it, then?'

'No, she's no football fan. Neither is Grace. Right, I'll let you go. Take care, Mum, and try not to get into any bother. Tim would be on the next plane.'

They disconnected with a laugh, and she breathed a sigh of relief.

Michael looked at her, aware of the relief etched on her face. 'Everything good?'

'Yes, you're called Andy, and you were some random fan who got carried away after the goal was scored and hugged me. Mark accepted that quite happily, because he's a massive fan, but Tim's different. He's a bit half-hearted about football, and doesn't understand the feeling of a goal being scored. He does now.'

'So we're okay again?'

'I think so. Jenny didn't see it. But, don't forget, she's seen my phone. She knows there's an MG out there who sends me cheeky texts. And who gets cheeky texts back from me,' she added with a grin.

'Why do I get the feeling you're a little bit scared of Jenny?'

'Not scared, more…wary. Don't forget they lived in Leicester, not Lincoln, so I don't really know her all that well. I'm getting to know her better now they're in Lincoln.'

'Right, pass me your phone. Let's stop her seeing anything else that's private.'

He set the passcode on the phone and handed it back to Anna. 'It's 0112, like the safe. Do not tell anyone that code. I'm going to change mine to the same number so we can access each other's phone, but nobody else can. Is that okay with you?'

'Yes, that's fine. It makes sense, doesn't it?'

'It certainly does. So is life, our lives, back on track now? Can we breathe again?'

'We can,' she said. 'For the moment.'

'Well, I hate to say I told you so, but didn't I say that football match would be no good for us? Didn't I try to talk you out of it?'

'You did, my love. I'll go on my own next time, and then we won't get into trouble.'

He frowned. 'Oh, no, you won't. I want to know more about this snog with Westwood! You're a married woman, you know. You can't go around snogging goalies. No, I'll have to go with you.'

She laughed. 'Admit it, Michael Groves. You thoroughly enjoyed it, didn't you? Going again has got nothing to do with my potential infidelity, you bloody enjoyed it!'

Chapter 47

Jenny had listened to the conversation between Mark and Tim with interest. Apparently, they had seen Anna in the crowd on the kop, and they had initially thought she had gone with a man.

She decided not to draw attention to anything by asking to see the playback; they knew she had no love for the game. Mark had set it to record back in England; she would watch it at her leisure when the children were back at school and Mark back at work.

She put it out of her mind for the rest of the holiday, deciding Mickey Mouse was far more interesting than Anna Carbrook and her MG. She would deal with her when she got back home.

Everyone was dejected waiting at the airport for their flight. Tim and Steve had accompanied them; everyone was miserable, knowing it would be a while before they met up again. They watched the four of them go through to the departures area and slowly began the walk back to the airport car park.

'We need to go and see your Mum,' Steve said, staring one last time out of the window at the huge machine that would take the Carbrooks back to England. 'I didn't say anything when you and Mark got all wound up about the football match, but I'm sure she knew that man. She's a very wealthy woman, Tim, so maybe we should go over in a couple of weeks, check things out.'

Tim stared at him. 'But, you said nothing...'

'I'm saying it now. I didn't want to say anything while Mark was there, and I wanted to rearrange some free time for us so we could go. I've done that now. We'll book our flights when we get back. Is that ok?'

'I knew I was right to worry. Let's hope she can put our minds at ease when we go there.'

'Tell her we'll stay with her. That way, we'll soon know if there's a man in the offing. There'll be something of his there.'

Tim nodded. 'Thank you, Steve. You knew I was still concerned, didn't you?'

Steve frowned. 'It was obvious. I hope there is nothing. But, if a man has clicked on to the fact she has quite enormous wealth now, we really do need to know who he is. She's gone through enough this year. I would hate to see it get worse.'

They exited the building and headed towards where they had left the car. Tim threw the keys to Steve. 'You drive. I've got too much to think about.'

*****

The Carbrooks arrived home just after 6.00am, and Jenny ushered Adam and Grace off to bed. Mark checked everything was okay then sat down with his wife to enjoy a cup of tea.

'I'll put a wash load in, and then I'm off to bed as well,' she said.

'I'll stay up a bit. Just need to unwind. I bloody hate Tim being over there. He's my brother. It was Dad's fault, you know.'

Jenny stared at him. He never said a bad word against Ray. She had always thought he idolised his father, believing he could do no wrong. She waited, curious to know what he would say next.

'Yes, he refused to believe Tim was gay. Couldn't imagine him having feelings for Steve, because that wasn't what real men did. The furore that night was unreal. Mum kept trying to intervene, and in the end I got Tim out of there and took him to Steve's house, where Steve was telling his parents he was going to move in with Tim.

'The situation was a bit different there, I can tell you. They were delighted, really liked Tim. Tim was in a bit of a state, as you can imagine, so I stayed for quite a while and then headed off home. Dad had disappeared, and Mum was in the bathroom, bathing her injuries. She was in a mess; he'd hammered her for sticking up for Tim.

'Caro came downstairs when she heard me come in; she was still a kid, and had heard it all. I comforted her best I could and got her back in bed. Next day, Dad turned up saying he was really sorry, but Mum had to go get patched up at the hospital. That wasn't the first time he'd hit her, but it was the most serious. It changed her. I think, in her mind, she became his employee rather than his wife, until that day she walked away.'

'So Tim left?'

'Yes. Dad never spoke to him after that. Within six months, Tim and Steve had moved to Florida, and they're happy and doing really well, in spite of Dad, not because of him.'

Jenny sensed a change in Mark. He had always said he could never work with his dad, but she had thought it was just a clash of personalities. She hadn't realised the depth of his anger towards Ray, because of his treatment of Anna. She felt vindicated for what she had done to rid this family of a monster. And she appreciated how Mark was starting to open up, to confide in her about the important things he had buried while his father was alive.

Jenny waited, but he said nothing else. He seemed lost in thought and then suddenly stood. 'I'm going for a little walk. Won't be long.'

She nodded. 'I'll sort the washing, and then I'm going for a nap. I'm setting an alarm though, don't want more than a couple of hours or I won't sleep tonight.'

With Mark's departure, the house became quiet once more. Jenny stared out of the kitchen window for a while, and then went to open the suitcase filled with dirty laundry. She started the machine and sat back down at the kitchen table, clutching a second cup of tea, staring into space.

She needed to contact Anna, invite her to come over. They had bought her gifts, and Jenny knew she would want to see the children. The letters would come with her, and she could get them safely stowed away until the investigation died a death. Gainsborough clearly had no idea where to turn next, and it was looking as though it would be one of life's mysteries—the Lincoln serial killer who just stopped killing.

Jenny moved into the lounge and switched on the television, checking that the football match had been recorded. It had, and she switched it off again; she would save that bit of viewing for when she was on her own.

With the washing machine humming in the background, Jenny went to bed, sleeping almost immediately.

*****

Heading back into the kitchen some two and a half hours later, Jenny found Mark had mowed the back lawn and was now sitting at the table eating biscuits and drinking tea. He smiled at her.

'Sorry about this morning. Bit of heart searching going on, I think. Just ignore me. I've finished the back lawn, going to tackle the side now and get that done, then I'll see how I feel. If I'm tired, I'll have a nap. If not, I'll try to make it through to tonight before sleeping.'

'Okay,' she responded with a smile. He looked exhausted, no matter what he might be saying. She figured he would be in bed by six.

Jenny made some lunch, and then called Adam and Grace. Grumpiness was written all over their faces; they were obviously still tired.

'Okay, here's the deal,' she said. 'If you both smile, I will feed you. If you don't, you'll have to help Dad mow the side lawn. Without pizza.'

They both smiled.

*****

Both children had opted for baths rather than showers before bed; ensuites in every room were definitely blessings, Jenny decided. Mark looked drained, and she made him go to bed at the same time as the children. He almost fell asleep in the shower, and finally succumbed the instant his head touched the pillow.

Jenny tidied everything away, put yet another wash load into the washer, and then switched on the television. She scrolled down the recorded programmes and pressed for the football.

At first, she was tempted to fast forward, but then realised she didn't really know at what point they had seen Anna. She hadn't wanted to let anyone know she was concerned so thought it best not to ask. She watched intently.

Jenny winced as two Arsenal players were stretchered off in the first twenty minutes, but kept her eyes peeled as the cameraman swept through the crowd. He concentrated on the Arsenal supporters; their team was being decimated, and he was catching the expressions of the fans admirably.

And then came the twenty-seventh minute, with a cracking shot on goal from Ross Wallace. She saw it a further three times before the camera swept along the spectators, this time focussing on the Kop fans.

And there was Anna. The exhilaration showed on her face as she turned to the man next to her, who was already holding open his arms. His head moved slightly, and in that brief moment, Jenny sucked in her breath and held it.

She exhaled slowly and rewound the recording to the ball going into the net. The split second Anna came on the screen she froze the picture. She moved along a frame at a time and saw him. The man she had seen in Anna's car park was the man at the match.

But, of more consequence than that piece of information, was she knew him; she knew who MG was.

He was the genetic father of Mark and Tim. The angle of his head as he turned, combined with the same design Sheffield Wednesday scarf Mark always wore, left her in no doubt she was looking at an older version of her husband. What she couldn't understand was why the brothers hadn't seen it; she put it down to they were there to see the football, she was there to see the fans.

Jenny moved closer to the screen and took several pictures on her phone before closing down the television. She sat on the sofa, zombie-like. She tried to remember the conversation she had had with Anna when Anna was confessing to the affair she had had when the twins were conceived; what name had she said?

Jenny felt sure she had only said a first name, but she couldn't bring it to mind. It clearly began with M – had she said Mark? Had she dared to call one of the twin boys after the man who had fathered them?

She closed her eyes and let her thoughts drift to the scene. They had been sitting in Anna's lounge in her first apartment, sitting on camping chairs because she had no furniture. And she had made Anna talk. It had been a reluctant conversation at first, but then Anna had really opened up, telling her that Michael...!

Michael! That was the name Anna had given her. But, Anna had said he was dead. He didn't look very dead in his Wednesday scarf; in fact, he looked very much alive. Anna obviously hadn't trusted her enough to be honest about everything; she didn't want Jenny to know Michael was still alive and contactable. Michael and Anna were reunited, and if Anna loved him as much as she had said she did, then might she just tell him secrets he really shouldn't know?

Her worries had now increased tenfold.

Chapter 48

Michael placed the cup of tea on her bedside table and then sat by her side. He leaned across and kissed her.

'What shall we do today?'

'Well...'

He looked at her, his head to one side. 'Well what?'

'Shall we test the waters?'

He looked puzzled, not sure how to respond. 'What waters?'

'Well...'

'Well waters? At Buxton? I assume they're tested all the time.'

'Now you're being pedantic, Michael Groves.'

'I am?'

'Yes. I know someone who might not throw up their hands in horror at the idea of us being together.'

'We're not just together. We're married.'

'I know. You're being pedantic again.'

'Okay. Perhaps you can be more explicit?' He smiled at her.

'Don't patronise me, Mr. Groves. I have powers you know nothing about.'

'You have powers I know a lot about,' he whispered and leaned over to kiss her again. 'Shall I get back in bed for us to test out these powers?'

'No. You're out of favour now. Now listen to me.' He looked dejected, and she tried not to laugh. 'I want to go to Doncaster.'

'To the market? The races? The retail outlet?'

'No. I want to see Charlie and Dan. With you.'

'With me?'

'Yes. With you.'

'Okay…' The word was long and drawn out. 'Today?'

She nodded. 'If they're in, yes. I'll have to ring first.'

'And what does she know?'

'Nothing at all. I'll sort of play it by ear as to how much I can tell her, but I'd like her to know you. We're unconditional friends. Always have been. Can we go?'

'We can do anything. Are you going to get out of that bed, woman? If you laze around, we won't be going anywhere.'

She looked at her bedside clock. 'It's seven o'clock.'

'I know, but today could be a good day. I don't want to waste a minute of it. I actually thought the first people to know would be Lissy and Jon, because that would make life so much easier, but, heyho! What do I know?'

'We'll practice our confession on Charlie and Dan, and then perfect it on Lissy and Jon.'

'And our kids?'

'Not yet. It's not time for that yet. That's why I'm testing the waters. Charlie's sensible; she'll say all the right things.'

He looked at her thoughtfully. 'Are you absolutely sure? Once you talk to Charlie, it may change your relationship.'

'It won't. She was so pleased when I walked away from Ray…'

'Yes, but it doesn't mean she'll be pleased you walked straight towards me. She might even think you left Ray for me, that we were having an affair before you walked out.'

'If she thinks that, then I'll put her straight.'

She swung her legs out of bed and then headed for the bathroom. Michael watched her go, a worried look on his face. He wasn't convinced this was the right thing to do. He heard the shower start up and went into the kitchen to make breakfast.

Michael knew he'd never been so happy; he hoped the trip to Doncaster would do nothing to spoil that.

Charlie confirmed they were in, and she was looking forward to the visit. Anna had simply said, "there are two of us," so he guessed Charlie's mind was now in overdrive. They stopped off to pick up some flowers for her, and forty-five minutes later, they were walking up to the front door.

Anna was bouncing at the idea of seeing her two closest friends; Michael felt sick.

Charlie and Dan came to the door together, both smiling. Anna introduced them to Michael, simply by acknowledging he was a friend.

They sat around the kitchen table, getting to know each other, with Charlie throwing in the odd question in an effort to find out who the mystery man was.

'So where did you two meet?'

'In Lincoln,' was Anna's simple response. It wasn't the right time to expand on that yet.

Charlie refilled their coffee cups and sat back down. Dan and Michael seemed to be getting on really well, and Dan offered to show Michael his shed.

Michael looked at Anna. 'Do you mind?'

Anna laughed. 'Oh, you'll be safe enough with Dan. Go and look, but I'm warning you, it's the scariest shed you'll ever see.'

The two men disappeared, and Charlie sat down.

'Okay, that was pre-arranged. Now spill. Who is he? Just don't tell me he knows you're a very wealthy widow.'

'Of course he knows I'm a wealthy widow. He's a considerably wealthier widower.'

Charlie breathed a sigh of relief. 'Well, that's that out of the way. I like him. Do you?'

'Yes.'

'And?'

'We're good together. But, the kids don't know about him, just you. Even Lissy and Jon don't know, and they live next door.'

'Then, I'm honoured. I'm just a bit concerned it's too soon, and after such an abusive relationship...'

'I met Michael thirty-six years ago.' Anna spoke quietly. 'I haven't seen him for the last thirty-five years or so, but I've never forgotten him. Do you like him?'

'Anna, I don't know him, but if you like him, that's okay with me. He seems to be getting on very well with Dan. Thirty-six years ago? Were you and him...?' She made a sort of half wave in the air, and Anna laughed.

'Maybe.'

'And I assume you and him are...'

'Maybe.'

'What's with this "maybe" lark? Have you found a new love, or not? And did you find this new love before Ray was bumped off, or after?'

'Exactly. That's why we're keeping it quiet. It's what everybody will think, but I contacted Michael when I was at my lowest point after Ray's death. But, everybody is going to think differently, aren't they? The kids, the police – even you!'

'The police?'

'Well, they haven't found anyone yet for the murders, so it follows that members of families are still on the list of suspects – not just my family, but the families of the other two victims. I don't think we're seriously considered as suspects, but if Gainsborough found out I'd mar...met Michael, it would put a different slant on it, wouldn't it. I just needed someone to know I am happy, and that someone is you. Are you okay with that?'

'Of course I am! I just worry about you; you know I do. You looked so lost at Ray's funeral, as if the weight of a million tons was on your shoulders – and now, you're happy again.'

They heard Dan and Michael come through the back door, and Charlie stood. 'Let's go and sit in the lounge. It'll be comfier there. And I can do my own quizzing of Michael,' she added with a laugh.

Anna knew she wasn't joking.

It seemed Michael and Dan had a lot in common; a shared un-love of football, a shared love of DIY, and a shared love of vintage motor cars.

The vintage car stored in the garage of Michael's Lincoln home came as news to Anna.

'Perhaps,' she said drily to her husband, 'you might like to show me this miracle of engineering next time I'm at yours?'

He grinned. 'Didn't think you'd be interested.'

'I would,' Dan said.

'Then, please, come over. Next weekend? We can be there, can't we, Anna?' He looked to her for guidance.

She nodded. 'That would be lovely. If you came Saturday, we could make a weekend of it, stay through to Sunday.'

Anna had never once invited them to stay at Lindum Lodge. Charlie was shocked.

'We'd love to,' she said, before Dan could respond.

They produced assorted diaries, and Charlie filled in Michael's address in her address book. 'Can't wait,' she said. 'Is it a big house?'

Michael laughed. 'It's very big, quite secluded as it's set pretty far back from the road. It's one of those houses you look at and think, "I wish I lived there."'

Charlie stood. 'I'll go and get us some lunch started.'

Anna followed her into the kitchen, leaving Dan and Michael to talk cars.

'Is it serious?'

'Yes.'

'How serious?'

Anna hesitated. She didn't know what to say. She ran a hand through her short blonde hair and opened her mouth, but no words came out.

'Anna?'

Finally, Anna spoke. 'About as serious as it gets.'

'You love him?'

Anna nodded. 'Always have.'

'For thirty-six years?' Charlie looked shocked. 'But, why the bloody hell did you marry such a moron as Ray?'

'I can't really explain now. When you come to Michael's next weekend, we'll have plenty of time to talk, and I'll fill you in on what's happening and what happened. You're going to have a lot of questions, and today isn't the right time. I just needed you to meet Michael, to let you see things have changed in my life, and I'm happy.'

Charlie reluctantly agreed, and they took assorted sandwiches and salad bowls through to where the men were.

Anna and Michael left in the middle of the afternoon and drove back to Sheffield.

'Did you get the third degree?'

'Oh, yes, she wanted to know everything. And it can only get worse next weekend,' she added with a laugh.

'Look, Anna, I don't mind what you tell her. She's clearly very concerned about you, so if it helps ease her mind, for goodness sakes tell her we're married, that I'm not after your money, because I've got a bob or two myself, and I love you and have done for a very long time.'

'Well! Say it like it is, Michael! To be honest, I'd already decided to tell her after I'd talked it over with you. So we'll have champagne next weekend then?'

He laughed. 'Too damn right we will.'

*****

By the time the weekend came around, Anna was feeling sick, excited, and apprehensive; she had no idea how Charlie and Dan would react to the news, or what questions to expect.

Living a life of secrecy was taking its toll on her, and the phone call from Jenny hadn't helped. She had invited Anna over to stay; the children had brought gifts back from Florida for her, she said. Although Anna had said she would love to visit, it could only be for two days, because she had a dental appointment in Sheffield on the Wednesday. They agreed to her staying Monday and Tuesday, and Jenny had finished with, "And don't forget to bring the letters, will you?"

Talking it over between them had resulted in them deciding Michael would return to Sheffield on Monday morning. Anna would go straight to Lindum Lodge, following their weekend with Dan and Charlie.

Their visitors left Doncaster, armed with flowers and wine, and arrived to a warm welcome. Charlie felt suitably chastened when she thought back to her first worries about Michael; he certainly didn't want or need Anna for her money. She loved his home, and her mind projected to the future when maybe Anna and Michael would become partners properly. Anna would love this house.

Michael disappeared with Dan almost immediately, each bearing a mug of coffee. They had gone to inspect Michael's Riley 11, his classic car Anna had still to see. She could wait; let him share his proud owner moment with someone who understood such desires!

She walked with Charlie around the immaculate garden. Michael freely admitted to liking gardening, but he killed more than he grew, so had now given up and employed a gardener. The lawn was massive, the cottage garden appeal of the borders impressive. Most of the flowers were finished now, but it was apparent just how spectacular they had been throughout the summer.

Anna and Charlie wandered back to the lounge, and still the boys hadn't reappeared. They sat down and finished their coffees, then Anna took her upstairs to the bedroom allocated to them. It was a beautiful room, decorated in lemon and white. The weak winter sun lit up the interior, and Charlie smiled.

'Oh, this is lovely, Anna. It's immaculate.'

'Well, nothing to do with me. He not only has a gardener; he has a cleaner. He cooks for himself, though,' she finished with a laugh.

'Good for him.'

'He's doing tonight's meal. We had initially thought we might take you out, but decided it would be better here; it's easier to talk sitting around a coffee table after, isn't it?'

Charlie made no comment, just looked at her friend.

She put away the few items of clothing they had brought, and then Anna showed her around the rest of the upstairs rooms. There were many. Charlie saw six bedrooms on that level, and then a further two in the attic space, all beautifully decorated and dressed.

'Does Michael have children?'

'Just one, Erin. She's in South Africa at the moment, I understand, and no, she doesn't know about us, any more than Mark, Tim, and Caro do. Michael would tell them in a heartbeat, but I'm not ready yet.'

'Not ready to commit to Michael, or not ready to tell them?'

'You're fishing.'

'I'm not.'

'Then put the rod and line away.'

Charlie held up her hands in laughter, and they went back downstairs. Dan and Michael were in the kitchen, making fresh coffees for all four of them.

'It's beautiful,' Dan said.

'The house?' his wife responded. 'It certainly is.'

'Not the house! The car. I need one, Char.'

'Michael! This wasn't supposed to happen! I was quite happy accompanying him to classic car shows, but living with one wasn't in the plans.'

'Sorry.' Michael looked sheepish. 'Next time you come, we're going out in it. I'm just waiting for a part coming, or we could have driven it today.'

Charlie tutted, but knew she had lost. His Christmas present would be a car.

After lunch, Dan and Michael disappeared once more into the garage, and Charlie and Anna sat and talked, with Anna skirting around any difficult subjects. She did briefly touch on how changed Jenny was, but Charlie thought it was probably down to having to deal with Mark's grief at the loss of his father.

'And how is Caro? Settled into the new job?'

'Yes. I don't hear from her very much, but when I do, she says they are both happy but not living together. Her job is quite stressful, and there has been a lot to learn, but she's glad she took it. She absolutely loves Paris, but don't we all?'

'We certainly do. And Tim? Isn't it strange how twins can be so different?'

'What do you mean? They look alike. Not so much as when they were growing up, but even now, you couldn't mistake them for anything but twins.'

'I didn't mean in looks. I meant their personalities. Mark was always the serious one, the one who felt he had to please Ray. Tim never seemed to like his dad very much. Tell me to shut up if you want, I don't want to upset you.'

'No, it doesn't. And you're probably right. I guess I'm a little too close to see it that objectively. Tim definitely walked away from Ray that night, anyway.'

They both knew the night in question. *I'm moving in with Steve. We're partners now. I love him.*

Charlie stood and moved around the room. In one corner was a beautiful ornate display stand, antique, polished to a beautiful finish. It was covered in framed photographs. She picked up one of the pictures and looked at it. It showed a much younger Michael and his wife, with Erin about three years old.

She stared at it for long moments. 'Would this have been taken around the time you met Michael?'

Anna moved across to her and looked closely at the photo. She nodded.

'I guess. I think Erin was about three when I first knew her.'

Charlie replaced the photograph.

'Anna, if ever any of your children come to this house, you have to remove pictures of a younger Michael.'

Anna flushed. She had also seen the uncanny resemblance between the twins and their genetic father. 'I...'

'Don't say anything. I won't. Ever. Just take care.'

Anna's mouth turned down. This hadn't been the subject planned for discussion. Charlie continued to walk around the room, looking at things with a craftsman's eye, logging ideas into her brain, to be brought out and used in future times.

Dan and Michael returned, their greasy hands evidence of their activities. They chatted and washed, and then Dan joined Charlie and Anna, while Michael began to prepare the evening meal.

It was a lovely afternoon with much laughter as Dan began to discuss his plans for his own classic car.

'Where are you going to put it?' his wife asked.

'In the garage!'

'You can't get in the garage for all the other *important stuff,* as you call it.'

'I'll clear it out.'

Charlie laughed.

'But, where will you put all the clearing out rubbish you can't bear to part with?'

'I'll build another shed.'

'Dan!'

'Okay, I'll get rid of some stuff.'

Charlie sighed in exasperation and Anna laughed. 'Is it really good, this car?'

'It's beautiful,' Dan said solemnly. 'Michael needs me with him when we take it out for its first spin, just in case.'

'Just in case what?' Anna queried.

'I don't know. Just in case.' He looked affronted Anna didn't understand the importance of his being there for the Riley's inaugural trip out of Michael's garage.

Michael interrupted the conversation by bringing wine glasses and bottles of wine in. After that, they talked about more mundane things, and Michael eventually summoned them to the dining room.

It looked spectacular. The antique table had been dressed by Anna earlier, and Michael had added a silver champagne cooler. The candles flickered and glowed, and they sat down to enjoy the meal.

There was a lot of laughter; the wine was flowing freely, and after the main course, Michael removed the large plates. He then opened the champagne and topped up everyone's champagne flutes.

'Okay,' he said, taking a long look at Anna who nodded and smiled. 'We have a toast to propose. Please raise your glasses and toast my beautiful wife, Anna. Mrs. Groves, I love you very much. Thank you for being my wife.'

There was a silence that lingered in the air and then Michael, Dan and Charlie took a sip of champagne each, followed by Anna. She simply said, 'Thank you.'

'Anna?' Charlie stared at her friend. 'Is this a current Mrs. Groves or a future Mrs. Groves?'

'Very much a current, Charlie. Apart from our random witnesses, you are the only people who know. It has to be secret for now, but, yes, we're married. The ceremony was in Sheffield on 18th September, but we don't want it to be public yet. However, we do want you two to know.'

Dan stood. 'I am so chuffed for you two.' He raised his glass in the air.

'To Mr and Mrs Groves, a long and happy life together.' He drank. 'And I'm sure that when Charlie's mouth closes, she'll say the same thing.'

The tension collapsed, and Charlie burst out laughing.

'Well, Anna, you're certainly full of surprises these days. Seriously, I'm really pleased for you.' She, too, raised her glass. 'A long and happy life together.'

She walked around the table to Anna, who stood as she approached. They hugged each other, and Charlie whispered, 'Be happy' in Anna's ear.

'I am. Happier than I thought possible.'

Bizarrely, Anna's mind flashbacked to the night when Jenny had returned to her apartment from Lincoln, and she had been covered in blood. Ray's blood. James Oswoski's blood. Her happiness plummeted, and Charlie looked at her.

'Anna?'

'Oh, it's nothing. I just for a second thought about how Ray's awful death has led to this, to Michael. I'm fine, honestly. It's the alcohol.' She laughed shakily.

Michael stood. 'Come and sit down, sweetheart. And for heaven's sake, put on your wedding ring! You can wear it now. I'll go and get the dessert.'

They finished the meal with Anna fully restored to her normal self, and Charlie eager for details of the wedding day. She could see the happiness glowing out of Anna now there was no need to hide the marriage. Michael seemed to be a good man, and she couldn't help but reflect that if Anna had been able to be with him from the start, then the boys would have grown up to know the true love of a father. She hated the idea of Tim leaving because Ray couldn't cope with his son's sexuality.

She wondered if Michael knew. If he did, it must be difficult for him not meeting up with Mark and Tim. The damned police needed to pull their fingers out and find the chap who had killed the people in Lincoln, and give Anna some peace and to be able to come clean about this new relationship.

And then she thought about this uncanny resemblance between Michael and his sons. It wouldn't just be about telling them they were married. Erin would acquire half-brothers, who were also step brothers.

Oh, Anna, Charlie thought, *you don't make life easy for yourself, do you?*

They moved back into the lounge to have coffee and yet more wine, listen to some blues music, and generally talk and laugh. It was a good evening.

Three out of the four would always remember it as being a good evening.

Chapter 49
Sunday, 13 November 2015

Jenny carried the clean bedding through to Anna's flat and began to make up the bed. Mark had taken the children swimming to give her chance to get Anna's room ready, and so it was proving to be a very quiet Sunday.

She gave a final tug at the quilt, and went out to the kitchen to get the vase of flowers she had bought for the room. She placed them on the coffee table. Then, she stood in the doorway and looked around. Perfect.

Although she envisaged it being an awkward couple of days, Jenny was looking forward to Anna coming. Adam and Grace loved having her with them, but it was time for her and Anna to talk. By the end of the visit, Jenny had every intention of knowing who the mystery man was, and if he was a threat to her safety and security. She also needed to let Anna know just who the lead actor in this play was. She had been the one taking all the risks, and she would be the one to call all the shots from now on, starting with those damn letters. She had a feeling Anna wouldn't hand them over voluntarily, so if Anna made no reference to them, she would leave everything until Tuesday when the children were at school and then demand them. They would be taken to the bank on Wednesday.

She smiled at the sign on the door that said, *Nanny's Flat*, along with a tiny Minnie Mouse. The children had chosen it to bring back from Florida, and she had to admit it looked good. She was sure Anna would love it.

She felt troubled by her feelings about Anna. She had lost her all those years ago because Ray, the husband from hell, had raped her, and she had to put distance between them. And she had missed her. Anna was back in their lives because Ray was out of their lives, but she knew her mother-in-law had built a barrier.

And then there was this bloody man. This bloody man who had clearly fathered Mark and Tim, she had no doubt about that, which meant Anna had lied when she said he was dead. Why had she lied? Did Anna think she would try and track him down? Did Anna really think she would go up to some random man and say, 'Hey, I'm married to your son!'

Perhaps the reason behind Anna's silence about the man was she had been seeing him before she left Ray. Perhaps all that bunkum about the anniversary cards being the catalyst that had set her free was simply that, bunkum.

Jenny's mind was whirling, and she felt out of control. She would have to take that control back, and it would happen when she got those letters back. She knew Anna would never go to the police, would never leave Adam and Grace without their mother. She sat at the kitchen table and dropped her head. She felt tears begin, and she reached for the tissues.

She would not cry. She would not allow Ray, in any form, to destroy any more of her. She dabbed at her eyes, but the tears didn't stop.

And that was how she was when Mark and the children returned home, smelling of chlorine and excited by the morning they had had.

Mark frowned. 'What's wrong, sweetheart?'

'Nothing, I'm absolutely fine. Just a moment, that's all. I'll make us a cup of tea.'

Mark sent the children to put their wet swimming clothes and towels in the utility room and put his arms around his wife. 'Would a hug help?'

'Oh, it would, it would,' she said, and laid her head against him.

'What's caused the tears? Thinking about Dad?' Mark still felt very raw about the brutality of Ray's death.

Jenny nodded. Better he thought that than continue to question her. He hugged her a little tighter and then led her to the kitchen table.

'I'll make us a drink. Is everything ready for Mum coming tomorrow?'

'Yes, all done. And it looks lovely.'

'What time is she coming?'

'She said about 10ish.'

'Then I'll wait and see her before going into work. I just need to see she's doing okay. It would be good to have closure on this bloody case for all our sakes, but it's just not happening, is it?'

'We don't know what's going on behind the scenes,' she said. 'Really, Gainsborough tells us nothing, other than the bare minimum. He could have a suspect in mind right now, but we wouldn't find out until he'd arrested him.'

'You're right. Fingers crossed he gets him soon.'

He reached across and squeezed her fingers. 'Feeling better?'

She nodded. 'Yes. It was just a blip. Don't worry about me.'

They sat without speaking for a while, and then she stood to go and sort out the wet swimming clothes. As she went through the door to the utility room, Jenny turned to Mark. 'Have you ever considered Anna might meet someone else?'

'What? Mum? No, I hadn't. It's too early, surely.'

'You're right,' she said with a dismissive wave of her hand. 'I meant in the future.'

'Well, I can't see it, not really. She didn't have a particularly good life with Dad, he was a proper control freak; surely she wouldn't want to be tied down again. In fact, I think she would be quite scared of having another relationship. He might have been Dad, but I could see his faults.'

Not all of his faults...

'She might not see it as being tied down. She might fall in love.'

'Maybe. Don't know how I would feel though.'

She looked at him for a few seconds, and then turned and went in to sort the laundry.

Why was it only she had seen the obvious connection between the man and Anna at that damned football match?

******

Tim and Steve waited at the airport for the flight to Heathrow. They had opted to combine the trip back to the UK with business, and were spending the first four days in London before heading up to Sheffield. There they would stay until the New Year, spending Christmas with Anna and the rest of the family.

They wanted to use the element of surprise, and so decided to leave telling Anna until Wednesday morning, the day of their arrival in the northern city.

They filled the long flight with work. A meeting scheduled for two days ahead meant careful planning and reports to be finalised, and the flight hours passed quickly. They occasionally chatted about their proposed stay in Sheffield, in turn feeling anxious and apprehensive; they hoped Anna wouldn't see through their plan. They just needed to know she was safe. In the end, they had both agreed there was a connection between Anna and the man at the football match, and it needed to be monitored, dealt with.

*****

Michael took it upon himself to make breakfast for the four of them, and the atmosphere was easy going, friendly and warm

Anna felt a sense of relief she had now told Charlie and Dan about her marriage; at least she had somebody she could be open and honest with. Except for the fact she was an accessory to murder.

Once again, the image of her tiny safe holding the letters flashed into her mind. She was dreading going across to Lindum Lodge the following day, because she knew Jenny would be expecting her to bring the letters with her. That definitely wasn't going to happen. Not in a million years.

Jenny might feel more secure for having the letters in her possession, but Anna felt safer for having them with her.

The four of them went to a pub for lunch, and then Charlie and Dan headed back home to Doncaster. All four agreed it had been a good weekend, and they made tentative arrangements to spend New Year's Eve at the Armitage home in Doncaster.

'Coffee?' Michael asked, after hanging both their coats in the cloakroom.

Anna nodded. 'Yes, please. Then can we talk, because I don't know what to do.'

'Of course.' He looked at her carefully. He had been aware of her disturbed sleep during the night and could guess what was on her mind.

Anna wandered into the lounge and curled up on the sofa. She smiled at him as he pulled a small table towards her and placed her mug on it.

He chose not to sit next to her and faced her by sitting in the armchair.

'What's on your mind?'

'I want to come clean.'

'About us?'

She felt uncomfortable for a second. 'Yes. About us.'

'Are you sure? Once said it can never be taken back. It's only a couple of weeks since you said we had to wait two years before telling anybody.'

'I know, but seeing the way Dan and Charlie have taken it... it gives me hope maybe our children will be the same. How do you think Erin will react?'

'My beautiful, laid back daughter? She'll ask me if I'm happy, and when I say ecstatic, that will be enough for her. She has never been the problem. It's Mark, Tim, and Caroline who worry me. For a start, do we tell the boys I'm their real father? If we're going to confess to our marriage, they will want to know when and where we met. We can't start out with a lie, so we have to tell them around thirty-six years ago. Then, they'll look more closely at me, and they're all going to see what's obvious. Does Charlie know?'

Anna nodded. 'Yes, she saw the photo of you and Pat, with Erin, who was about three. That one there.' She pointed to the display stand. 'She knew as soon as she saw that.'

'So, it's really not just about telling them we're married, and that it's a secret, and we're very sorry we didn't invite them to the ceremony, is it? There's so much more we have to consider. I will say this, we can talk forever and a day, but ultimately, the decision about what we do is yours. Erin will be pleased she no longer has to worry about me; you stand to lose everything, except me, if they don't react how you want them to react.'

She looked at him. 'I couldn't bear it, if I lost you.'

He laughed. 'Not an earthly chance of that. I've waited all my life for you. But, you've so much to think about. Do we come clean about my being their father, or do we wait until somebody sees the resemblance? I don't think we really have a choice. For what it's worth, I think we have to make it clear from the start. This has to have an effect on your relationship with all three of them, because even Caro will have an opinion on it – you've said in the past she was very much for her father.'

'To be brutally honest, Michael, I have absolutely no idea how any of them will respond. But, you're right. We have to tell them everything, because it's been a hard three months since our wedding. It feels like we're hiding, and I don't want that. The only decision now is, do we wait until after Christmas or risk spoiling Christmas for everybody? If we wait, it means we don't get to spend our first Christmas together, and if we don't wait, we run the risk of totally spending it together without anyone else.'

Michael moved across to the sofa to sit with her. Placing an arm around her, he pulled her close. 'Shall I just leave you to think about it? Whatever you decide, I'm with you.'

He was leaning across to kiss her when they heard the front door open. Anna looked at him questioningly.

He began to stand as Erin walked through the lounge door. She crossed to her father and kissed him.

'Hi, Dad. I'm back.'

'Hello, beautiful daughter.' He smiled. 'You're not due back till next Friday.'

'Change of plan. I'm going to Holland next Friday now.' She turned and approached Anna, holding out her hand.

'Hi, I'm Erin.'

Anna laughed. 'I know. The last time I saw you was 1979, just coming up to your third birthday.'

'Really?' Erin turned to her father, and he smiled.

'Really. Anna used to clean for us when your mum was first starting to be ill. She left when Mum was officially diagnosed, and we had carers and a team of specialist cleaners brought in. I don't imagine for one minute you can remember that far back.'

'Sorry, Anna. Did he say Anna?'

She stood. 'Yes, I'm Anna, and it's lovely to finally meet you. Your dad is immensely proud of you, and I guess I know a lot more about you than you know about me.'

She grinned. 'So you two an item, then?'

'You would be okay with that, would you?'

Anita Waller

'Anna, if Dad is happy, I'm okay with that.'

'Then, yes, we are an item, as you so delicately put it.' Anna laughed.

'Sit down, you two. I'll get us a drink. You staying the night, Erin?'

'If that's okay.'

'It's fine. Alcoholic drink it is.'

He disappeared into the kitchen and returned with three champagne flutes and a bottle of champagne.

Erin's eyes widened. 'Well! This can't be because the prodigal daughter's returned home. What's going on?'

'It's because I didn't introduce you properly to Anna. Erin, I'd like you to meet Anna Groves, who was Anna Carbrook until September 18th.'

There was a moment of silence, and then Erin turned to Anna. She raised her glass and said, 'Congratulations, Step-mum and Dad. Are you happy?'

'Very.' They spoke in unison.

'Then, that's good enough for me.'

Erin fired questions at them, and they laughed their way through the answers, relieved to have got one part of the problem out of the way, but knowing decisions had now been taken out of their hands.

Erin was asked to keep quiet about it for a week, giving them chance to tell all the Carbrook family.

It was only as Michael said the words, 'Carbrook family,' that a look of puzzlement crossed Erin's face.

'Why do I know that name?'

Anna visibly flinched. 'My husband died in March. I had already left him, so our marriage was non-existent, but he was still legally my husband. He was murdered. I was at a very low point, and I contacted your dad for the first time in thirty-six years. I don't know why. I just needed to talk to someone who wasn't involved with me. He never hesitated, and he's been

262

my rock ever since. We decided to marry, because we don't know how much life we have left to us. We want to live it together.'

'Ray Carbrook. That's the name. I'm so sorry, Anna. I didn't intend bringing it all back for you. Have they caught anyone yet? Wasn't it a multiple murder case?'

'Yes, three people all killed by the same person, but as far as I know, they haven't got him yet.'

'They will,' Erin said with confidence. 'They always do.'

They chatted and drank champagne for a while, with Anna filling Erin in on their home in Sheffield they would normally have been in, and then Erin went out to her car to bring in her luggage. An hour later, she said goodnight; she needed sleep, and disappeared upstairs to her room.

Michael and Anna decided she would make arrangements to go the following weekend to Lindum Lodge, accompanied by him. She wouldn't break the news of a companion to Jenny and Mark until Friday, so it didn't initiate questions when she was on her own. She knew Jenny would wear her down.

They went to bed feeling scared and excited about finally being able to live openly at last; Anna slept much better than she had the previous night.

Chapter 50

Monday, 14 December 2015

All three of them left together the next morning; Michael headed off back to Sheffield and Eric, Erin went home to her own place across the other side of the city, and Anna headed for Lindum Lodge.

She pulled on to the parking area and noticed the company van was there. She was pleased because it probably meant Mark had waited to see her.

And he had. 'Morning, Mum,' he said, and bent to kiss her cheek. 'You okay?'

'I'm fine. Are the children expecting me to pick them up from school?'

'Try getting out of it,' he laughed. 'Last words this morning were, "Tell Nan we'll see her at the gates."'

'Good. I love getting them. It's been a long time since I did school runs.'

They enjoyed tea and biscuits, sitting comfortably together around the kitchen table before Mark had to leave for work.

Following his departure, Anna went to her own flat and laughed aloud at the plaque the children had bought for her door.

Jenny heard her laughter and smiled. 'Do you like it?' she called.

'It's wonderful. Did they choose it?'

'Yes, They've bought you some other touristy bits as well, all chosen by them, so just pretend they're awesome when you get them,' she said, walking towards Anna.

'I won't have to pretend.'

'Oh, you will. If I said articulated wooden alligators and stuffed Mickey and Minnie Mouses... mice... you might very easily have to pretend.'

She took Anna's small suitcase from her, bringing it into the flat.

'I'll leave you to unpack and then do you fancy a run into Newark for a change? We could have some lunch, a walk around the shops, and come back in time for you to do your duty by the children.'

'That would be lovely. I'll change my shoes, then, if I'm going walking.'

Jenny left her to get ready and headed back to the kitchen.

Anna was puzzled. She had half-expected Jenny to be waiting with hands outstretched for the letters, but she was being really chatty and welcoming. She found out her flat red shoes, picked up her bag, and within minutes, they were on their way to Newark.

Anna had always liked the town, not least because of the good memories it held for her. These memories had now increased; she and Michael had spent many hours in 'their' cafe. She just hoped Jenny wasn't taking her to the same place.

She drove them to a pub, one she said they had found one evening when she didn't fancy cooking.

It was good. They both ordered a ploughman's lunch and thoroughly enjoyed it. They chatted as if there were no murders, animosity, or letters between them.

They walked around Newark for a couple of hours, fitting in yet another coffee before returning to the car. And still, Jenny said nothing.

It was almost with relief Anna eventually escaped from Lindum Lodge to collect Adam and Grace from their respective schools.

Jenny made a huge meat and potato pie for their evening meal, and afterwards, they played a game of Uno. Mark never enjoyed losing, and the children shrieked with laughter when he was the first one to be disqualified.

Anna went to her flat later, and still Jenny hadn't brought up the subject of the letters. She went to bed around 10.00pm, after sending Michael several texts and telling him she would see him the following evening. He confirmed Eric was fine and looking forward to his mummy coming home.

Chapter 51
Tuesday, 15 December 2015

Anna was up and about early on Tuesday, and took Adam and Grace to school. On her return, she went to the kitchen where Jenny handed her a cup of coffee. They chatted and decided to go into Lincoln; Jenny had a couple of Christmas presents to collect and hide before the children came home from school.

Anna went to her flat to change into her boots; it was cold outside. She was pulling them on when her door opened.

'While you're in here,' Jenny said, 'you can pass me my letters, if you don't mind, Anna.'

'I haven't brought them.'

'Pardon?' Jenny's tone was hard.

'I said I haven't brought them. They're locked safely away in my safe. I think it's the best place for them.'

'I said I want them back.'

'Well, Jenny, you can't have them back. It's as simple as that.'

Anna could feel the tension in the air rising. She felt sick.

'I need them.' Jenny's voice was cold as ice.

'Why? I don't trust you, Jenny. If you destroy them, there is nothing keeping anyone else in this family safe. I said I'm keeping them, and I mean it. After five years, I'll hand them over, but they stay in that safe for now.'

Jenny reached across and picked up the vase of flowers, then hurled it at her mother-in-law. Anna ducked but not fast enough.

The vase hit her on the side of her head, and she cried out in pain. She twisted around and lunged towards Jenny.

'You bitch,' she screamed, and tried to pull on Jenny's hair. She was hurting and could tell that blood was pulsing down her face. 'Are you going to add me to the list now? Four murders? You still got the bags and plant ties, have you, Jenny? And the knife?'

'Anna, you're a liar and a fucking hindrance. Who's the man at the football match? I know it's Mark's father, so tell me his name!' Jenny was screaming in frustration. The row had escalated beyond all comprehension, and neither of them heard the front door opening.

'Okay, so he is Mark's father. But, what that's got to do with you, I don't know. You want to add him to the list as well?'

Jenny once more lunged towards Anna who was unable to see clearly, because the blood was flowing freely down her face.

Anna sidestepped with difficulty, grabbed her bag, and ran. Jenny tried to stop her, but desperation lent wings to Anna, and she ran towards the front door. She bumped into Mark, and he stared in amazement at the sight of his mother covered in blood, followed closely by his wife, screaming obscenities at her.

Anna pushed him to one side and ran out of the door. She fumbled in her bag for her keys, and within seconds was leaving the parking area, her tyres screaming.

She hit the road for Sheffield at some speed. Tears were now mingling with the blood, and she tried to clear her vision. She couldn't stop crying, but she needed to put distance between herself and Jenny and Mark. She guessed Mark wouldn't be able to follow her; he would have his hands full with Jenny.

Anna was soon on the A57, and as she approached the Dunham Bridge toll booth, she fished in the drinks holder where she kept loose change to make sure she had the right money for crossing the bridge.

She was still sobbing as she reached the booth, and as she handed the money over, the attendant stared at her in horror.

'Hang on a minute, love,' he said. 'There's blood all over your face. You need help?'

She shook her head and put her foot down hard. She needed Michael. She had no idea what she would tell him, but she needed him. Her sobs increased, and the blood was still blinding her left eye almost totally.

She swung around a bend in the road, not seeing the speedometer registering 85 miles an hour, and as she approached the crossroads, she was out of control.

She screamed. There was no way to avoid the oncoming truck. Anna's world descended into darkness.

*****

Michael was looking forward to the evening. He would cook Anna a nice meal, and they could share a bottle of wine and discuss telling the Carbrook family of their marriage.

He took the steaks out of the freezer and put them on the kitchen work surface to defrost. He couldn't remember ever being this happy and blessed the day Anna had called him. Eric the fish would always have a special place in their hearts.

He picked up the newspaper and sat down to do the crossword. The buzzer sounded, and at first he ignored it. But, then it was repeated, and he went across to answer it. Cautiously.

'Yes?'

'Mr. Groves? It's the police. Can we have a word please?'

Uneasily, he pressed the door release button, and then went out into the vestibule to wait for the lift, hoping neither Lissy nor Jon would walk out of their door.

There were two of them, a man and a woman.

'Is there a problem?' he asked and then felt stupid. Of course there was a problem. They wouldn't be there if there wasn't a problem.

'Can we go inside, please, Mr. Groves?'

He waved them through, and all three of them sat down.

'What's wrong?' he asked once more.

'Is your wife Anna Groves?'

'Yes...' He swallowed.

'I'm sorry, Mr. Groves, but she's been killed in a road accident on the A57, this side of the Dunham Bridge. We're very sorry for your loss.'

He stared at them. 'It can't be her. There must be some mistake, because she's not coming home until tonight.'

'Does she drive an Audi R8?'

'Yes.'

He passed a small piece of paper across to Michael. 'With this registration, sir?'

Michael looked and nodded.

'Then I'm sorry, sir, it is your wife. We recovered her handbag at the scene. Her driver's licence was in it, and when we checked the car registration, it came up with this address.'

Michael felt tears flow unchecked down his face. Anna, gone? How could that have happened? She was always such a careful driver.

'Whose fault...?' He had to ask.

'As far as we can tell, and from eye witnesses, your wife was going very fast and drove straight into a truck at a crossroads. The driver is in a critical condition in hospital, but is expected to live. We are hopeful he can give us more information. Can we notify family for you, Mr. Groves?'

Michael shook his head, deeply in shock. He owed it to Anna to handle this.

'No, I'll notify everyone.'

270

'Then can we get someone to come and stay with you?'

'I'll be fine. If you'll go now...'

'Of course, if that's what you want.'

Michael showed them to the lift and went back inside.

He sat for over an hour, unsure of what to do first. Clearly, he had to get to Lindum Lodge, but that wasn't going to be an easy thing to do. They would have no idea who he was.

And then he remembered the letters. He would have to take them with him; they belonged to Anna's children. She had written them for when she died.

He moved zombie-like into the bedroom he had shared for such a small amount of time with his love and keyed in the code she had told him. The safe clicked open, and he took out the large brown envelope.

It was sealed with sealing wax, and at first he thought he would just leave it and hand it over in its entirety to Mark and Jenny. Nobody else was in England.

Michael changed his mind. He would take all of them with him, but he wanted to keep them until he met up with the name on the envelope, and could explain just how much he had loved Anna.

He broke the seal and peered into the envelope. He could see three envelopes, and he tipped them out on to the coffee table.

He picked them up and stared. There were no names on them.

Murder Number One. Murder Number Two. Murder Number Three.

His brain went into shutdown. He stared at the envelopes for a long time and then stood to get a drink. He felt sick. He poured a glass of water and carried it back to the table.

Three murders. What had Anna known? Who was she protecting? Tim had been in America, so it left only one person to protect. Mark.

His eldest son.

Chapter 52

Michael drove to Lincoln via Newark; he couldn't bear to use the A57, and guessed it would still be closed at the crossroads while forensics did their work. His brain was reeling. Three murders could only mean one thing; Joan Jackson, Ray Carbrook, and the other chap with the Polish sounding name. Mark must have written everything down and given them to his mother for safe keeping. But, why had Anna said they were to be opened in the event of her death and not in the event of Mark's death? He clearly must have misunderstood her, and now, it was up to him to put things right. If she'd had a secret, he would keep that secret also.

He pulled up outside Lindum Lodge, leaving his car on the road. He sat for a while without getting out; he was about to do something so difficult, and he needed his brain to be in top gear for it. The letters were in his inside pocket. He had to see Mark on his own.

He had to make sure Jenny was out of the room. He didn't want her to hear or see anything during the conversation he had to have with his son. He planned the scenario; he hoped it would go according to plan.

Jenny opened the door, thinking it would be Anna coming back for her things. Mark had stayed at home, in an attempt at smoothing things over between his wife and his mother; they just needed Anna to come back.

The shock showed in her face when she realised just who was on her doorstep.

'Jenny,' he said. 'My name's Michael Groves, and I'm Anna's husband. Can I come in for a few minutes, please?'

She looked nervously behind her. Mark was approaching the door. 'Hi. Can I help you?'

'I need to speak with you.' Michael felt helpless, out of his depth. This was his first meeting with his son.

'Who are you?' Mark was looking at him, curiosity written into his features. 'Do I know you?'

'In a manner of speaking. I'm Anna's husband. We were married in September. Please, can I come in?'

Mark stood aside, but Jenny stayed where she was, half blocking his entry. He waited, and eventually, she moved.

He followed them into the lounge and began the most difficult conversation of his life. He saw Mark's face crumple as he learned of his mother's death; he saw Jenny turn ashen, and she stood and moved to sit with her husband.

'Where?' The word came out of Mark as a croak.

'The crossroads, just after Dunham Bridge.'

Jenny was staring at both of them. She didn't know what to do. She needed to get to Sheffield and get in that damn safe, that was for sure.

Mark's head dropped, and he began to cry quietly. 'Jenny,' he said between sobs, 'what the fuck was so important in that argument it's caused this?'

Jenny put her arm around him, and he shrugged her away.

She stood. 'Mr. Groves, Michael, would you like a cup of tea. I think we all need one.'

He said thank you, and she left to go into the kitchen.

Michael leaned forward and spoke quietly to Mark. 'Mark, listen carefully. I am your father. You were conceived just before your mother married Ray. Look at me, and I know you'll know I'm telling the truth. But, that's irrelevant, except for one thing. I won't give you up to the police. I believe Anna died protecting you, and as my son, I'll do the same for you. I don't know why you did what you did, but I suspect it was to save your mother from your father, from any more abuse. These belong to you, I believe.'

He took the three letters out of his inner pocket and handed them over.

Mark held out his hand and looked at the words written on the fronts. Then, he looked at Michael, his eyes blank. 'What...?'

The door opened, and Jenny came through with a tea tray in her hands. She saw the envelopes in Mark's hands.

She dropped the tray and screamed.

Epilogue

Michael, Mark, and Adam had enjoyed staying overnight at Nan's apartment in Sheffield, boys together.

But now they were enjoying watching the Owls, all three of them season ticket holders. Michael had bought his in memory of Anna, and Mark had bought one for Adam, in memory of Ray.

Michael had decided to keep the apartment so they could stay over when they went to home games; it made life a little more exciting for Adam. Grace went to her other grandparents when they had their boy's weekends.

Life without Mum and Nan had been hard at first, but they were slowly carrying on with life.

After Jenny's spectacular scream and collapse on that heart-breaking afternoon, Michael and Mark had read the letters. It became clear immediately Michael had completely misread the situation.

Mark had asked him to leave, and Michael had slipped a business card into his hand.

'Call me when you need me.'

Mark had merely nodded.

He then read the letters one more time and turned to his wife. She was softly crying in the corner of the sofa.

'You have ten minutes to get out of here,' he said. 'If you're still here in fifteen minutes, I'm ringing the police. I'll hang on to these, just in case I ever need them. Leave your credit cards, and anything else concerning money. You are leaving with nothing. I never want to see you again. I shall tell the children you've gone with another man. I shall blacken your name to them, and to everyone else who asks. You will never see any of my family again. Is that clear?'

She nodded, too distraught to speak.

'In exchange, I won't go to the police. However, if you attempt to contact any of us, I will make Gainsborough a present of these.'

Jenny did as instructed, and left.

*****

After the match, Michael took the three of them for a meal, and then they went back to the apartment. Mark had dismissed facts in the letter pertaining to the fatherhood of Adam, the son who was also his half-brother. He chose to forget the half-brother bit. Adam was his son. Michael had taken on the role of grandfather – they would explain true relationships when Adam was much older.

They walked across the car park singing hi ho Sheffield Wednesday, remembering the singing before the match started. They entered the vestibule and disappeared from view.

A woman with newly dyed dark brown hair cut very short sat in her car and watched. She heard the song, saw the camaraderie, felt the closeness between the three people in her line of sight. Felt the anger in her, so very deep inside her. One day, she would show them just who was in charge here, one day.

One day, when she had the letters back where they belonged.

With her.

Anita Waller

Acknowledgements

A huge thank you to Sheffield Wednesday Football Club, who helped me with dates, fixtures, results, and general information as I 'borrowed' this MASSIVE club for part of my story. Up the Owls!

Thank you also to Karen Tighe, who read the first half of the novel and encouraged me to continue with it, despite breaking off after 35,000 words to write Angel.

Mike Miklosz, my Lincoln helpmate, also came through with information about the upper class part of Lincoln, for which I am truly grateful – it saved me having to invent area names.

And thank you to Dave for keeping out of the kitchen while I write!